The Long Weekend

# FIONA PALMER

## The Long Weekend

 hachette
AUSTRALIA

Published in Australia and New Zealand in 2021
by Hachette Australia
(an imprint of Hachette Australia Pty Limited)
Level 17, 207 Kent Street, Sydney NSW 2000
www.hachette.com.au

A catalogue record for this
book is available from the
National Library of Australia

ISBN: 978 0 7336 4611 9 (paperback)

Cover design by Christabella Designs
Cover photographs courtesy of Dreamstime and Shutterstock
Author photo courtesy of Craig Peihopa
Typeset in 12/17.8 pt Sabon LT Pro by Bookhouse, Sydney
Printed and bound in Australia by McPherson's Printing Group

*To Anthea Hodgson and Rachael Johns*


'You have been my friend,' replied Charlotte. 'That in itself is a tremendous thing.'

– E.B. White, *Charlotte's Web*


'I knew when I met you an adventure was going to happen.'

– A.A. Milne, *Winnie-the-Pooh*


'I have your back. I don't mean only when it's easy. All the time.'

– Veronica Roth, *Divergent*

# Prologue

Joy flowed through her like a rushing creek. It was more than the excitement of Christmas, more than falling passionately in love, more than anything she could imagine. It was raw and powerful.

Was it a tiny hand or foot that pressed against her belly where she rested her hand? Did this growing human know she was his mother? Could he hear in her voice the love she already felt for him? She often spoke to her child, imagined his features. Would he have her eyes? Her chin?

Or maybe he would take after his father. Her mind clouded. A father he could never know. No matter how many times she did the calculations, the numbers didn't change, the dates didn't change. No amount of force, of wishing, of praying could change the fact that this child was not her husband's son.

# 1

## Beth

'PLEASE, BETHY, FOR ME?'

The vise-like grip on her hands was not threatening; if anything, the slight tremble betrayed Poppy's desperation. It was the first time in a long time she'd shown so much determination. Poppy had never been a fragile person. Growing up, her big sister had been brave and happy, energetic and kind. A true reflection of their parents, especially their mother. But trauma had left its mark, in the curve of her shoulders, the timid movement of her body and the permanent shadows in the creases of her eyes, like dark stains on her soul.

'But I can't leave Hudson and Dad.'

Beth Walton glanced over at her son on his elephant-print play mat, his wooden blocks strewn around him. Drool oozed down his chin, soaking into his blue jumpsuit, his cheeks glowing red as he focused on chewing a block as if he were a puppy and it was a tasty bone. Poppy's surprise visit had interrupted Beth's routine and she'd forgotten to put on his bib.

'Especially now he's teething. His temp's all over the place and he's cranky,' added Beth.

'Dad's always like that,' said Poppy, scrunching her nose up enough to move her black-framed glasses.

'Ha-ha.'

'Look, it's only for a weekend,' Poppy continued in her best imploring tone. 'I'll stay here and look after Dad and Hudson. I'll clean the house, I'll do everything. *Please*, sis, you know what this means to me!' Her shoulders dropped along with her grip on Beth's hands. 'I can do this, Beth.'

Poppy rifled through her bag and took out a pamphlet.

'Just take a look. You get to spend the weekend in Dunsborough. Geographe Bay! Think of it as a weekend away. You haven't had any time off since having Hudson and you need a break from Dad.'

*And from you.*

Beth brushed away the thought as Poppy raced on.

'I'll pay for it all. You won't need to do anything but rock up and enjoy yourself. You might even find that you enjoy writing.'

Beth scoffed but took the pamphlet anyway.

*Jan Goldstein's Writers' Retreat Workshop.*

*Help get your creative juices flowing in our gorgeous surroundings with renowned bestselling author Jan Goldstein. Enjoy invaluable time learning skills from one of the writing greats, along with tips and pointers to help with that new novel, memoir, blog or whatever other creative outlet beckons.*

*Book your spot now at this highly sought-after workshop. Places limited.*

It went on to list prices, and Beth choked on her own breath. 'Shit, sis, are you sure you want me to do this?'

Poppy's blue eyes glistened as she blinked the tears away. Her lips moved but no words came. Instead she nodded, swallowing hard.

Beth felt herself crumble. Years of standing tall, trying to be strong for everyone while fraying at the edges bit by bit, had taken its toll. Every now and then she couldn't help but let her facade slip. And she knew it was even worse for Poppy.

Beth reached for Poppy's hand, her thumb gently brushing along a scar. 'Are you sure you want to go through with this?'

Closing her eyes, Poppy nodded again. 'I need this, Bethy. I need to put things right, and I can't do it without you. And frankly, it's just not fair. It's wrong!'

The growing steel in Poppy's voice gave Beth hope. For years now Beth had watched Poppy retreat into a shell of self-protection. She only left her apartment for groceries and her full-time job at the cafe a few blocks away. Poppy didn't drive, of course. She barely spent money on anything. Beth glanced down at Poppy's blue Adidas runners, her second pair this year, but they were still cheaper than a set of tyres. No wonder she could afford to pay for the swanky retreat.

'Look, read this again.' Poppy retrieved the ill-famed novel from her bag and shoved it at Beth.

Beth pulled a face, but Poppy only pushed it harder into her hands.

'Read it. If it doesn't piss you off, then fine, you don't have to go. But if it burns your blood like it does mine, then please ... *please* help me do something about it. You know I can't go to the retreat, but you can.'

Hudson started to cry and kick at the blocks at his feet while trying to jam his fist into his wet mouth. His face was instantly stained with tears, and before Beth could even call his name Poppy had swooped over and picked him up.

'Hey, hey, my boy. What's up? You tell Aunty Poppy your problems,' she said, kissing his head and rocking him in her arms.

The afternoon light was filtering in through the corner window. Poppy glanced at her watch, no doubt calculating how long she had left before it was too dark to walk home. Beth had given up offering her a lift home, or anywhere for that matter.

'Look,' said Poppy as Hudson stopped crying and gazed up at his aunt in fascination as she waved her beaded necklace across his hands, 'I'd love to have some time with Hudson. Plus you work too hard. You never take a break. I see this as a win–win.'

Beth rolled her eyes. She was still getting the raw end of this deal, but with the book heavy in her hands and the beautiful landscape depicted on the pamphlet drawing her eye, she knew she would say yes. She could never deny Poppy.

'I'm writing you an alphabet book,' Poppy cooed to Hudson. 'It has all your favourite animals and toys, and when it's done I'll come and read it to you as often as I can. And I've started another book about a little boy and a magic football. I think you'll love it.'

Hudson smiled up at Poppy. At nearly eleven months, he'd grown so much since Beth had felt his kicks inside her belly and held his tiny body in her arms, and yet he was still so new to the world. She was in awe of everything he did, from babbling to laughing to pulling funny faces, or his joy at the simplest things. But it wasn't only Hudson who was mesmerising in that moment. To see Poppy so animated and full of love, talking to him as if he understood every word. To see Poppy really happy made Beth's eyes prickle with tears. She blinked them away before they could drown her. She knew what this meant to Poppy and she knew she could do this for her sister.

'I've decided,' she said. 'I'll do it. I'll go.'

# 2

## *Beth*

BETH PASSED THE SIGN FOR BUSSELTON, WHICH MARKED AS far south as she had ever travelled.

For the tenth time she glanced back to Hudson's empty car seat, still adjusting to being alone in her blue hatchback. She'd listened to 'Baby Shark' and 'Five Little Ducks' on her Hudson playlist for about ten minutes before realising. It had been so long since she'd listened to adult music that she didn't even know what was current, so she put on the radio. But more than two hours later, as she turned onto Marri Road, spying glimpses of homes nestled in green paddocks she felt like she had finally adjusted to being alone and feeling like a person, not just a mum. She'd had brief respites from Hudson – a solo trip to the supermarket, or a few walks while Poppy babysat – but nothing as long as this, or as far away. She wasn't sure what was scarier: the feeling of being like a yacht losing its anchor, or the idea that she might not even know how to exist without Hudson. Even the clean navy fibres on her T-shirt seemed to shine without stains and drool. And her light-wash jeans, usually hidden in the back of the cupboard, hugged her legs as if in thanks to finally be worn again. She felt a little guilty, but she also felt free.

Maybe Poppy was right, this weekend break would be good for her. Three nights – her first away from Hudson. Her stomach dropped a little whenever she thought about him waking up and not seeing her. It had taken ten minutes to say goodbye to her boy, standing by her car with Poppy waiting while Beth hugged and kissed and smelled her wriggling son. Her dad had quickly tired of waiting to wave her off and limped back inside.

'Beth . . .' Poppy had grumbled more than once.

In the end Hudson had got fed up and started to push against her chest, feet kicking and grunting his displeasure. With one last kiss on his wet red cheek she'd handed him over.

It was hard to drive away and her eyes may have watered a bit, but common sense told her that she might be overreacting a little. She planned to call home the moment she arrived but until then she would stick to her promise of not touching her phone.

Going on this writers' retreat felt ridiculous. Poppy was the writer. She was the one who'd spent her childhood reading and creating stories, always doodling on scrap paper and writing in diaries. There wasn't a day Poppy didn't have a book or two on the go. Beth had been more outdoorsy, probably due to their dad's influence; he was always outside fixing something or volunteering at the local footy club where he helped manage the team. Beth tagged along as often as she could. But a lot had changed since then. Everything had changed.

*Christ, how am I going to get through this? I can't write a shopping list to save myself!*

Google Maps told her she was very close to her destination and the butterflies started to take flight in her belly, self-doubt creeping in like the dark on a setting sun.

'Don't stress,' Poppy had said earlier that day. 'All sorts of writers of all levels of experience go to these things. Just pretend to write something. Or use this.' Poppy shoved a USB into Beth's hands. 'I've written a few things you can play around with, in case you have to share or read something out.'

'What do you mean, *read something out*?!'

Beth had nearly keeled over, as if suddenly she was back in high school standing at the front of her English class having to recite a poem she'd been made to write. It would be different if she was asked to talk about how to use a tennis ball to release discomfort in the shoulder, or how to stretch out tightness in the hamstrings. Being a physiotherapist had been her dream job until Hudson came along; being his mother – as trying as it could be – was so much more. Only recently she'd started working again a few days a week, combining both loves. Writing had always been Poppy's thing.

Poppy had spent the next five minutes reassuring her that it was unlikely, and that even if she were asked, she could refuse. Beth tried to look reassured, for Poppy's sake, but inside she was a mess of nerves. Reminding herself that she was doing it for her sister helped, but only a little.

Without thinking, she took a hand from the steering wheel and felt the long scar that ran diagonally from under the left side of her nose, down across her lips and to nearly the bottom of her chin. It wasn't her only scar, but it was the one people noticed first. Another stretched along her forehead and through her eyebrow, separating it like a parted sea. Her long mousy hair fell across her face to the right, mostly covering this scar; it wasn't intentional, but nor did she bother to change it.

Beth wasn't ashamed of her scars; she didn't try to hide them under make-up or shield her face when talking to people. But she couldn't stop the irritation that rose when people stared or when men looked past her to the next, flawless face. She didn't mind the little kids, because they didn't know any better. Once a little boy asked her if she'd been attacked by a werewolf or Wolverine, and she'd run with that explanation for a while. In a way her scars had made her invisible to some people, while others openly stared with curiosity. Then there were those who screwed up their faces and gasped.

Being invisible was by far the better alternative.

'Oh wow.'

Her mind was drawn back by the landscape that had changed around her. Tall trees, maybe marri or jarrah, stood high on either side of the road as she slowed to turn off on to a narrow driveway. Google Maps informed her she had arrived at her destination, but she was still climbing up the steep driveway, twisting left and right around massive trees that arched over her, shielding her from the sun and hiding the sky. Finally, the hint of a massive building appeared through the trees. This wasn't a run-of-the-mill house dwarfed by the landscape, cocooned in its rainforest-vibe surroundings, this was the biggest home she'd ever seen, all natural wood and wide windows, imposing and glistening like a magazine spread. Soft cream walls shone and a tin roof mirrored the silver–blue sky; rustic brown bush poles held up a second-storey balcony that made for a grand entrance beneath. Beside the house was another structure, the shape of a big shed but with large see-through panels in the walls – a pool house perhaps? The compacted dirt road opened up before her, forming a turning circle around a well-maintained garden with a mix of native shrubs and roses. Off to the side of the house was ample parking for at least six vehicles.

*Hmm, I see why you chose this place for the retreat.*

A black ute with big rims and chunky tyres was the only vehicle parked near the house. Two long bags were strapped to the roof rack. Surfboards? Beth wondered. When she climbed out of her car the smell of the damp undergrowth hit her; it was like new life and felt invigorating in a way she couldn't explain.

She turned in the direction of the house and her mouth fell open. Feeling like a sprite, she glided past the house, drawn by the view. The tall trees seemed to part like textured curtains, just enough so she could see the ocean, endless to the horizon. It was so still, like a picture, and yet she could hear the rustle of leaves and the gentle sway of branches, reminding her she wasn't standing in front of a painting. White caps tickled the tops of the waves but the ocean was too far away to hear them crash against the beach. Yet Beth swore she could.

'Not bad, hey?'

Beth jolted to her right to see a man lazing on a chair a few feet away.

'Sorry, I didn't mean to scare you.' His easy voice, calm and relaxed.

Beth didn't want to stare – she knew what that felt like – but this man was . . .

*Whoa.*

Her eyelids closed as she tried to form coherent thoughts. *Beautiful.* That's what her mind came back with. This man was beautiful. She forced her eyes open, and there he was, like a blinding light in his tight black T-shirt, every muscle defined and highlighted, and dark denim over his long legs to the black Converse on his feet.

Beth subconsciously ran her hand over her good jeans. 'Um, hi. Is this your place?'

'No. But I'm the first one here, it seems,' he said with a languid smile.

Shivers ran down her back at his smooth, sexy voice. It had been a long time since anyone had made her react like this, not since Hudson's father. And look how that turned out, she reminded herself. Nowadays, the only excitement she got was from sneaking in some screen time to dream about a Hemsworth or a Jamie Fraser. Real-life men who looked like this one had let her down; it was easier to admire the fantasy kind that could never hurt her.

Beth crossed her arms and turned back to the ocean, trying to take a more relaxed pose, opening her stance as if the surroundings were all that engrossed her while she tried to control her racing pulse. Adrien had been handsome but not as well shaped as this guy. The bulge of his muscles stuck to her eyes like the dots from staring at the sun, unable to blink them away.

'Are you here for the retreat?' he asked.

Her hair cascaded across her face as she nodded.

'Cool, me too,' he said as he jumped smoothly up from the chair and extended his hand. 'I'm Jamie Dunham.'

Her eyebrows shot up. *He's a writer? You've got to be kidding.*

Hesitating for a fraction, she stepped towards him to shake his hand. His muscles rippled as his sizeable hand closed around hers. Her first thought was that he looked like he belonged on a football field rather than at a writers' retreat, but then she realised she was hardly in a position to judge. His mahogany hair was cut short and neatly styled, unlike Beth's; her split ends hadn't seen a pair of scissors since she was in her teens.

'Yes. Hi Jamie. I'm Beth,' she said, retaining her last name. She winced slightly, suddenly feeling like a fraud. She had stepped into the lie now. Beth the aspiring author. What a joke.

'Your first writing retreat?' he asked.

Beth nodded again. At least that was true.

Jamie's brow knotted together for the slightest moment. Finally he'd noticed her scars. He was only human after all. Now he'd glance away in discomfort as most people did.

But his eyes found hers and didn't circumnavigate her face. Instead he let out a nervous chuckle.

'Me too. I feel a little out of place,' he admitted.

'Well, that makes two of us. At least it's nice here,' she added, her arms dropping to her sides as her breath rushed out.

'Yeah, I love this area. Yallingup especially. Good waves,' he said with a wink.

Beth smiled, unaffected by his wink. She had gathered herself and wouldn't fall for any of his charms, which probably came as naturally to him as someone checking their watch. She shoved her hands deep into her pockets and tried to think of something else to say.

'So, do you know what's happening? Is there anyone else here?' she asked, glancing around.

He shook his head. 'I've opened the locked box with the key and we all have information packages in our assigned rooms. Come, I'll show you to yours.'

Hurrying to keep up, Beth followed Jamie into the house through massive sliding doors between chunky bush poles. Inside, more poles added to an earthy feel but she was unsure if they actually held up the second storey or were purely aesthetic. The walls were cream, similar to the outside, but here the natural timbers and furniture became the feature. Artworks and canvases of native flowers adorned the walls. The floor was tiled in huge cream squares that drew the eye to the main event – a stunning staircase of timber and iron that wound up to the next level.

Jamie pointed skywards. 'The other two participants have the top floor, and we're down here. We have to share the bathroom.' He frowned. 'Sorry.'

'It's fine,' Beth replied with a smile, thinking of the bathroom she shared with her dad. She wasn't afraid of a lifted toilet seat or jocks left on the floor.

Jamie gestured to an immaculate open-plan kitchen, which again resembled something Beth had only seen in magazines or movies. Cream cupboards, black granite benchtops and stainless steel appliances, with a splash of jade green from the tea towels to the fruit bowl and the splashback. Definitely no kids visited here.

As his long legs glided down the cream passageway past more artwork, Beth quickened her step to keep up.

'Here you are.'

Jamie opened the door at the end and gestured to the corner, past the queen bed. 'A desk for your laptop. There's a printer in Jan's cottage but you can access it on the wi-fi. It's all in your information pack.'

Beth spotted the A4 envelope on the desk with her full name printed on the outside.

'You've been here a while then?' she asked.

'Maybe twenty minutes before you. There's not much in the pack, just our session times and some resources. Anyway, I'll let you settle in. I'm right next door if you need anything.'

Jamie slid past her and out the door, leaving an intoxicating scent, one that reminded her of the fresh woodiness of the lush trees and dense undergrowth outside.

Beth looked around her room for the weekend. It was bigger than her living room, the bed rich and plump with patterned blue pillows. It was like being inside an antique tea set, with the soft blue and white theme, and gold accents on the lights and desk lamps. A long window at the end of the bed gave her a view of the gorgeous tall trees and leaf-littered grounds outside.

*I could get used to this*, she said to herself, and took out her phone. She'd promised Poppy she wouldn't call in every five minutes, but suddenly, all alone in this big room in the silence, she needed to know that Hudson was okay. It hit like a brick that her son wasn't by her side, or even in the next room. He was hours away and it was suddenly sickening.

'What are you doing!' Poppy said as she answered the call. 'You've only been gone two hours!'

'I'm just letting you know I arrived safe,' Beth replied.

'Bollocks,' countered Poppy. 'You're checking on us. Hudson is *fine*. I'm quite capable of looking after my nephew.'

Beth sighed. 'You're right. It's just . . . This is harder than I thought,' she admitted.

'I know, you miss him,' said Beth sincerely. 'Hey, I promised I'd send you photos, didn't I?'

As if to prove her point, the line went dead and a photo came through of an eye-rolling Poppy with Hudson on her hip chewing on a rusk, slobber and biscuit all over his face and hands. Then a message: *We are FINE!!!*

She couldn't help a small smile. Looking at the photo helped her forget – almost – where she was and what she had to do.

'Just don't think about it,' she mumbled. 'Relax and pretend you're on holiday.'

'Good plan.'

Beth spun around to find Jamie standing by her door, hands shoved into his jeans.

'Do you often talk to yourself?' he asked, a slight curve to his lips.

'No, I was having a staff meeting,' she said, deadpan. He was hardly an arm's length away, far too close, but she fought the urge to step back.

Jamie's light laugh surprised her. 'Well, if you ever need more staff, I'm right next door. Do you need a hand with your luggage?'

Beth frowned. 'No, I'm fine, thanks.' She'd only brought an overnight bag – she planned to spend most of her days lounging around in tracksuit pants and watching Netflix while pretending to write.

Jamie was staring at her, but not at her face . . . her hair.

'Um, you have . . . um, something in your . . .' He reached out, fingers almost at her long unruly strands before he paused, uncertain.

Beth instinctively leaned away from him and examined her long hair. 'Oh,' she said with a nervous chuckle, 'it's a bit of rusk.'

Jamie's eyebrows shot up. 'Say what?'

Heat flamed her cheeks. 'My son is teething. It's his rusk, a hard biscuit he loves to chew on. It ends up everywhere.' She pulled the lumpy goo from her hair.

'You have a son?'

He sounded surprised. Beth frowned.

'I mean, you're so . . . young. To be married, I mean.'

Jamie crossed his arms and leaned on the doorframe, watching her as if he found her strange or confusing, an anomaly he couldn't work out. Beth's hairs on her neck prickled as she felt like he was searching her soul.

'I'm not married.' It was hard to keep the thorny tone from her voice.

'Sorry, *partner*,' he corrected, shuffling on the spot awkwardly.

'No, not one of them either.' Pressing her lips together, she tried not to smile as he squirmed, then when she couldn't take his unease any longer she went on to explain. 'I'm a single mum. And twenty-five isn't young – my parents had both their kids by this age.'

'Yeah, but it's not like that now. I'm almost thirty-two and my friends are only just getting married and thinking about having kids,' he said.

'I guess.' Beth shrugged in her best attempt at nonchalance and focused on tucking her phone into her pocket. 'Anyway, I better go and grab my bag.' With half a wave she shimmied past him and headed for the front doors.

As she stepped outside, she was blindsided by a ball of colour – from the fairy-floss lips to the deep tan, feathered honey hair and the most vibrant active wear Beth had ever seen. It was like meeting Rainbow Barbie, or almost being bowled over by her.

'Hi, sorry. I'm Beth.'

'Do you work here?' said Rainbow Barbie briskly. 'I'm trying to find my room.'

The woman's gaze skipped past Beth to flit around the house, her eyes darting from left to right.

'No, I don't work here,' said Beth. 'And I'm not sure which one is your room, but if you're here for the retreat, then I think you're upstairs.'

Rainbow Barbie pursed her plump lips and gazed up to the second floor.

'Okay, thanks,' she replied and headed towards the stairs, a bright yellow water bottle swinging from her manicured hand, each long nail decorated in teals, pinks and sparkles.

As Beth continued to her car, she spotted an older-style, sky-blue Volkswagen Beetle parked nearby, a yoga mat and a huge number of bags piled in the back.

A navy BMW four-wheel drive appeared from the driveway and pulled up alongside the Beetle, and Beth couldn't help but wonder who or what would emerge from inside. By the time she'd collected her overnight bag and jammed her laptop into her oversized handbag the owner of the car had climbed out.

'Hi,' the woman said with a nervous laugh. 'Are you here for the retreat? Am I in the right place?'

In the filtered sunlight, gold jewellery sparkled from her ears, her neck and her fingers. A big diamond glittered like a disco ball on her left hand as she brushed back salon-perfect waves. Her sleek fitted jeans looked like they came with a high price tag and her cream blouse flowed like soft milky silk.

Beth nodded. 'Yes.'

'Oh great. Looks like I'm the last one here. My son decided to tell me, *as I was leaving*, that he had crazy-hair day at school and I "absolutely" had to help him.'

The woman flashed blue-stained fingertips as she waved her hand, and Beth felt relief that, budget and wardrobe notwith-standing, finally there was someone at this retreat who she might have something in common with.

'Come inside,' Beth said with a smile. 'I'm pretty sure I can help you find your room. I'm Beth, by the way.'

'Hi Beth, I'm Alice. I'm so excited about this weekend,' she said, reaching for her leather handbag before locking her car.

'Wish I was,' Beth muttered without thinking.

'Oh,' Alice said with a surprised smile. 'You're not happy to be here?'

Beth forced her smile to return. 'Um, just a bit out of my comfort zone.'

As much as she could tell herself to treat the weekend like a holiday, she still felt exposed, as if her own secrets would be nudged from their hiding places.

Alice followed her inside and Beth felt a wave of relief after she pointed her in what she assumed was the right direction, then escaped to her own room.

Jamie's door was open. He was at his desk setting up his laptop, but his eyes flicked up to watch her walk past. Was he really an aspiring author? Maybe he was writing an action thriller, that would make sense. He did look like he could be a cop. Beth rolled her eyes as she realised the unfairness in her assumption of what an aspiring writer should look like. What did the others think when they looked at her? Did they think she had things to write about, a million stories hidden behind her scars? Still, she wondered what stories Jamie had to tell.

Beth threw her bag on the bed and shut the door, leaning against it.

*Damn you, Poppy.*

How on earth was she going to make it through this weekend?

# 3

## Jamie

HE'D NEVER BEEN THIS NERVOUS IN HIS LIFE.

Sure, he'd had butterflies on big occasions, but that was always when someone else was in the limelight. Sitting through his brothers' AFL draft picks, watching them run onto the MCG for their professional debut and then in grand finals. But this was different, this was him exposing himself, with nowhere to hide. Not even buying his own gym had come with this much anxiety. He was excited to be here – he knew what an opportunity it was to work with an author such as Jan Goldstein – but it came with the conflict of lies and secrets.

No one knew he was here. Officially he was off on a business trip for the weekend – meetings and talks with fellow gym owners about new equipment and the latest exercise trends. What made him uneasy was how quickly the lie had been believed by his family and friends. It didn't sit well, like a bad burger that kept repeating.

Pushing his hand through his hair, he sighed and focused on his laptop, which was trying to load. It was his holder of secrets, his keeper of keys, and like a diary, it held a lot of his innermost feelings. He glanced up as Beth walked past and shut her door.

He found her equally unsettling and intriguing. He'd trained plenty of older single mums at his gym – some freshly divorced and ready to get in shape and take on the world; others fragile and in need of the confidence to forge a new life for themselves – but he'd never met such a young and determinedly single mother before, especially not a woman who only brought one small bag for a weekend. He pictured her face. She had a haunting beauty . . . perhaps it was the scars?

With his laptop ready and charging, there wasn't much left to do, so he headed out into the open area near the stairs, where he immediately saw an activewear-clad woman trying to carry three bags, one off each shoulder and the other dragging along the floor.

'Do you need a hand?' he offered.

Her eyes lit up. 'Oh, would you mind? Thank you.' She promptly dropped all her bags. 'I'm Simone Kroft,' she purred, holding out her hand. 'And you are?'

It was like shaking a dead fish, and he was the first to pull away.

'Jamie. Where would you like these?' He scooped up all her bags, wondering if she actually had weights packed in them.

'Up here. Thanks again,' she said, strutting up the stairs.

Her multicoloured backside was right at Jamie's eye level and he sensed it was being swung side to side with extra gusto for his benefit, so he dropped his gaze to the floor and watched his feet instead.

'I'm in here,' Simone directed, heading down a neutral-painted corridor into the room on the far right.

On his left, wide glass doors opened onto a balcony facing the ocean. Jamie paused to drink it in, overtaken as he always was by the majesty of nature, imagining how beautiful the sunset would be.

'Just here,' Simone said again, impatience underpinning her words.

He stepped into the room and placed her bags by the base of her bed.

'Are you here all weekend?' Simone smiled, her body melting into a rehearsed pose.

'I am. Hopefully we can all take something away with us,' he said smiling, unaffected by a pretty girl parading in activewear. He'd seen it all in his line of work. 'What's your genre?'

Simone grimaced, her petite nose wriggling like she was about to do some magic. 'My publisher thought the retreat would be a great introduction to writing. They've contracted me to write a memoir.'

Jamie watched her, unsure how to reply, but Simone soon filled in the silence.

'I'm an influencer,' she boasted. 'I just tipped over the fifty-thousand mark on my Instagram page. It started as my weight-loss journey but I'm branching out into other areas of wellness and now companies get me to endorse their products.'

Automatically, she rotated to show off the label on her activewear.

'I was recently approached to write a book about my success, but I've never written anything that long before, so here I am, ready to learn.' She ran her hands through her hair, the skin under her arms crinkling like crepe. 'And are *you* here to write?' she enquired with a raised brow.

'Yes,' he said simply, 'that's the plan.'

She looked at him with a mix of confusion and curiosity, but he didn't enlighten her.

'So what do you do for a real job?' She pointed to his bulging bicep. 'Are you an athlete?'

Jamie narrowed his eyes and hesitated over his reply. 'I own a gym.'

Her pupils dilated and her plump lips spread into a wide smile.

He suddenly felt like bait jiggling on a line while the water thrashed with hungry fish. 'Are you right here, or do you have more bags to carry up?' he added quickly, glancing towards the door.

'Oh no, I'll be right with the rest. Thank you, Jamie.'

He didn't like the way she pronounced his name. *Jar-mee.* His mates called him Jay most of the time.

He paused by the door. 'Righto, after you,' he gestured.

She gave a giggle of appreciation as she walked past then headed back downstairs. Just as Jamie was about to follow, the other bedroom door by the stairs opened. A woman emerged, her movements suddenly familiar. The tilt of her head, the swing of her hips. Memories flooded back as they blended with this woman before him.

'Alice?'

She startled so much she nearly dropped her notebook.

Green eyes, so green, flicked to him. How could he ever forget those eyes?

'Jamie!' It was a surprised squeak, like a mouse darting out of a hole straight into the path of a cat. 'What are you doing here?' She was slightly breathless, cheeks tinged pink as she clutched her notebook to her chest.

Alice hadn't changed much in the past six or so years: she was still a vision, a thoroughbred, an expensive bottle of champagne. From the alluring scent of her perfume, to the perfectly cut and coloured hair and the face of someone who had always followed a set beauty routine, she screamed box seats, yachts and private schooling.

'I'm here to write,' he said, then managed half a smile. 'Who would have thought we'd meet again at a place like this?'

Alice's cheeks and neck glowed, and he knew she was remembering their past, just like he was. Her eyes darted to the stairs. No doubt she wanted to flee as much as he did.

'I know. How crazy is that?' A nervous laugh. 'I better get the rest of my stuff,' she said, moving forward timidly.

Jamie stepped back and gave her room to escape. She wasn't the only one rattled. He cracked his neck, his usual go-to move to release the tension, and wondered how the weekend would go now.

'I'll see you around.' She threw the words over her shoulder as she practically jogged away.

Jamie took a few moments to think. *Alice*. He breathed out slowly. It was all such a long time ago.

Shaking his head, he descended the stairs and went back to his room for a quick change into shorts and running shoes. He needed to clear his head.

'Can I have everyone's attention, please!' A commanding voice echoed through the cavernous house. 'I'd like to speak with you all together, if I may?'

Jamie headed to his door and met Beth in the corridor.

'It seems we've been summoned,' she said quietly. 'I feel like I'm back at school.'

'Hmm, wonder what this is all about,' he replied, slightly irritated at the disruption to his planned run.

Beth walked beside him, but not close. He could sense her wariness, got the impression she didn't like him much or maybe that she didn't trust easily.

Most women responded immediately to his smiles, even flirted a little, but Beth was different. He'd be happy with a half-genuine smile for now. He could see he was going to have to work hard to get beneath her exterior.

They were first to arrive to find a mid-fifties woman standing in the entry area as Simone and Alice came down the stairs.

'Thank you. I'm Nadine and I'm the caretaker of this home,' she said, clasping her hands together.

Simone bounced her way towards Jamie, coming to stand closer to him than was necessary, and not at all subtle. He didn't glance at her; he was here to learn and to write, and his years of mixing work with pleasure were long gone. Alice stood opposite him, her eyes avoiding his.

'I see you've all met and hopefully found your rooms. I've been informed Jan will arrive tomorrow morning and will reside in the self-contained cottage, so you'll have the house to yourselves. All meals will be delivered and a continental breakfast is provided in the kitchen.'

Nadine picked up some sheets from the side table and handed them out.

'Here are the menu and house rules. Feel free to explore – the pool is available and there are walking trails around. You'll find pamphlets in the kitchen that list the local sights.' She paused only briefly before finishing, 'Does anyone have any questions?'

No one replied.

Nadine smiled. 'You all have my number if you need anything. Extra pillows, rugs, bottle openers – which are in the wine cabinet near the fridge. Those wines are for you to enjoy, any food or drinks in the house are all for you. So please, do help yourself.'

Jamie was starting to understand the price tag of the retreat, but he would have paid it just to meet Jan Goldstein.

'I hope you have a fabulous weekend.' With that, Nadine exited, leaving them standing in a circle looking down at their menus.

'Meals look good,' mumbled Beth.

'Well, shall we meet back here at six-thirty, then?' asked Simone. Her long sparkly nails were scrolling through her phone as she spoke, clearly already distracted.

'I better check in with my kids,' said Alice and headed back to her room.

Beth had moved to a bamboo chair in the corner and was riffling through the pages. As she leaned forward, Jamie watched her hair fall like a caramel syrup in the light. Minus the biscuit clumps.

He mentally shook himself. The outdoors beckoned, so he quickly slipped out the front door before Simone could invite herself along. He wondered whether the exercise gear was all for show. So often it was these days.

Sticks and leaves crunched underfoot. He ducked past branches and stepped around the massive trunks. Jamie began to relax, the tension easing from his muscles as he explored the area around the retreat house. The smell of the earth mixed with the moist leaves of the undergrowth loaded every breath with energy, Mother Nature providing a natural drug that made him relish life.

After he reached the thirty-minute mark he stopped to add in some reps – fifty push-ups, sit-ups and squats – and then planked for two minutes before heading back. As he made to pass a massive marri tree, he stumbled upon Beth. Or, almost into her. Like a kid, she was squatting on the ground, intently examining a collection of gumnuts.

Beth looked up as he approached, taking in his appearance – dripping in sweat, clothes clinging to him – and the corner of her lip twitched.

'I can't say I know many women who sit and play in the dirt.'

The afternoon light picked up golden sun kisses along her skin and the puckered ridges of her scars as she smiled at him, studying him, her eyes cautious.

'I like being out here,' she said simply. 'And these gumnuts are cool. Hudson would love them.'

Beth picked up an urn-shaped gumnut from a collection she'd gathered at the base of the tree.

'Hudson. Your son? How old?'

'He'll be one in another month. I'm not sure I'm ready,' she sighed. 'Life doesn't slow down for anyone.'

Her last words were weighted with something he didn't understand but suddenly wanted to figure out.

'No, sadly time won't wait,' he agreed. 'You miss him,' he finished rhetorically.

She nodded and started to sift through the pile of gumnuts, arranging them in a little pattern. 'More than I thought possible.'

He wondered if it was her first time away from him since he was born. 'So, you're a creative soul, then?'

She stopped and gave him a blank stare. 'Me artistic, ha,' she scoffed. 'I'm a physiotherapist who doesn't have a creative bone in her body.'

He frowned. 'Then why are you at a writers' retreat?'

Jamie drank in her startled expression; it was as if he'd caught her out. But at what?

'My sister sent me here. For a break. I was forced,' she spluttered out rapidly as she stood, her hands filled with gumnuts.

It felt like there was truth in her words but not the whole story. Seeing her discomfort, he didn't push.

'So where do you work?' he asked instead, hoping to detain her longer. Being outside chatting to Beth was much more appealing than being inside with Simone. Or Alice, who was clearly avoiding him. Probably with good cause.

Moments ticked by, his question unanswered.

'Sorry, I was just curious,' he said. 'I run a gym called Xtreme on Latham Road, so physios are great to know.'

'Yeah, I know the one. I drive past it. That makes sense,' she added.

'Why?'

'What?'

'Why does that make sense?' he persisted.

She rolled her gorgeous blue eyes and breathed out heavily. 'I haven't seen many muscled writers.' She scrunched her nose. 'It's not an unrealistic assumption.'

'But it *is* a little judgemental,' he countered.

She shrugged, her eyes sparkling with a smile that she kept from her lips. 'You're probably right.'

Beth dropped the gumnuts and dusted off her hands as she turned and headed for the house. Jamie cocked his head watching her slow stroll, and smiled.

# 4

## Beth

THE COLD TENTACLES OF NIGHT LICKED AT BETH'S SKIN AS she meandered back to the house. When she stepped inside she still felt cold; clearly no one had thought to turn on the heating.

Digging out her maroon hoodie, adorned with the yellow stripes and logo of the Subiaco Lions, Beth headed to the open lounge area by the stairs and scanned the quaint collection of books on the shelf. She didn't have time to read these days. Only work-related texts. Not counting Jan's new book that Poppy had urged her to read.

'Okay, yes I know. I will try.' Alice was heading down the steps, phone pressed against her ear. 'I'll call tomorrow with an update.'

She ended the call quickly, sliding her phone away before she sank into the soft leather couch. The room was quiet, unnervingly so, and Alice just stared at her hands.

'How old are your kids?' Beth asked, taking a seat in the second two-seater couch.

'Mia's eight and Abe's six, almost seven.' She smiled as all mums do when speaking about their most prized possessions.

'You have kids?' Alice asked as she crossed her legs.

Her white canvas sneakers oozed Vans not Target. Beth too was wearing black Vans but she'd found hers in her local op shop, along with a few other worn-in favourites. Alice even smelled like wealth, expensive perfume filling the open room and also making Beth wonder if she'd remembered to put deodorant on this morning. Things got forgotten or interrupted easily when Hudson was around.

'Yes, Hudson. He's eleven months.'

At that moment Jamie appeared from the corridor and Simone called down a greeting from the top of the stairs. Jamie glanced at the two empty spaces. Alice tilted her head away from him.

'Mind if I . . . ?' He gestured to the spot beside Beth.

Beth nodded and he sat, bringing a wave of freshly showered man with him. She tried not to breathe too deeply as her body fought against falling towards the crevasse he'd made in the couch.

Alice cleared her throat and looked at her hands. Beth glanced at Jamie, who was watching Alice intently. Beth could feel the awkwardness.

Alice forced her lips into a smile. 'Did you find any good books?' she said, nodding towards the shelf Beth had been perusing.

'Nothing jumped out at me. But I haven't done much reading since having Hudson. I almost don't know where to start.'

Jamie was going to say something, Beth could tell by the way his chest rose, stretching against his grey T-shirt. In her peripheral vision she noticed the print on the front: a black outline of Arnold Schwarzenegger and the words 'Come with me if you want to lift', which she found rather appropriate and rather funny. But he didn't get a chance to get his words out because Simone's voice bellowed.

'Hey guys, do you all mind being in my Instagram photo?'

She didn't wait for their replies before taking up position to get a selfie of herself with them in the background.

'Oh, hang on, it's blurry.' She took a few more, swinging her head from left to right in various poses. 'Cheers, guys, that's great. I'll make sure to tag you.'

Simone, still wearing a rainbow, glanced towards Jamie, her eyes sizing up the gap on the couch. Beth was pretty sure she'd try to fit, but common sense prevailed and she popped down next to Alice.

Jamie let out a long, slow breath.

Simone launched into a monologue about her Instagram page, like a car salesman trying to reach a sales target, hands gesturing with each word and her smile never once leaving her face. 'So, if you want any information on the products, hit me up. Weight loss, collagen, beauty products . . . I have it all and it's *amazing*.'

Simone's gaze landed on Beth.

'Oh, wow,' she said, then after a beat she added, 'Collagen is really good for scars.'

'Miracle cure,' Beth mumbled under her breath as Jamie tried to suppress a chuckle.

Simone parted her glossy lips, and Beth clenched her teeth, knowing what was coming.

'What do you think Jan's like?' Jamie said quickly. 'Has anyone read her latest book?'

Simone sat on the edge of the couch, shoulders back, chest out. 'My publisher sent it to me,' she said. 'But I'm not even halfway through. I just can't seem to find the time.'

Beth's gaze flicked to Jamie, to convey her thanks for the subject change, which was a mistake. It was wrong for one man to be so perfectly sculpted. Chris Hemsworth sprang to mind. She'd never admit to anyone that she often got stuck on Chris's Centr page on Facebook, watching him work out. That was as close to dating as she got these days.

'I've read it,' Beth stated. 'First book in nearly two years. Have you? What did you think?'

Long eyelashes fluttered as Jamie blinked, contemplating his answer. An image of him reading popped uninvited into her head which she forced aside.

'I enjoyed it. It had Jan's usual flair for the dramatic, really pulled at the heartstrings. Her romance storylines are great, and the hint of mystery adds another element. She sure knows how to write an engaging story. Jan's always shortlisted in the Best General Fiction category in the Australian Book Industry Awards.'

He studied her intently, but not her scars. It felt as if he were reading her eyes, the arch of her brows, the kick of her lips, any sign that he could decipher.

'You didn't like it?' he deduced.

'No,' she admitted. 'Not really. Bits of it rubbed me up the wrong way.' That was an understatement. 'But like I said, I've hardly had time to read anything lately, so I'm not a great judge.'

'We'll have to rectify that.'

With a whoosh he was off the couch, and before Beth could figure out what he was up to he reappeared and plopped back on the couch beside her.

'Try this and tell me what you think,' he said, holding out a book.

Beth took it, her fingers running over the raised name. 'Susan Vincent. *Lie to Me*,' she read.

'I haven't read that one, but I've seen it everywhere,' said Simone, leaning towards them.

'I have. It's brilliant. We read it for book club last month,' said Alice, her eyes only on Beth. 'It's a bestseller.'

'Oh, right.' Beth smiled. 'I mostly only know about *The Very Hungry Caterpillar*. I don't often get to the fiction section.'

'Try it. I'm sure you'll love it,' offered Alice.

Beth noticed Jamie watching Alice intently, and when Alice also noticed her eyes dropped down to her lap and she seemed to shrink back into an invisible shell.

'Well, I suppose this is the right place for reading,' Beth replied, then turned to Jamie. 'Thanks. I might make a start on it tonight. The cover looks interesting.' She looked at the close-up image of the side of a woman's face with another person's lips to her ear, then flipped the book over to read the blurb. 'Scandal, lies, buried secrets. More than one person isn't telling the truth,' she read out, then shivered as if someone had walked over her grave. This book might be too close to her truth.

'Great, let me know what you think.' Jamie smiled. 'She's a friend of mine,' he added.

'Oh wow, you know Susan!' Alice said curiously. 'I've heard she's a bit of a mystery.'

'What do you mean?' asked Beth.

'No one has seen her and with her book becoming a bestseller everyone wants her even more. Mind you, that could also be part of the charm. You can't trust anything these days. They probably set it up that way to give the media something to feast on,' she finished.

Beth turned to Jamie. 'If you know her, is that true?'

Jamie was already shaking his head. 'No, Sue is a writer only and refuses to do any publicity. They were so desperate for her book they agreed.'

'How strange. I would want to do all the publicity I could,' Simone pitched in.

'Not Sue. She thinks her work should speak for itself. It's up to her publisher to sell it; she just wants to write. She's not the only author who's reluctant to do the media side.'

Beth wondered if there was more to Sue's reluctance. Was she like Beth and hiding scars, or was she carrying internal ones that gripped her with fear just being outside the house? Her mum sprang to mind, always being behind the camera, never in front of it. She didn't like being in the limelight. Beth could imagine writing a bestselling book would mean everyone would want a piece of you. Her mum would have said no to it all as well.

Jamie glanced at his watch just as they heard a commotion near the kitchen.

'Sounds like dinner has arrived,' Simone said, rubbing her hands together.

Alice was sitting quietly, poised but not contributing to the conversation.

'Are you writing a book as well, Alice?' Beth asked.

She gave her a small smile. 'I'm trying to. I've been working on one,' she said sheepishly, 'but I need some help.'

'That's exciting,' Beth said.

'And what about you? Are you writing a book?' Alice asked politely.

Beth froze momentarily but reminded herself to keep her lie simple.

'No, I'm here to learn from Jan,' she said in what she hoped was a casual tone, and then remembered that Jamie knew the partial truth. 'And a bit of a break as well. My sister encouraged me to come.'

'What about you, Jamie?' Simone cooed. 'What brings you here?'

Alice shifted in her seat, turning towards Simone as if she didn't want to know the answer.

Jamie threw an arm across the back of the couch. Beth was relieved it was the other side, yet also a little disappointed.

*Don't be an idiot, Beth.*

'I've always loved reading,' Jamie was saying. 'And when I saw this retreat it seemed like a great way to progress with some writing.'

Beth watched Simone hang off his every word and Alice avoid looking in his direction, all the while feeling somewhere in the middle.

'Are your family all readers?' Simone asked. 'Or is this a little side hobby?'

Jamie's laugh was laced with dryness. 'No, I'm the odd one out in my family. Both my older brothers are professional football players.'

'Oh my God!' Beth swung around so fast she nearly threw his book back at him. 'Damien and Reece Dunham are *your* brothers?'

Jamie smiled, glancing at her hoodie. 'You know your football.'

It was Beth's turn to gush. 'I can't believe it. I can't wait to tell my dad. Damien was one of his favourite players, he was devastated when he retired. What a brilliant career, though. Reece is talented as well. Do you play?'

Light danced in his eyes, clearly proud, but he shook his head.

'I never knew that,' Alice said suddenly, and then turned a shade of pink.

Jamie and Alice shared a glance, which she broke off quickly.

*I knew it! I knew something was up between those two.*

Now Beth's mind ticked over. Had they both come here under the pretence of the retreat because they were having an affair? Was that why Alice was being so aloof? And was Jamie being so chatty with Beth to throw them all off the scent? It made sense, especially with her track record with good-looking men. Their shallowness had left scars deeper than the ones on her face.

*Ha, maybe I should write fiction.*

Beth gritted her teeth and tried to rein in her wayward mind as Simone headed for the kitchen.

'Have you always been a footy fan?' Jamie asked Beth, while his eyes remained on Alice.

She doubted he would hear her answer – he was clearly sharing some sort of moment with Alice – but she replied anyway.

'My dad's been in various coaching roles at Subiaco, and I used to tag along when I was a kid. I liked being Dad's offsider. My sister was like my mum. They both loved reading, whereas I loved football and being around the players.'

'Ah, the physio bit makes sense now,' he said, but before Beth could reply, Simone's voice reached them from the kitchen.

'Dinner looks good, you guys. Come and eat.'

Beth left the book on the couch as she followed the others.

The food was set up on a massive eight-seat wooden table off from the gorgeous kitchen. It was surrounded by floor-to-ceiling glass windows, and the jade accents from the kitchen continued with the table runner and decorative bowls. This was a dining room you would want to eat in all the time.

'It smells divine.' Beth's stomach rumbled as she glanced through the window, spotting a walkway to another building. It looked like a secluded romantic guest house, in a similar style to the main house.

'That must be where Jan's staying,' said Jamie as he paused by her side.

Beth's heart began to race as she thought about what she had to do, had to at least attempt. It would mean waiting for the right moment. Figuring out a plan. Shit, she needed a plan.

*Oh Poppy. How am I going to do this?*

# 5

## *Alice*

HEAT PRICKLED ALONG HER NECK, WHILE HER MUSCLES FELT tense. This weekend was supposed to be about her, about moving forward, being stronger. Yet she felt awful.

It was all because of Jamie. Not in her wildest dreams did she expect to see him again, let alone at a place like this, with nowhere to escape. But she would not leave. This writing weekend had been on her calendar for a whole year, anticipated for so long that she would not give it up because of Jamie. If anything, his presence felt like a test. Or penance.

Trying to draw breath, she followed the others to the kitchen, her chest so tight she could barely think. Conversation was such an effort; avoiding Jamie took all her strength. It didn't help that he hadn't changed a bit, was maybe even better looking, if that were possible. He seemed less the young man with a fresh face now, more solid and mature like a fine wine.

*Why is he here?*

At first she wondered if he'd known she was going to be here. But that couldn't be possible, could it? Not after all these years.

*Unless . . .*

No. It had to be luck. What shitty luck.

The table was laid with finger food, pastries, meatballs, koftas and salads. Plates were stacked, and tongs sat alongside each dish.

Simone had her phone out, snapping away at the food, rearranging the table to get the right look. Alice hadn't realised she was staring until Simone commented.

'It's for Insta. It pays to get the best shot. I've done a few online courses in food photography.'

Simone then moved the flower arrangement in the centre of the table to the side of the koftas and took more photos, while Alice willed herself to remain friendly.

*Can we just to get to the writing part?*

She was dying to meet Jan and see what she could learn to help polish her book. Wasting time on idle chitchat with people she had nothing in common with merely annoyed her. Or maybe it was the added frustration of Jamie.

The table had eight seats and there were only four of them. Alice didn't want to sit until Jamie had, because then she could make sure she was the furthest from him. Trying to use up more time, she went to the kitchen, found wineglasses for everyone and filled hers with the local wine that had been put on the table with the food. She'd kill for a large glass of Möet or Veuve. After dinner she might try to find a bottle shop; she'd need something good for the whole weekend to survive the images that flashed through her mind. The longer she was near Jamie, the more they appeared, like an old school album full of bad hairstyles and fashions long dead.

'Anyone else like one?' she offered.

'Oh, why not? It's free,' said Simone.

Beth thought about it for a minute before nodding. 'A little one, please.'

Jamie shook his head to the wine as his impressive form found a seat. Simone swiftly crawled into the vacant one beside him; like Blu-Tack she was quickly gluing herself to his side. Feelings swirled – relief, annoyance, confusion.

Alice took the seat opposite Simone, while Beth sat opposite Jamie.

'This looks so good, especially because I didn't have to prepare any of it,' said Beth. 'None of it is remotely baby food either.'

Beth tucked a wayward strand of hair behind her ear, a small smile on her face that seemed to enhance her scar. Alice couldn't help but wonder what caused it; it must have been awful, to leave such damage, though it was clearly long ago because it had healed and settled.

'Is this your first time away from your son?' Alice asked.

Beth laughed. 'Am I that easy to read?'

'I think another mother can usually tell. Even now I keep expecting my two to bolt in demanding food or squabbling over a toy.'

Beth smiled sadly as she relaxed back into her chair. 'I miss him like crazy.'

'The first time is always the worst.' Alice sipped her wine before asking, 'Did I hear that you're a physio? Sorry, I didn't mean to eavesdrop . . .' she added with a quick glance at Jamie. She was so curious about him. Where had his life taken him?

Did he have a partner, wife, children? And yet prying into his personal life felt like a big no-no. How could a person feel so many emotions at once? She just felt so hyper-aware. Maybe writing in her journal after dinner might help to ease the ball of pain at the base of her skull.

'I am,' Beth answered. 'I just work part-time, though. I don't like leaving Hudson in childcare for too long. Although sometimes I take him to work and our receptionist helps keep an eye on him.'

'That's nice,' Alice said, aware of Jamie's eyes on her. 'Sometimes I wish I had a profession. I'm just a mum.'

'There's no such thing as "just a mum",' replied Beth quickly but kindly. 'My mum always said it was one of the hardest jobs going around – and unpaid. That it's demanding and thankless most of the time but utterly rewarding, and I see what she meant.'

Alice's mouth curled into a smile, and she felt a little lighter as she looked down to her plate. She'd stuck to the salads and a kofta, but even so, she knew she wouldn't eat it all.

Simone had put one of nearly everything on her plate but spent more time talking than eating. For someone so eager about the food, she'd hardly touched it, bar a few nibbles.

'So, what else is available at your gym? Do you still train clients as well as run it? Do you cover nutrition too?' Simone was firing questions at Jamie like an automatic weapon. She was locked onto her target as if Jamie were the only one at the table.

As Jamie spoke about his gym and personal training, Alice felt her face heat up. It didn't help when he flashed his steel-grey eyes at her; she knew they were both were thinking the same thing.

'We focus on strength, conditioning, rehabilitation, lifestyle,' he said smoothly.

Alice's mind went to the gym as she remembered it, wondering if it was still the same or if he'd overhauled it when he took over. She did a drive-by once not long after, maybe to get a glimpse of him and those eyes. But it had been torture and she knew it wasn't helping her to move forward. So she'd cut the cord and never gone there again. It had turned out to be the best decision she'd made in a long time, though it didn't make up for some of the bad ones.

Alice quickly checked the time, sliding her gold watch across her wrist to read the diamond-studded hands. Dale had told her to call at eight so she could talk to the kids before bed. The time couldn't come soon enough.

Alice slipped some kofta into her mouth and smiled. If this were some kind of test, then she would pass. Sudden confidence surged through her along with the need to get back to her room and write it all down.

Simone and Jamie were deep into a discussion on exercise and what worked your core better. Alice didn't know Simone, but it seemed like she was pumping Jamie for info, her eyes squinting as if taking it all down on a mental notepad.

'Do you sell any products in your gym? I have some great shakes that would sell like hotcakes there if you're interested,' Simone purred.

Jamie's eyes darted around, clearly looking for an escape.

'What do you think? We could work out a partnership?' Simone pushed.

'Did anyone go over tomorrow's schedule?' Jamie asked in Beth's direction.

Beth shrugged. 'Jan's session is at nine for two hours, and then again in the afternoon at two. Does anyone have a one-on-one with her?' she asked, looking around the table.

'I think I do, actually,' said Simone, tapping away on her phone. 'I'll just read the email from my publisher. I have a feeling they've asked Jan to help me plan my book.'

'You're very lucky,' Alice said, though she sensed Simone didn't agree. 'I'd love to have Jan help with my book. I don't even have a publisher. I think I need to finish it first before I send it out. How did you find your publisher?'

'Oh, mine found me,' Simone said breezily. 'I got an email out of the blue after *Sunrise* ran a segment on how big my Instagram following was, which only made my page triple. So amazing.' She paused, as if trying to remember the question. 'Um, yeah, it was Bass and Bird who sent a message, saying they were interested in producing a book. They offered me money upfront too.'

'Most contracts do,' said Jamie. 'If you have to pay, then it might be dodgy.'

'Oh, really?' Alice said. She had come across publishing sites like that. Thank goodness she hadn't pulled the trigger yet.

Jamie looked at her. 'I read an article about it once,' he said. 'Be careful. But there are also some great websites that can help with your writing. Obviously, Jan could give you advice too.'

'Um, right,' Alice replied, feeling like a spotlight was suddenly on her. She stood and collected her empty plate and glass.

With long strides she quickly put her things in the dishwasher before filling her glass to the brim.

'I'm going to head off and do some writing. Night, all.'

Back in her room, she settled herself on the bed with her drink.

She sighed deeply as she took a long sip before reaching for her leather-bound journal. Pages of ink flashed past until she reached a crisp new cream page. She wrote the date and day, then started.

*Today I saw Jamie.*

# 6

## *Beth*

ALICE'S ESCAPE HAD BEEN BETH'S CHANCE TO FOLLOW SUIT. She collected the book Jamie had given her, leaving Simone's voice – which could match a dentist's drill – filling up the empty spaces of the large house. As she closed her door and threw the book on the bed, she giggled at the thought that sounds of Jamie and Simone having hot sex might resound through the wall, but then she reconsidered. In the short time she'd known Jamie, he hadn't shown that kind of interest in Simone – or any interest, for that matter. At dinner, he'd seemed as exasperated as Beth felt. Alice, on the other hand, now that was a different story. Beth had watched him watch Alice throughout dinner, and not in simple curiosity but more familiar, personal. There was history between them, Beth was sure of it.

Soft pillows cocooned her as she kicked off her shoes and settled on the bed with the book. Even though she just wanted to call Poppy she decided to read a few chapters first. That lasted one chapter. Desperate to hear her son's voice she marked her page and grabbed her phone.

'Hi Poppy.'

'So, tell me all about it,' she said, her excitement buzzing down the line. 'Have you see Jan yet?'

'What? No "Hello, my darling sister, how are you?",' Beth teased.

'Oh come on, just give me the goss.'

'Tit for tat: how's my boy?'

Poppy breathed an irritated sigh. 'He's sound asleep with his lion. Hold on . . .' Beth's phone buzzed. 'See?'

Beth pulled her phone away from her ear to see the photo Poppy sent. Hudson tucked up in his cot, his plump lips and long eyelashes made her heart ache. Soft angel hair curled at his temple and the desire to kiss his forehead was intense. His stuffed lion lay next to his outstretched arm. He loved that toy, given to him by his pop who was keen to make him a Subiaco Lions fan.

*My boy.*

Her heart felt like it might burst.

'He's been great as usual. Scoffed dinner, just like Dad does. Loved his bath. I read him two books and now I'm sitting back with a cup of tea, hoping my dear sister will share the juicy details of her day with me.'

Beth groaned loudly so Poppy got the full effect.

'What are you doing now? Not mingling?'

'No, you'll be quite surprised but I'm on the bed about to read Susan Vincent's *Lie to Me*.'

'I don't believe it.' Her attempt at sarcasm brought a smile, reminding Beth of the old Poppy. In those moments, she could almost forget the trauma that hovered beneath the surface.

'It's a good book though,' Poppy went on. 'I loved it. I'm glad you're taking time to read and relax. Who else is there? Have you seen Jan?' she pumped.

'No. I won't see Jan until the session tomorrow. But I think she's arrived. She's staying in a cottage next to the main house, not with us.' Her stomach roiled as she gripped the phone tighter. 'And before you ask, *no*, I haven't sorted a plan yet and *no*, there's no point doing anything this early on.'

Poppy's reply was deflated. 'I know.'

Beth needed to change the topic. She didn't like letting her sister down, or adding to her frustrations. It had taken so long to draw Poppy back into her old skin and Beth still carried the fear of her sister lapsing back into the dark. The days of tiptoeing around her were mostly over, but sometimes Poppy's eyes would go lifeless, as if her soul had departed and was wafting away. Hudson had been a new tether, his arrival improving both their lives beyond measure after losing their mum – even if it magnified her absence knowing he'd never experience the wonders of a doting grandmother.

'There are three other people here for the retreat,' she said with as much brightness as she could muster. 'I think only two are really here to write though,' she added, then went on to describe Simone, her rainbow outfit and her publishing deal. Then she switched to full gossip mode to explain everything she suspected about Jamie and Alice.

'I'm pretty sure they already know each other,' she finished. 'I haven't worked it out yet, but there's something weird going on there, I just know it.'

'Gosh, this is more entertaining than the book I'm reading.'

'Well, that's all I have to share. I'd like to go have a shower, crawl back into bed and read more of this book,' Beth said through a yawn.

'Okay, okay, I'll leave you alone.' She paused. 'Thank you, Beth. I . . .'

'I know, I know. It's okay. I'll talk to you tomorrow. Give Hudson a kiss for me.'

'I always do.'

Beth collected her things for a shower. The bathroom was beyond Jamie's door on the opposite side. Light spilled from his room as she quietly stepped past. Was he hunched over his laptop writing, his hair flopped forward across his brow? Or maybe on the floor, shirtless, working his way through a million push-ups? She shook her head. Maybe it was best she didn't even try to imagine.

Light cream tiles filled the large bathroom from floor to walls and the black tapware gave the room an expensive elegance. Moisture still clung to the corners along with a warm, spicy scent. Images of a naked Jamie showering in this spot not long ago invaded her mind; clearly this was not going to be the same as sharing a bathroom with her dad.

When the hot water splashed against her skin, Beth forgot all about Jamie. For the first time in a while she enjoyed having this time to herself without worrying about Hudson. Instead she could stand under the shower until her fingers resembled pink prunes.

Beth slipped on her usual night attire – singlet and track pants – then stepped out of the bathroom, just as Jamie flung open his door.

His sleepwear left nothing to the imagination. Shorts. He wore only shorts. Tiny black workout shorts. Maybe he'd only thrown them on? Maybe he preferred to sleep naked? Or had he been doing those push-ups, just as she'd imagined?

Sculptured muscles caught the light, bouncing off the firm silky skin over his six-pack. Dark curls gathered at the waist-band. Her eyes felt like they were burning, unable to process this real-life image – which was ridiculous, because being a physio and growing up in a football club she'd seen her fair share of muscles and naked flesh. Was this a hormonal issue leftover from giving birth?

'Hey,' he said. 'Started the book yet?'

Beth focused on his face, but that was just as distracting as the rest of him.

'Yes,' she said, trying to remain calm. She'd had years of practice hiding her emotions behind her scarred face, like a constant shield. 'It's good so far,' she admitted.

'Cool.'

She felt his gaze give her the once-over, his right eyebrow cocked for a moment before he nodded towards the kitchen.

'I'm going to fill up my bottle.' He was in fact holding a large metal water bottle. 'See you in the morning.'

Then he left. He may also have winked but Beth wasn't sure. It felt like her eyes were playing tricks on her.

*Bloody hell.*

Thumping her door shut, she scooted back into bed and picked up the book. The distraction of the story helped quell her nerves about tomorrow. Beth had never been brilliant at acting, never picked for the school play unless it was to be a tree or another non-speaking part. By Year Seven they'd placed her behind the curtains, either operating them or helping with costume changes or set design. So how in the hell was she supposed to act like she was an aspiring author? She clearly had no qualifications.

A set of abs appeared in her mind. Okay, maybe the flutter was not all worry about tomorrow but the unsettling naked body belonging to the man next door. She didn't want to find him attractive, history had proved caddish behaviour and shallowness thrived in attractive men. Maybe she should thank him for that; any thoughts stuck on him meant not thinking about Jan and what Beth had to do tomorrow. She pressed her finger and thumb into her eyes as the niggle at the base of her skull grew like tendrils, waiting to slither through and overwhelm her, threatening her calm. Okay, she wasn't really calm but the only thing that could distract her from all these thoughts was the book.

*Read the book, Beth!*

Finding her mark, she did just that.

# 7

## Simone

THE BLOCK OF CHOCOLATE WAS CALLING TO HER. SIMONE opened the packet of dark salted-caramel and stared at it. It was a constant war to fight the desire to eat. Especially when emotion was attached to it. She squeezed her eyes shut and tried to imagine that skinny woman in her yellow dress, waited for the anger to come, felt it squeeze at her heart until it overtook the longing to taste the sweet chocolate. Teeth clenching, she opened her eyes and shoved the chocolate back into the side drawer.

*Tomorrow you can have one square after a thirty-minute jog.*

Her phone lit up, vibrating on the bed, but she ignored it. Instead she pulled the towel off her head, dumping it onto the carpet before shaking out her damp tresses. The room, which she'd nicknamed the grey box, had cloudy tones throughout from the floor, walls and bedspread. The only other colour was white, which highlighted the furniture, architraves, and the extra pillows and throw rug. Simone sighed as she looked around. She was done with dull.

Her phone rang again, and this time she didn't bother to look. 'Not now, Mum,' she muttered as the phone rang out.

At nearly twenty-seven she hated the fact that the most calls she received were from her mother. Again, it rang, like a persistent reversing truck. Cecilia's face took up the whole screen: the bottom half by her jowls and the top by the heavy bags under her eyes.

'What, Mum?' Simone snapped, finally answering. She tucked her legs underneath her and screwed up her nose as her excess skin gathered around her waist like a hitched-up dress. At least in her activewear she could tuck it in; high-waisted tights were very forgiving, unlike sleepwear. The reminder of what she had been was a constant, uncomfortable annoyance.

'Don't speak to me like that,' her mum retorted. 'I need to know what that spicy chicken's called that you always ordered from Mr Woo's Chinese. I've got a craving for it.'

Simone rolled her eyes, hating the way her belly groaned.

'It was number sixteen.'

'Thank you. Was that so hard? Oh, by the way, there's a bad smell coming from the laundry. I need you to have a look when you get home. When will you be home?' Cecilia asked.

Simone reined in her sigh. She knew her mother wasn't asking because she was missing her only daughter. She must need something. *Simone, get this. Simone, get that. Simone, empty the bin. Simone, pay the power bill. Simone, I need some money. Simone, is dinner ready?* She'd really started to hate her name, especially the way her mum would screech it in two drawn-out syllables. This book contract was her saving grace. Years of listening to her mother say, 'You owe me' and 'Don't leave me like your rotten father' made her feel stuck, but lately she was doubting she owed her mother anything. She was starting to make a successful business for herself. Finally she could move out of the house she'd grown up in, had shared with her mother for so many years, and if she could just figure out how to make this book a success, it would make her enough money to get her own little place. She felt a brief thrill thinking about it, and refused to let guilt ruin it, like her mother tried to ruin everything.

'I'll be home Monday sometime,' she said, her future freedom so close she could force calm into her voice.

'Can you stop by Woolies on your way? Vanilla Coke is on special – get the two-litre, not the smaller one – and a few other things. I'll send you through a list.'

'Whatever,' Simone said crisply. 'Look, I have to go and get ready for tomorrow. Some of us have to work.'

'Okay. Have fun.'

'It's not fun, Mum. It's work.' Simone hung up.

Straightaway her phone dinged with screenshots of the Woolworths catalogue with items circled. Simone flicked them away and opened her Instagram account. No new followers. *Damn it!*

She really needed to find something extra to keep her public presence growing, she couldn't let it slide now. Images of living with her mum for the rest of her life appeared like a horror movie, the fear gnawing away at her resolve.

*I must make this work.*

Searching through her photos from tonight's meal, she selected the best ones to upload. Then she watched the video she'd made on arrival, showing the house. The sparkles on her nails shimmered in the light as she pressed play again, checking every aspect of her outfit and facial expression. Happy that nothing was out of place, she set about applying filters and adding hashtags before she uploaded it.

She gazed at the photo of her and Jamie at dinner. It was the wrong angle and it showed some lines on the side of her face near her ear, but Jamie looked smoking hot. Her followers would love him! In the end Simone found a filter that hid some of her wrinkles, making them both look fabulous. Her pout was on point. Maybe she should ask him if it was okay to post? But she had asked the group earlier if they minded being on her Instagram page and no one had said otherwise. Quickly her finger pressed the screen. Done.

If this post took off, she'd have to get more photos of Jamie. She wouldn't mind seeing that for herself. He was definitely boyfriend material, and he seemed really sweet, but she wasn't getting any vibes from him. Maybe he was gay? But her followers didn't need to know that. If Jamie was a hit she'd have to get some more photos, maybe even workout videos? Would he allow that? Or would he want to be paid? She could tag his gym, surely he wouldn't mind a bit of free publicity.

Simone's preferred locations for selfies were gyms or river foreshores. And most good-looking blokes didn't mind having their photo taken with her. They loved any excuse to show off their muscles. A flirty smile and a little ego boost went a long way.

Visiting Jamie's gym was now on her to-do list. He'd asked her at dinner if she wanted to come in and try some of their classes. Yoga, stretching, cycling and walking she enjoyed, and Zumba. Dancing was great fun. Losing weight had made exercise so much easier; at first it had been hard but with her food cravings it was essential. Luckily walking had always been a great way to get out of the house and have some time to herself.

Simone sighed and glanced at the ring-bound notebook with its colourful cover and matching pen. Where to start? How to start? She used to read a lot as a kid, using it as an escape, but as her world changed and her mum's demands increased, she'd had no time to read. If she was truthful, the image of her mum reading all day long while shouting commands was probably what put her off. Then when she could afford a phone it became all about social media. A pastime turned into a money earner. She never would have believed it would grow into a book deal.

Vanessa, her publisher, had said to start jotting down bits of her life, childhood memories, anything significant as she went through her transformation. How hard it was to lose the weight and then how her Instagram page had taken off.

Simone squeezed her eyes shut. It sounded so easy, but it wasn't. How on earth was she going to put a spin on it so her book would sell the tens of thousands of copies her publisher was hoping for? She needed the sales, and the money, but she didn't want to tell *her* story. Her childhood wasn't something she wanted to commit to paper, and sure, she'd lost weight but . . . how did she go about picking and choosing what to write? What could she bear to share?

Maybe she could make one up? It seemed to work in the past, why quit now?

With her pen at the ready she stared at the page and then started to doodle a name in the corner.

*Jamie.*

Before she'd lost weight, no boy like him had ever looked her way. All through school she'd been invisible. Sporting a wardrobe of cheap Target T-shirts and tracksuit pants hadn't helped, nor the fact that her parents weren't the type of people to encourage outings; they simply weren't get-up-and-go people. And then her dad left.

As a teenager, the only way to meet boys was to show an interest in sports, to look good or to actually have a social life. Simone never got that chance. It was hard to meet boys but just as hard to find friends, which was why she'd had book friends.

Simone looked up from the page, wondering how Vanessa and the wider world would react to a story about a house-bound kid reading and eating her way through her teenage years. But before the image could take hold she shook her head, straightened her shoulders and refused to continue that thought.

Life was different now. She liked how she looked, and she'd found a way to connect with people. Men noticed her on the street, and she only wore the best clothes and accessories. Any money earned through the sale of her Alive products or her online presence went towards expensive brand-name activewear and designer clothes. People looked at her differently when she strutted past in skinny jeans and tailored shirts – she was no longer invisible. The only way she planned to move was forward.

She drew a heart around Jamie's name. He had no rings on his fingers or tan marks where one might have been. She would ask him tomorrow if he was single; she hadn't wanted to scare him off tonight. Neither Alice nor Beth had asked him either; if anything, those two looked less than impressed by the breathtaking man before them.

Simone wasn't afraid of his hotness; she'd been out with a few good-looking men lately. Keeping them was the problem. She'd made sure not to bring them home, telling them she preferred to spend time at their places. If only she could master this writing business.

With a sigh, she threw the pen and book down and went to the bathroom she was sharing with Alice. As she turned on the blow-dryer, she hoped Alice wasn't going to need a shower anytime soon. The bathroom was still filled with moisture from her shower, the bath mat still a wet mess on the floor. She nudged it away from the vanity so she could stand in front of the mirror. It was a fancy-looking bathroom, classy in white, black and grey, not like their green bathroom at home with the matching green mould on the ceiling. She silently vowed that when she got her own place it would be mould-free and the paint wouldn't be peeling off the walls. Everything would be fresh and new and expensive. And hers.

The bathroom downlights were harsh, showing every fold of loose skin around her waist and under her arms. When the money came through for the book, Simone would seriously look at having surgery to get rid of her excess skin. It made it hard to go all the way with guys, knowing it was contained only by her clothes.

*Ugh.*

She adjusted the band on her spotted flannel pyjamas until the excess skin was held down underneath, invisible, making the rest of her stomach look taunt. With a smile, she resumed drying her hair while studying her other features. Once her hair was dry she set about applying all her creams.

'Hi, Simone. Do you mind if I brush my teeth?'

Alice was at the doorway, toothbrush in hand.

'Yeah, sure. I'm nearly done here.'

Alice was wearing Peter Alexander sleepwear, Simone could tell. She'd seen that black satin set on the website when she was looking for her own during a sale. The Krofts loved a sale. If Simone had to take one thing from her mum, she was happy it was that.

'Wow, that's a nice collection of creams. Are they the ones you sell?' Alice asked as she ran her toothbrush under the water.

Simone felt a prickle of heat; it was always worse under her arms, as if her body remembered how much it used to sweat.

'I, um . . . no, these aren't part of the brand. We don't have much of a selection of the face creams and anti-wrinkle, but I've found these ones are amazing.' She gave Alice a small smile. 'After I lost weight my skin was quite stretched and . . . well, it needed lots of help to regain some elasticity.'

Alice smiled in return as she finished brushing her teeth. 'Sorry, I didn't realise. So you're an, um, Instagram influencer?' she asked.

Simone paused mid stroke. 'Yeah, I guess I am now. I started out selling Alive products after a friend put me onto them. She sold them and signed me up and I used their shakes to help lose weight. As I started to make progress, I posted it on Instagram. I got more and more followers as my weight dropped, and then all of a sudden I had an online business. It was like a snowball effect: the more followers I got, the more people joined Alive. I did a few local radio interviews and then GWN news ran a story. It really exploded when I went on *Sunrise*. People now send me all sorts of stuff for free to endorse and they all love the products from Alive.'

'I've never heard of Alive,' Alice said. 'But you look amazing, so it must be great.'

Simone tried not to wince and plucked up a big smile to cover it as she switched to sales mode. 'It's an Australian company, prides itself on nutritional products that are as close to nature as possible and locally sourced. I've got a pamphlet if you'd like to take a look?' Simone knew she sounded hopeful, but a sale was a sale, and she needed every one.

Alice smiled at her through the mirror. 'I'll have a look tomorrow. Sounds good. Night, Simone.'

In that moment, all Simone wanted was to be Alice. Her poise, her grace. The woman oozed class, the one thing Simone knew she couldn't buy. As the scent of expensive perfume evaporated, Simone decided: she would focus on the collagen powder range for Alice. If she could tap into Alice's wealthy friends, she could build her business exponentially.

Talking about the products was something she knew well, but writing a book . . . not so much.

Simone put the lid back on her face creams and anti-wrinkle gels, looking at the bench overflowing with bottles, hair product and creams. Flicking off the light she padded back to bed, eyeing her writing book with disgust.

On the floor by the bed, two of her suitcases lay open with clothes spilling out. Underneath her Lorna Jane hoodie she spotted the book Vanessa had sent her. Jan's book. Its glossy cover and thick pages took her back to her youth, a connection she didn't like to revisit. But for tonight she would brave it, because reading Jan's book seemed a hell of a lot easier than trying to write one.

Simone grabbed it and settled into bed, trying to ignore the call of the chocolate. She opened the book.

*Chapter One.*

# 8

## Jamie

MAGPIES WARBLED ONLY METRES FROM HIM, UNFAZED AS he crunched his way through his sit-ups on the front verandah. It was still early, the house quiet except for Beth's room. He'd heard her moving about as she creaked open her door and left her room before the sun had come up.

Light was starting to filter through the trees now, with winter gone and spring well on its way towards summer. And yet morning dew hung heavy on the undergrowth, saturating the air with the scent of moss, tree bark and eucalyptus.

After he finished his set, he lay flat along the hard wooden boards of the verandah and let his body and mind relax, drawing in the smells around him and the sounds of birds chattering and swooping from branch to branch, along with the rustle of leaves as the breeze whistled through the trees. As he breathed, moss-covered trunks and rotting jarrah leaves in the undergrowth left a damp mulch taste on his tongue. After a while, he felt as if his body were lifting from the boards and floating through the

treetops as light as a feather. The outdoors had always brought
him a sense of peace. His brothers had always been gung-ho,
never stopping, but Jamie had enjoyed afternoons in the garden
with his mum, helping her weed or plant seedlings. She would
say, 'Listen to the pigeons,' or, 'See that honeyeater,' and make
him lie on the lawn and soak up the afternoon sun. In a way
his mum had taught him about meditation, how to take time
out to just be in the moment. To focus on the senses and free
the mind from all the weight of the world.

He heard Beth's soft footfalls and rolled onto his side,
propping himself up on an elbow as his ears strained to pick
her location. Glancing at his watch, he noted the time. She'd
been gone a good forty-five minutes.

As if his thoughts had brought her to him, Beth burst from
the bushland, a blur of black like a crow flying low through
the greenery.

She changed gears from a jog to a walk, then began to stretch
as she headed towards the house. She hadn't seen him, and he
didn't try to make himself known, content to watch her from
afar. Black tights and a black racerback singlet with a jumper
tied at her waist. Her silky strands swished from a high ponytail.

After she vanished inside, he went for a quick run to get his
heart rate up again. He loved the feeling of his body working
hard, his heart pounding, pushing it as far as he could. A gym
junkie, his brothers called him, but they'd also spent their fair
share of time doing the same – a necessary part of their job,
they said. He never quite understood how they thought it was
any different for him.

'We don't enjoy it like you do, Jay,' Damien had told him.
'It's work.'

It was true, Jamie did enjoy it. He felt invigorated after a workout. He loved being the master of his body, shaping it, taking good care of it. The gym was a way to help others feel the same, and being able to spend his days with like-minded people was ideal. But that was only one side of him. He was his mother's son and had found a well of creativity bursting from within, needing a release, which he'd found through words. Since embracing this newfound avenue it had grown, and was now more of a compulsion. He liked how it balanced his life. One half at full pace, the other slow, imaginative and thought-provoking.

Beth was in the shower when he got back but he didn't have to wait long. Her towel was hanging on the rack and her small blue toiletry bag sat beside the sink. It had been nearly two years since he'd shared a bathroom with a woman. Letisha had never been especially tidy; in a few minutes she could cover a bench in make-up and creams, straightening iron and a blow dryer threatening to topple off the edge.

His heart still squeezed when he thought of her. When would it stop? Sometimes he was hit with longing, other times anger, and then he hated the fact he could still get churned up about her. Especially after all this time. It reminded him of his own failings. It made him feel weak and regretful. Alice was another dark mark, like a small melanoma growing on his skin, only he didn't know how to cut it from his past. Maybe that's what he was doing with his writing? A method to help explore and understand.

The water in the shower didn't get hot enough for his liking but it did the job, and he dressed in his favourite going-out jeans and button-up blue shirt, ready to make an impression on Jan. As he went in search of coffee, his chest vibrated with nervous energy.

Alice was in the dining room, sitting at the table with a coffee and a bowl of muesli. He paused, wondering if he should leave her be. He didn't like the way she shied away from him but he understood why. He wanted to tell her not to be embarrassed . . . it was all in the past. But he just had to figure out how to say it.

'Morning, Alice,' he said as he went straight to the coffee machine on the kitchen bench.

'Hi, Jamie.'

Her reply was a whisper but at least she'd acknowledged him.

When his coffee was made, he sat at the table, leaving a seat between them. Alice twitched a bit but didn't leave, her bowl still half full.

Jamie leaned forward, his arms on the table, hands around his cup of magic. 'So, shall we have a chat and clear the air, or would you rather continue pretending we only just met?' he said softly.

Her eyelashes fluttered as she breathed slowly, then she turned to him, meeting his gaze. She was still as gorgeous as he remembered, in that highly polished and put-together way of hers. Always perfect, always smelling great. But this Alice was different to the one he'd known, certainly not as confident around him as she used to be.

Images of the take-charge woman in his old office assaulted his mind, and then other, more dangerous memories flashed. He closed his eyes so Alice couldn't read them. He didn't want her running off again.

'I'm not trying to avoid you . . . Jamie.'

His name was forced, tacked on at the end.

Alice pushed her long fringe back, her cream silk blouse like liquid as she moved uncomfortably. The rings on her fingers glistened as a warning, but Jamie was not interested in going there; he just wanted to clear the air.

'Good,' he said. 'We don't have to make this awkward. I know it's a shock, but we don't have to repeat mistakes. All I'm asking is that you relax.' He pushed down his own jitters, clasping his hands together to hide the tremble. 'I'd hate to ruin your weekend.'

Her lips curved in a weak smile. 'Thanks. It's not you, it's more me, and . . . well, having to think about the past and the feelings it churns up.' She sighed heavily. 'I wasn't in a good place back then.'

Jamie nodded. 'I think I started to realise that at the end.'

The coffee machine rattled into life and they both jumped. Jamie swung around to see Beth at the machine, pulling a face.

'Sorry, I didn't mean to startle you both. Just chasing my morning fix.'

Her face flushed scarlet – clearly she'd heard more than she needed to of their conversation – before she tipped her head forward, using her hair as a curtain.

Alice was focused back on her breakfast, and he knew their discussion was over. For now.

'Were you planning to have breakfast here, Beth?' he asked, trying to keep his voice light.

'Um, I suppose. Why?' She raised a brow as she brought her coffee to the table and sat between them.

'I'm going to duck out to find a cafe for a hit of smashed avo and bacon. Cereal just doesn't fill me up enough.' Jamie leaned back as his stomach grumbled on cue.

'Oh, that does sound nice.' Beth was eyeing off Alice's cereal, a little unimpressed.

'You're welcome to join me. Beats eating alone.'

Beth glanced at her watch. 'We have over an hour till the first class.' She paused. 'Sure, that'd be a bit of a treat – a real cafe with real food and no screaming children throwing food.'

'Well, I can't guarantee that won't happen,' he said with a smirk, which elicited a smile from Alice and Beth.

Alice's green eyes held his for a moment before dropping down to her breakfast. Had they possibly jumped a small hurdle? He hoped so.

After their coffee, Jamie and Beth climbed into his ute.

'My God, what do you have in that?' he said as he glanced down at the handbag resting at her feet. 'And I thought you'd packed light for the weekend,' he said with a laugh and a shake of his head.

Beth's brow creased. 'I *am* a mum, remember. I have to be ready for any occasion: spew mop-up, poo overflow, changes of clothes, nappies, wipes, toys, teething rusks and spare food for a start.' She opened her bag and pulled out a shirt. 'And that's just for me.' She smirked.

Jamie negotiated the roads to a cafe he'd googled earlier, a grin dancing on his lips.

'My mum had a Mary Poppins bag too. No matter what we needed, she had it.'

'A Mary Poppins bag, I like that. It feels bottomless at times, especially when I'm digging for my car keys. Dad calls it the Tardis.'

'Ha, love it. I think I'd like your dad.'

'Oh, he would love you. That's why I'm not going to mention you at *all*. I'll be hounded about your brothers. I'll never hear the end of it.'

'It wouldn't bother me, I love talking about those two idiots. I wish I saw them more often, but they're settled over east with their families. I miss them.'

'You still have your parents nearby?'

'Yeah, my parents won't leave WA until I'm happily married. Mum's made my happiness her primary mission in life.'

He rolled his eyes as he pulled up at the cafe. 'I love her to bits but she has a big romantic interfering heart.'

He got out, and as he watched Beth close her door, a thought hit him. He didn't realise he was frowning until Beth spoke quietly.

'You okay?'

He looked up at her. 'Yeah, sorry. Miles away.'

'Boring company?' she added with a hint of amusement.

'Never,' he replied, shooting her a smile. As they stepped into the cafe, he bent down to her ear to speak over the noise inside. 'I was just realising that you're the first woman I've had in my ute since my last girlfriend.'

Those eyebrows shot up again. He couldn't tell if she was concerned or shocked at what he'd said.

'Is that like, since last week?' she remarked.

He threw his head back and laughed. 'No, it's been about two years.' He shrugged. 'Probably too long.'

He scratched his fingers through the faint stubble as he followed Beth to a nearby table.

'I'm probably not one to comment,' she said as they sat. 'But I'd think it takes as long as it needs. Better than rushing into something you're not ready for.'

'I didn't know you were a counsellor *and* a physio,' he said playfully.

'It's a bit like being a hairdresser or a barman, the jobs go hand in hand,' she said with a smirk.

'Can I take your order?' asked the waitress before Jamie could reply.

As they waited for their eggs and smashed avo on sourdough, both with a side of bacon, they fell into a comfortable silence, just listening and watching the bustle of the cafe, until Beth suddenly yawned then slapped her hand over her mouth.

'Sorry,' she said, then added with a smile, her scar pulling a little at her lips, 'That's actually your fault.'

'What did I do?' Jamie feigned indignation.

'I got halfway through that book last night. Couldn't put it down until nearly midnight. I haven't been that absorbed by a book in years.'

'Oh, great,' he said, feeling his smile broaden. 'I was hoping you'd enjoy it.'

Their breakfast arrived quickly, considering the tables were all occupied.

'This is *so good*,' Beth said through a mouthful.

She didn't seem to care that he was watching her eat. She didn't try to take baby bites or be dainty as she used the last bit of her bread to mop up her egg.

'What?'

'My dad does the same thing,' he said, nodding towards her plate with a smile.

'I think I'd like your dad,' she said.

'And I think he'd like you too.' It was true, he would. 'I've never—' Jamie stopped himself before he said what was in his mind: that he was yet to bring home a girlfriend who was really into footy, not just humouring him. Then he realised the implication and clamped his mouth shut.

'You've never what?' she asked, watching him intently as he internally squirmed.

'Oh, nothing.' He glanced at his watch with forced casualness. 'We better head back and get ready.'

Beth shot him a wary look. 'Ugh, do we have to? I mean, I'm just so nervous,' she added quickly.

Jamie's brow creased. Beth flitted between suspicion and . . . well, something else he couldn't put his finger on. What was she hiding? He cleared his throat. 'It won't be that bad. Relax. Jan is just like everyone else.'

Beth's eyes shone with a ferocity that made him lean back. Long eyelashes blinked and he saw the emotion fade, but not completely. Had he done something?

She tilted her head. 'I hope you're right.'

He followed her out to his car and they drove back in a strained, uncomfortable silence.

'Thanks for the ride,' she said, opening the door. Then she paused and patted the dash, throwing him a look that would have set him on his arse if he wasn't already sitting. 'Two years, hey. Interesting.'

She smiled before walking back to the house, shoulders square, strides long.

*Interesting indeed.*

# 9

## *Beth*

INSIDE THE FORMAL DINING ROOM, THE TABLE HAD BEEN set with jugs of water and glasses. A bowl of mints sat in the centre, and sheets of paper were placed neatly in four spots on the table. At the end a screen had been set up opposite a projector. Beth pulled out a chair and sat beside Jamie.

Alice and Simone were already seated in the remaining chairs opposite them.

Alice clapped her hands. 'Wonderful,' she said brightly. 'I can't wait to get started.' She picked up the sheet in front of her.

Beth's teeth ached, her skin feeling clammy. Simone was twitching on her seat, but Jamie seemed intent on ignoring her blatant attempts to get his attention. He was busy scribbling something on the notepad. Not that she could read it, he was protecting it like a footballer mid pack holding the red Sherrin to his chest.

Alice continued, rattling off Jan's bio from the sheet in her hands.

'Jan Goldstein, born in Perth in 1951, is one of Australia's favourite authors, capturing the imagination of the huge general fiction audience. Her books are regularly shortlisted for the Best General Fiction in the Australian Book Industry Awards, and her first novel, *Everything You Never Told Me*, went on to sell over one million copies worldwide, and was translated into many languages. Her second book, *The Hidden Life of Adeline*, debuted at number three on the *New York Times* Bestseller list. Jan hosts a series of retreats that are highly regarded by the industry and many of her students are enjoying publishing success.' Alice beamed at them. 'Did you hear that! I wonder if one of us will make it?'

'Anything is possible with hard work.'

Beth snapped her head to the left so fast she might have given herself whiplash. She'd seen Jan's photo of course, it was on the back of her book and in the pamphlet, yet now it was like seeing her for the first time. Though not especially tall, she was an imposing figure, well-dressed in black trousers, black shirt and a charcoal jacket. Her white hair reminded Beth of the wig worn by Sia, but Jan's fringe was cut high above her eyebrows. Her hair was short at the back and longer towards the front, level with her chin. Her lips were painted with the brightest red lipstick Beth had ever seen on anyone over the age of forty.

Vibrant green eyes flicked around the room, giving her face a brightness to offset the harshness of her lines. She was nearly seventy. There was no smile, no obvious emotion, just a concrete expression. It gave Beth more reason to dislike her. Jamie shot her a frown as she squirmed uncomfortably, her anger simmering under her skin like a menopausal flush. Were her cheeks as hot as she felt? Jamie poured some water into her glass. 'Thank you' she mouthed before gulping it down.

'Good morning everyone,' Jan began as she took her position at the head of the table but remained standing. 'It's lovely to be here. Let's start with an introduction so I can get to know you all. Your name, and a bit about why you're here and what you hope to achieve.'

Jan's voice was a deep rasp that matched her hard-edge vibe. A bent bony finger pointed at Beth and she felt all eyes flick to her. She swallowed and glanced down. Heat flushed her skin again.

'Um, hi. I'm Beth. I'm here to get better at writing.'

Jan raised an eyebrow, as if Beth's answer was barely a pass but because it was the first day of class she would let it go. To her relief, everyone else's answers were much the same.

'It can only get better,' Jan said once everyone had mumbled out their brief introduction. 'Hopefully I can inspire you all to live and breathe writing, to be passionate and eager.'

Beth almost scoffed. *What a load of rubbish.*

'Okay, on to the slides.' Jan motioned to the screen and pressed a button on a tiny remote.

'You would have all read my bio by now, so I'll cut straight to the program for this weekend. This course will provide you with the tools to show emotion in your characters and evoke emotion in your readers.'

The screen turned blue with the words 'Getting Started' in white across the centre.

'We will work through overcoming obstacles like fear. Fear of a blank page, fear of rejection, fear of putting yourself on the page and having to share that with the world. I will show you techniques to stay motivated, to be dedicated and to finish.'

Jan's face remained emotionless, like a stern headmistress reading the school rules, quite a juxtaposition to the woman supposedly teaching 'emotion'. Beth was sure the others would share her sentiments if they knew. Should she tell them? They were engaged, watching Jan like an understudy would the lead. Would it be cruel to sever that? Or would it be cruel to keep the illusion? There was a weight pressing against her chest, it had been there since she'd arrived. If she was honest, it was the weight of Poppy, not wanting to let her down and now these three others were another brick. Even though she didn't really know them she couldn't help worrying about them too.

'Next, we will work on story and plot, but as this workshop is not focused on fiction, I'll keep it brief. I will spend time with each of you individually as we progress so we can discuss your current works.' Her thin arm pointed to the projector and she clicked the remote. 'Emotional writing,' she boomed, causing everyone to flinch.

Did Jan's lip just quiver? Did she take great delight in getting the reaction she hoped? The room became noisy with movement: Alice clicked her pen, writing down the headings; Simone sat up quickly and blinked as if only just noticing the screen; Jamie coughed to hide an involuntary squeak, while Beth had hit the underside of the table with her knees.

'Emotional writing is what we will focus on. I will be mining your feelings.'

Beth pressed her lips together, her eyes smarting. 'We will delve into the theory behind it all, how to capture emotion on the page, which every story needs whether it's a work of fiction or a biography. As a writer, you want to evoke emotion from your characters as well as the reader.'

'Be prepared for hard work' popped up on the screen but Beth was busy watching Jan. Her movements were minimal; nothing was jerky or erratic. What was going through Jan's mind right now? Just the presentation or other cunning things?

'And also if we have time I might cover the importance of self-editing.'

Jan leaned back on a heel, striking a pose. 'I want you all to be relaxed through these exercises, let go and let your words flow. Do not expect to write perfectly from the beginning. Most of you will write quite badly at first. Let it be bad. Don't aim for perfection or you will just find yourself with writer's block.' She turned, not quite giving them her back, and pointed to the words. *Just Write!*

'I've seen so many people get bogged down through trying to make their first draft a final draft. Let me be clear, there will be many drafts. Three, five, ten, even more. Structural edits, copy edits. You will have plenty of time to go back over your work and polish it so *please* think of the first draft as the rough bones. At this point, it's important to just get your story on the page. Give your mind the freedom it needs to create without all the editing noise.

'Has anyone here sent anything off to a publisher yet?'

She stared them down, waiting for any little morsels to be coughed up. No hands moved but all eyes darted around the room.

'I'm getting close to sending something,' said Alice.

'Good. Be prepared for rejection. You will need to overcome the fear of sending your work out into the big wide world of criticism. Rejection doesn't mean the work is bad, it can mean wrong timing, wrong genre, wrong publisher . . . so many variables. Keep trying. I always say that a rejection can be helpful if it draws attention to what needs improving – your plot, your characters; you can always put the feedback to good use.'

Simone put up her hand. Jan gave her a curt nod.

'Were you rejected?'

'No,' she said quickly, then her lips pursed as if disagreeing with her answer. 'Although if I'm honest, my fourth book was rejected.'

Eyes boggled at this new information.

'How can that be when you're already published?' asked Jamie.

'There are no guarantees. If your work isn't up to scratch, it will get rejected. No matter how many books you've written.'

Jamie opened his mouth again, but Jan tuned back to the screen and pressed her clicker.

'Be disciplined, set targets and stick to them.'

Jan continued bringing up screen after screen of helpful information.

Beth jotted down notes, just so she looked like the others in the room who were madly scribbling. Often she would find herself staring at Jan, waiting for the cracks to show, but her demeanour didn't sway from professional and poised for the whole two hours.

'If you want to write a strong, moving piece you must make your readers *feel*. Emotion is complex. We never experience a single, isolated emotion. Instead, they wash through us, continually changing, each with many layers of conflicting thoughts and feelings.'

Jan scanned the room and then pointed at Simone. 'What was your name again?'

Simone sat up and quivered like an excited puppy. 'Simone.'

'Would you like to read this out, please?'

Being singled out put a smile on Simone's face as she obliged.

'Amy finds racy pink underwear, which isn't hers, down the gap in their couch.' Simone glanced around the room. 'Ooh laa laa.'

'I want you all to list the emotions that Amy might feel and express. Dig deep and think of the unexpected. You might show emotion, like the clenching of fists to show anger, but you haven't made your reader feel anything. You need to elicit an emotional response and you can do that through your characters thoughts. Now have a go, write down what you can in a few minutes.'

Pen in hand, Beth thought hard about Amy. Poor Amy, was she married or just dating? Did she have a husband or a wife? Beth smiled as she enjoyed trying to think outside the square. She jotted down her thoughts then spotted Jan wringing her hands with a sly smirk. Indignation boiled in her blood, flipping her mood like a switch. Her pen scratched across the page, over her words and thoughts, until the ink blobbed and the paper tore through. Her hand was shaking.

*There's emotion for you, Jan.*

How visceral her reaction, from enjoying the task Jan had set only to realise she'd probably been played like a fiddle. Groomed for what Jan wanted and needed.

'What emotions did you come up with, Simone?' Jan asked.

Simone beamed and gave her examples.

Beth wondered if Simone's was the only name Jan could remember.

Jamie stuttered out a few words, followed by Alice, but Beth remained defiant.

'Good. Here are a few more.'

The screen filled up with words. Beth tried not to, but automatically she read through the list. It felt like she'd be betraying Poppy if she participated in any way. Her loyalty was with her sister, first and foremost.

Next Jan asked them each to relate a story to the group. 'Any story. It could be something you heard from a friend that caught your interest, sad news, or something that happened at home that you thought quite funny. Don't feel embarrassed, we're all here to learn, so be kind.'

Beth flinched at Jan's words. *Be kind!* It was hard not to feel the burning anger shoot up her throat, and it took all her self-control not to throw daggers at the woman who had hurt Poppy. *Who had hurt them all.*

Alice put up her hand. 'I'll have a go. Last week my six-year-old son had snuck into the pantry.' She hunched her shoulders as if she was creeping up behind him. 'I crept closer, ready to give him a scare and a stern talking to because I knew he was after the icing sugar in the cupboard as he'd seen it go on the top of the cakes I've made. "Abe!" I yelled, causing him to spin around. He knew he was in trouble; his eyes were huge but defiant. He held a hand full of powder in his hand. We both stared at it. "Don't even think about it," I said. Then he shoved the handful right into his mouth.' Alice laughed. 'You should have seen his face – he had plain flour not icing sugar. He started to cough and tears ran out his eyes in confusion while trying to spit it all out. I think he learnt his lesson,' she finished with a grin.

'Good,' said Jan. 'Alice, you pulled me in with the humour.' Jan turned to Beth, her face expectant.

*Oh great.* Beth needed a story, but what? 'I can't think of anything worth sharing,' she said honestly. 'No one wants to hear about my son teething.'

'That's true,' said Jan matter-of-factly. 'But what if you said one day your son had started to choke on a teething ring? He started turning blue and you couldn't get it out of his mouth. And your phone was misplaced and you couldn't remember where you left it and your car had a flat tyre that you still hadn't got fixed. Your son is turning bluer and struggling for air. You scream for help and run around the house with him struggling in your arms but no one hears you.'

Beth felt her heart race as if Hudson were truly in this predicament, already feeling the panic work its way under her skin. Jan had just recounted every mother's fear.

'Do you feel that sudden involvement? The emotions? What is she going to do? What would you do in this moment? You can take a simple story and heighten it – don't make it easy for your characters, embellish. Maybe in real life you'd have the phone in your pocket, but who says that has to happen? *You* are the creator. Raise the stakes, force the reader to squirm. No one wants to read a boring, everyday story. We all want something engaging.'

They all nodded.

'Now, let's put some of these new skills to the test. I'm going to give you three words and I want you to create a story with them,' Jan instructed. 'I want you to grab the reader's attention, make them sit up and want to read on. The words are: guts, razor and salesman. Go.'

Alice and Jamie set to the task with vigour while Simone met Beth's eyes, and Beth sensed that she also wished she were anywhere else. But reluctantly they both managed to scribble something down. Beth thought about the words . . . What came to mind was a salesman with a big gut, but she dismissed that as nowhere near interesting enough. Unless a razor fell out of his bag at work? Beth smiled and jotted her thoughts down. Time went fast, and no sooner had Beth got to the bottom of her page than Jan was calling a halt.

'Would anyone like to read what they wrote?'

No one put up their hand.

'It's good to share,' Jan encouraged. 'It helps others to see a different viewpoint as well as learning from you. Please think about sharing. Later I could read some out anonymously, if you're all okay with that?'

Beth watched her carefully as she spoke, wondering if this was Jan's routine of grooming them for what she needed. Little nudges in the right direction so she could take the best bits.

'Okay, for the last exercise before we break, I'd like you to dig deep into your emotions. Writing is about connecting the reader to your story, and the best way to do that is through . . .'

'Emotion,' replied Jamie, Simone and Alice eagerly.

Beth dropped her head so no one would see her eyes roll. Jamie and Alice were like the top of the class kids, out to impress the teacher with their straight backs and smiles. Simone was watching them like a happy puppy, almost bouncing in her chair, wanting to fit in with the cool crowd.

'Yes, emotion. If you cry while writing your words, I can nearly guarantee that you'll make your reader cry. If you laugh, they will laugh. And to draw the best emotion from you I'd like you to write a piece that is deeply moving.' Jan paused for effect.

'When I say deeply moving, I mean your big, deep, dark secrets. Things you've thought but never voiced. I've run some journal-writing courses for grief counselling and you'd be amazed at the emotion in those pages as well as the relief it gives the writer. If you attempt this exercise honestly, you'll be rewarded with wonderful results. This retreat is a safe haven; nothing leaves these walls. When you've written your piece you can email it to me and I'll critique them for you. Everything is confidential.'

Jan paused, letting these last words sink in. It was almost as if she expected them to be humbled by what she was offering them. A personal critique by Jan Goldstein. Beth clutched her glass, gulping water to hide her involuntary scowl. She glanced at Jamie. He was watching her, frowning.

'And if I have your permission, I'd love to read out some snippets, all anonymous of course. There's a level of trust involved, but that's what writing is about. You are putting your heart and soul into your words and then letting others read them. You have to be brave. So this is a start, a way to push you out of your comfort zone and tap into the deep emotions you all have within you.'

Eyes shot around the room. Alice was chewing on her bottom lip uncertainly; Simone was a translucent white, which was amazing under that fake tan, and Jamie seemed guarded. Beth found him the hardest to read, probably because of his perfect lips and cheekbones, or those distracting eyes of his. *Don't be fooled again by a handsome face.*

Beth angled her body away from him, even if that meant it was towards Jan.

'So, you have until two this afternoon to write me something amazing and personal. Dig deep and let that emotion spill out onto the page. Good luck.

'The instructions on how to connect to the wi-fi printer are on the table. Also, remember not to put your name on it, that way not even I'll know who it's from so it's completely anonymous. I think you'll be surprised at what this will unearth.'

And with that Jan left the room.

As Beth stood, a shiver ran up her spine. Nothing about this was right.

'Well, that was interesting,' said Jamie, turning to her. 'What did you think?'

Beth chose her words carefully. 'It was fun trying to write something with the words she gave us.' *What a load of baloney,* was what she wanted to say. Except so much of Jan's lesson had been eye-opening, and if Beth had been a writer, no doubt it all would have been helpful. The glow on the others' faces was enough to tell her they'd all been inspired. Alice had dropped her wall and was chatting excitedly to Simone, and Jamie's eyes sparkled like something heavy was starting to shift.

'Are you going to write something *amazing and personal?*' she asked him, trying to keep the derision out of her voice. '*Dig deep and let that emotion spill out onto the page?*'

Alice and Simone paused next to them, keen on his reply.

'Yeah, why not? This is what we're here for, to dig deep. And emotion is the heart of a book. I think Jan has a point. Trying to draw out our own emotions through personal experience is a great way to add it into our writing. The same as an actor will wallow in a sad memory to make themselves cry on cue.'

'That's so true,' said Alice, nodding at him, her smile relaxed.

Beth felt that zap of familiarity run between them as they glanced at each other. She wasn't making it up, something was there. Especially after the deep conversation she'd interrupted this morning. Twitchy legs shuffled on the spot; suddenly she was annoyed at everything.

'That makes sense. I'm not writing fiction, but I get how it's still relevant. I can still bring emotion to my words.' Alice tapped her pen against her lips.

'I was reading Jan's book last night,' said Simone, 'and I was bawling my eyes out at that crash scene.'

Beth's jaw clenched and she resisted the urge to touch her scars. Any talk of crashes made her nauseous, even now.

'I'm keen to go get something down, so I'm going to make a start,' Jamie said. 'Meet you all back in the kitchen for lunch around one, give us two good hours to write?'

'Sure,' said Simone with a huge smile.

'Good plan,' said Alice, meeting his gaze.

Beth noticed the peace offering. Perhaps their earlier conversation in the kitchen had eased tensions as Alice was certainly more relaxed around him.

It had answered one question but thrown up so many more. How did they know each other and why was it strained? The idea that they'd secretly used this retreat to meet up for an affair didn't fit now. Beth suppressed a laugh at the way her mind was working – maybe she was cut out to write a whodunnit!

Her mum had always said she was unusually attuned to what was happening around her.

'Beth?'

Jamie was staring at her, a bemused smile on his face.

'Oh, sorry, what?'

'Let's go write some magic,' he said.

'Ah yeah, let's,' she agreed, trying to find some enthusiasm to match Jamie. Content with her reply, he left for his room.

Alice and Simone headed for the stairs.

Beth checked her phone and found more photos of Hudson, eating breakfast, food in his short curls, one with him kissing his grandfather goodbye as he left for work and one on the floor with his toys. She dialled Poppy's phone as she headed to her room. Jamie's door was ajar, he was at his desk, laptop out and fingers typing away already.

The phone rang twice before Poppy answered. She didn't bother with niceties.

'Tell me everything!' she demanded.

# 10

## Simone

SIMONE HAD TAKEN NOTES THROUGH JAN'S PRESENTATION, and slowly it had made sense. All the books she'd read growing up had taught her as much and she felt confident she could have a go at writing a piece of fiction. If only that's what she'd been contracted to do.

She opened her laptop and started to transcribe her notes. On her phone with two thumbs she could probably out-type her fellow participants, but getting all her fingers to cooperate at once on a keyboard was harder. There was never much to say in her social media posts, her photos did most of the talking, but this was different.

Simone typed her notes up before she began to think about what Jan had requested from them. Something with real emotion. Should she write about being bullied as a child and teenager? It would be something to put in her book at least. She'd prefer to share that rather than the rest of the truth.

Simone lay back on her pillows and closed her eyes as she let her mind wander to the schoolyard.

'Here comes Cartman,' yelled Josh. 'Clear the way!'

Attention from the hottest boy in Year Six would usually be welcome, but not this kind of attention. She crossed her arms as she walked down the hall, her backpack pulling heavily on her shoulders with all the books she'd picked up from the library. More like waddled down the hall, as Josh said, just like Cartman from *South Park*.

Josh flicked at her beanie as she passed, his laughter ringing out down the narrow corridor. The only reason she wore the beanie, beside the weather being cold, was because it helped hide her oily, limp hair.

At least she didn't have to walk home today. Mum said she'd be waiting with the car and they'd go do their fortnightly shop. It was Simone's favourite day, not having to walk the fifteen minutes home, and shopping with the hope of some treats.

Outside the school, Simone waited by the kerb for ten minutes before the familiar white Ford Festiva pulled up. Everyone else had gone and there was only the odd teacher heading to their car.

'Come on, get in. We haven't got all day.'

She tried to shove her bag in the foot well, but it was a tight fit so she had to lurch it over onto the back seat. They drove to the closest Woolworths, next to Target.

'Mum, can I get a new jumper, please?' she asked hopefully, her fingers crossed in her lap.

'There's nothing wrong with the one you have on,' said Cecilia, without even looking at her.

'It's too small,' she pleaded. The plain red jumper clung to every lump and bump. She hated free dress day. Although the uniform wasn't any better; it was hard to find second-hand ones in her size.

'We don't have the money.'

Simone frowned. 'Could we try the op shop?'

Sometimes she could find brand-name clothes for a few dollars. A month ago she'd found some hot-pink jelly sandals. They were two sizes too big but the cool girls wore them, so Simone had begged her mum. The fact that she could grow into them and they would last years was probably the only reason her mum let her have them.

She'd felt amazing the first day she'd worn them to school; she'd come home with a collection of blisters and then had to wear the sandals with socks, but it had been like putting on a red cape and finding a superpower. Tanya, almost one of the popular girls, had commented on her nice shoes, and Simone had floated through class on a high.

'If we have time,' Cecilia mumbled.

Simone wasn't allowed to push the trolley; her mum draped herself over it like an old lady with a Zimmer frame.

'Grab that twenty-four pack of Coke. Actually, grab two while it's on special,' she ordered.

Simone struggled to lift the box of cans into the trolley.

'Get four loaves of the white bread, and those bacon-and-cheese buns.'

Simone threw in packets of chips, toilet paper, jars of peanut butter and jam, mince, milk and biscuits as her mum directed.

'Oh, Tim Tams are on special, grab some of them.'

'Can we get some Shortbread Creams?' Simone asked, her favourites. 'They're two for one.'

Her mum nodded, never able to pass up a special. Simone hid her smile as she placed the packets into the trolley.

'Hi Cecilia, hi Simone. Shopping day?'

Simone beamed at Nora, their neighbour from across the road. She was a tall skinny lady with salon-curled hair. Mum called her Nosy Nora, said she was always looking over the fence watching everyone with her dark beady eyes. Mum didn't like her at all, but Simone loved the way Nora always waved and said hello to her in a cheery voice. Sometimes seeing Nora was the best part of her day.

'Harry back yet?' Nora asked.

Simone's ears picked up at the mention of her father.

'No, maybe next week,' Cecilia replied 'He's out in red-dirt country driving a truck. He's loving it.'

Her voice had gone up an octave and she was smiling. Her mum rarely smiled.

Simone wondered excitedly if her dad was coming home next week. He was supposed to be home last week, which was what her mum had told the woman in the second-hand bookshop, that he was finishing up his job on the seafood boat.

It had been exactly five months since she'd seen her dad. Simone hadn't heard from him – no phone calls, no cards. He'd missed her eleventh birthday. If she ever asked her mum, she got the same answer. 'He's off trying to find work. Stop asking me; he'll turn up when he can.'

'I see,' said Nora, cocking her head sideways.

'Right, well, happy shopping,' she said, continuing down the aisle.

Her mum muttered something under her breath, but Simone couldn't make it out. She thought about slipping some Froot Loops into the trolley, but her mum would probably eat them all in front of her as punishment. Instead she was told to get Rice Bubbles.

'Don't forget the conditioner, Mum,' Simone said.

Cecilia had short spiky hair that she cut herself to save money. She hardly ever washed it, but Simone needed to wash hers every week to stop it from looking greasy, and because she wanted it to be more like Tanya's: perfectly straight and a blonde that shone like gold in the sunlight. Tanya was popular and nice – well, nicer than the others.

'Get the two-in-one brand, you know the one.'

'But Mum, it's not as good. I need the separate conditioner to make my hair silky.'

'It's not going to make it silky – you're hair's as coarse as a rat's-nest, Simmy. Nothing will fix that.'

Simone waited until her mum had turned away before she pulled a face, then she picked up a bottle of their usual stuff and threw it into the trolley. It wasn't fair, she never got to have anything she wanted. All the other kids had fancy clothes and cool bags. Their parents would pick them up from school on time every day and hug them when they walked out the gate. Simone couldn't even get hair conditioner.

Up and down the aisles they went, Simone slapping her feet heavily in her sullen mood while her mum searched for specials. Finally they headed to the checkout, then back to the car. Simone liked it better when her dad was home; he did all the heavy lifting that now she had to do. Her mum had a bad back, and her legs ached as well.

'Good girl, Simmy. Drop them into the kitchen and I'll go through it.' Cecilia liked to stack all the food away herself once they were home. 'You can pop these in the bathroom and go do your homework,' she added.

Simone knew she wanted to hide away some of the chips and chocolate in her bedroom. Sometimes her school snacks would disappear too and she'd be left with just a peanut-butter sandwich for lunch. But her mum never kept count of the Cokes, so Simone could sneak one every now and then. Especially when she bought so many. Dad used to have his beer stacked alongside the Coke; now the spot seemed empty. It made her miss him.

She sulked off to her bedroom, kicking aside the old books, magazines and discarded clothes along the passageway. Her room was a dull yellow like rotting banana, and the carpet brown. It was like living in a shoe box – her bed was pushed against the wall to make room for a desk her dad had found at an op shop; it was fake wood with stains. A set of cream drawers sat the end of the bed against the wall, the bottom drawer out on the floor, its front broken with her clothes piled over it and onto the floor. It had been like that for a year. The only colour came from the school artwork she'd stuck on her walls and some of the stickers she'd collected.

She upended her school bag onto the floor and reached for the closest *Sweet Valley High* book. This one had a pink cover and was titled *Outcast*.

*That's fitting.*

From under her bed she pulled out a couple of biscuits from the packet and flopped onto her unmade bed, shoes and all, and settled in. It was a good hour of uninterrupted reading before her mum was yelling from her room.

'Simmy? Simmy? Can you get some spuds on for dinner?'

It was asked as a question but she knew it was a demand. Simone dragged herself from her bed and lingered by her mum's door. Her room wasn't much different, apart from a double bed and a big wardrobe. Cecilia was propped up on pillows, book in hand, and there were three more on the bedside table, along with her various medications. More books were scattered across the floor amid clothes, though none of her dad's. Simone had checked. She couldn't understand why he needed to take all his clothes, but then again he only wore the same couple of pairs of worn jeans and blue, grease-stained work shirts. The smell of fuel and grease was a scent she never thought she'd miss, but she did. Her dad used to work at a local mechanic shop. She remembered snuggling up on his knee and he'd tell her how a carburettor worked, or the pistons. Not that she understood it, she just loved the sound of his voice and the way his chest moved against her back as he spoke. His stained nails and grease-etched hands would mould shapes in front of her, as if he were building a motor right there on her lap. It didn't make sense that he was up north looking for different work.

'Three potatoes?'

Her mum nodded. 'I'll be out in a minute to start on the sausages.'

Sometimes Simone had to help her mum off the bed but most times she managed. Dad being gone had changed her – she was always grumpy and seemed to take it out on Simone. Nothing made her happy these days, unless it was a Coke sale or finding new books at the library.

Simone had the potatoes cut up when her mum appeared, her spiky hair stuck flat at the back from the pillows. Cecilia turned on the TV that sat on the kitchen bench, ready for them to watch *Neighbours* then *Home and Away*.

Most nights they had meat and three veg. Or pasta – their favourite was a bacon Alfredo and Simone loved taking the leftovers for school lunch. Even cold it was delicious.

'Mum, can we please try the op shop tomorrow?' It wasn't far away, maybe she'd let her go by herself. 'I really want to try to find some jeans, everyone's wearing them.' And a cute top. Something better than her plain blue or green tent T-shirts.

'It won't make you popular,' Cecilia retorted. 'You have to be rich or pretty to be popular.'

Simone twisted the bottom of her jumper, staring down into the potatoes. Her mother's hurtful words felt like a kid pointing and laughing, or stealing her beanie or slapping her books from her hands. Her dad always called her princess, yet her mum seemed to love pointing out all Simone's flaws. Just once, couldn't she try to be on her side? Rub her back and make her feel better like she'd seen other parents do. 'Still, I want to try. I might find a cheap jumper that fits.'

'Just you wait, that optimism will die off.' Cecilia rolled her eyes as she put frozen beans into a pot. 'You can go, but you're walking. Driving the car today has set off my back, I need time to recover.'

'I don't mind walking,' Simone said, trying to contain her excitement.

'Don't you boil them potatoes dry,' her mother warned. 'You'll never keep a man if you can't cook.'

# 11

## *Alice*

ALICE HAD WRITTEN SOME EMOTIONAL WORDS FOR HER book, knowing she had to put it all on the page if she was to be honest about her journey. It was hard, and she wondered if some would have to stay inside her, buried deep. There were days she thought about the things she had done and the mistakes she had made, and on those days she hated the feelings that came with them. Shame and regret.

Alice sat at the small desk in her pastel room, laptop open on a blank page, but her eyes were drawn to her phone. Mia's mop of chestnut curls and toothy grin smiled back at her. At eight she was a little chatterbox, loved all things rainbow and horses, and bossed her little brother around like a mother hen.

Her children were now her greatest comfort, and yet in some moments they churned her stomach with guilt. It made what Jan said about emotion so true. '*A kaleidoscope of emotions at any given moment.*' That's how it felt sometimes, so many mixed emotions in any given minute.

Alice flicked the screen, bringing up a photo of Mia holding Abe's hand as they walked to the playground. She flicked again to a close-up of Abe's cheeky face, his blue eyes so full of innocence and fun. The two were getting along so much better now, and she'd often find them in the games room playing shops. Well, more like Mia playing shops and telling Abe what he had to do. 'You get the shopping basket and pick out what you want, then you bring them to the counter and I'll serve you.'

Mia was like a director on a movie set, always taking charge and setting the scene. Alice knew things would change when Abe was old enough to demand they play his games.

The desire to cuddle them close, to smell them, to hear their voices, made her heart ache. Was she losing control? A dark fog felt like it was pushing into her light, making her body tremble with the scary sensation it brought with it.

*Jamie.*

Seeing him only undid everything she had tried to build up in the years since he'd been in her life. Her old life. It was years ago and yet it felt like yesterday. She could still remember the first time she met him.

It was summer 2014 and everyone – her family, friends, husband – had been encouraging Alice to regain her fitness regimes.

'It's time you got back to the gym, honey,' her mum had said the day before. 'Take some time out for yourself.'

It wasn't that they said it outright, but she wasn't back to her pre-baby weight and knowing this was another brick around her ankle dragging her down in the endless sea of sleepless nights, screams, and nappies.

'After Paris was born, I hit the gym and got back to my pre-baby weight in a matter of months.'

'Are you still wearing your maternity jeans?'

'Did you see the gym has a new HIIT class, Alice? You should check it out.'

Alice fumed whenever she drove away from yet another lunch or coffee catch-up with her friends or her mum. It was always their eyes that did the most damage, gazing over Alice's stomach or legs. She'd only gone up one size, and even now she was nearly back to size eight, but she wasn't as toned as she was before she had Mia and her fitness was non-existent. So, just to please everyone – or perhaps to spite them – she sorted a babysitter for Mia and booked into a gym that was miles from her home. The last thing she wanted was to go to her old gym and have everyone talking, her friends gawking; it was too much to deal with. These days all Alice craved was time alone. Even if all she did was stare off into space.

The Xtreme Gym had come highly recommended online and so she'd joined up and booked in for a class. Already being by herself in the car was exciting, and she found herself thinking about which days she might go each week.

A big yellow building appeared, 'Xtreme' painted in huge black letters on the front, and she manoeuvred into its ample car park. The light caught her damage-inflicting diamond rings as she plucked them from her fingers, depositing them into the console compartment. Wearing her favourite Lululemon three-quarter navy tights and a pink tank top – which still fitted just fine – and with her gym bag slung over her shoulder, she headed to the glass doors at the front.

The reception desk was attended by a woman wearing a polo shirt with the gym's logo above her name, Erica. 'Morning,' she said with a smile.

'Hi. I registered online recently and signed up to do the yoga tone class,' said Alice as a man walked out from a door behind the reception.

He smiled and wished her a good morning, but Alice could hardly breathe much less reply, looking at the man and his piercing blue eyes. As he continued on to one of the side rooms she noted his muscles and dreamy backside.

She turned back to the receptionist, mouth suddenly dry.

'We call that the Jamie effect,' she said with a chuckle.

'I, um, see why,' Alice replied weakly.

'The lockers are in that room, showers are communal but they have doors, the yoga room is opposite and class starts in five minutes. Here's a key; you get your own locker.'

Alice took the key, thanked the woman and went into the locker room. Exactly where the Jamie effect had gone.

He was wielding a mop of all things, which only made him more divine.

'Hello again,' he said, smiling.

Did he always smile so much? He certainly had the lips for it.

'Hi,' she replied while trying to find her locker and then get the key in. For some reason she was shaking.

'Need a hand?' he offered, putting the mop aside and striding over to help.

Having this pure man, his scent strong and intoxicating, so close made Alice forget why she was here. She held out the key; there was no way she'd get it unlocked with him standing so close.

'These can be a bit finicky; you have to give them a wiggle,' he said.

His hand enveloped hers, but his eyes never left her face. Alice couldn't move. It had been an age since her libido had worked, an age since she'd even thought about sex – to the point she thought she might be broken. And yet, right now she wanted nothing more than to undress this man and have her way with him. It scared and exhilarated her at the same time. She should rejoice in the fact that her libido was in fact alive and kicking. Her whole body was zinging.

Jamie took the key, slowly, and with a little jiggle, opened her locker.

'See, just like that.'

Then he put the key back in her hand, skin touching skin, every part of her sizzling.

Somehow, Alice found her way to the yoga room and an empty area to place a mat and her water bottle. She didn't remember getting her bottle out of her bag, nor putting the bag in her locker. It was all a blur. Her mind had been stuck on Jamie as he continued to mop the floor.

'All right, everyone, let's start with some deep breathing.'

The instructor clapped her hands and they all stood on their mats and began.

Alice didn't see Jamie again. She took her time after the class, telling herself it was merely to check out the timetable and amenities, and then on impulse she signed up for the beat class in two days. She walked out the door feeling as if she'd been injected with some sort of life-altering serum.

When she returned for the class, early, in her best black and silver yoga set, she lingered by her locker, but she didn't see him.

Then, at the end of beat class, Alice was chatting to the instructor, wiping sweat from her forehead, when she stepped back and rolled on a discarded dumbbell.

The floor was hard, pain shot into her ankle, and there was shouting and commotion.

'I'm fine, I'm fine, please, it's nothing,' she tried to reassure them all, her already sweaty cheeks flaming hotter than they had all class.

Suddenly she was levitating off the floor as strong arms lifted her up. Her mouth dropped open, ready to tell them off for the unnecessary rescue, when she met his eyes and her mind went blank. Just like that, she forgot what she'd been about to say.

Jamie carried her into the locker room and gently sat her down on the bench, then he looked at her ankle.

'You'll need an ice pack.'

Moments later he returned and tenderly wrapped the ice pack around her ankle.

'It's not that bad, honestly,' she managed to squeak out.

He turned, kneeling by her side, and was so close she could feel his breath on her face.

'I'll be the judge of that,' he said simply, then held out his hand. 'I'm Jamie.'

She shook his hand and smiled. 'Alice.'

'Nice to meet you, Alice.'

Their hands paused and lingered, skin against skin.

Alice didn't know how long they gazed at each other, all she knew was that electricity was pulsing through her and she was pretty sure he was feeling it too. She could no longer feel the ice on her leg – she couldn't feel her legs at all. She couldn't feel anything except for his hand that still held hers and the way he studied her, as if he might kiss her.

Alice didn't think. Pink lips puckered up slightly as she leaned towards him – and he leaned back.

'Oh sorry,' she said quickly, pulling her hand from his and feeling more stupid than she possibly ever had in her life. 'I didn't think,' she hurried on. 'I'm so sorry. I thought there was a vibe. God, I'm sorry.'

Now she was rambling. *Please stop!*

'Hey, hey,' he said reaching for both her hands and squeezing them. 'It's okay. And there *is* a vibe, believe me.'

His stared at her, silently, until Alice forgot to breathe.

He brought her hands up towards his face.

'And I'd like nothing more than to kiss you,' he said in a whisper. 'But I'm ever the professional while I'm at work.'

He placed a kiss onto her hands, slowly, gently. The pressure of his soft lips across each finger made Alice tingle between her legs, a sensation she thought she'd lost.

'Oh.'

He dropped her hands and checked on her ankle.

'How's it feeling?' He smiled. 'I need to go and sort out some paperwork, but I want you to rest up here for a bit, okay?'

She nodded like a good girl, though her body was anything but.

She watched as he left the room, then had to quickly rearrange her expression as Erica bustled in.

'Here's your water bottle,' Erica said brightly. 'You can take the ice pack with you, return it next time you're in.'

'Okay, thanks but I think it'll be fine.'

Erica shot her a look. 'I'll be in trouble if I don't make sure you head home with that ice pack still in place. Do you want a hand to your car? Can I call you a taxi or book an Uber?'

Alice shook her head. 'No, thank you. I'll be fine. Really.'

Without Jamie in the room her body and brain started to function again; she could breathe and think. Standing up, she tested her ankle; it was a little tender, she had to admit, but a warm shower would help. The water made her forget about her ankle and instead she relived the moment when she nearly kissed Jamie. What was she thinking? Her body sprang to life at the mere thought of it. It was a thrilling feeling – something she hadn't felt in a long time and it pushed any guilt away.

After she carefully dressed, she made sure the ice pack was tucked into her sock. Her ankle was still sore as she hobbled out to her car in the grey of impending night. Streetlights were on and shopfronts glowed with enticing colours.

'Alice.'

Her fingers paused on the car door handle as her heart bounced all over the place.

'Jamie?'

He was wearing a black hoodie now. Long legs strode towards her, a purpose to them. He didn't stop until he was right in front of her, and she backed up until she was pressed against her car, feeling suddenly dwarfed by him.

He leaned in. 'I just want you to know that I really did want to kiss you before,' he murmured low and gravelly.

His voice sent tingles all the way to her toes and her fingertips. She smiled.

'And . . . I've finished my shift.'

Her eyes went wide as his words registered. 'Oh.'

The word had scarcely left her lips when he replaced them. It was a wow kiss. Intoxicating. Alice was alive, like a flare in the darkness. And the best bit – she forgot everything. Jamie quietened the noise in her head; it was eerily quiet and it only made her crave more.

His hair was soft against her fingers as she buried them, pulling him closer. He deepened the kiss, his hands caressing her face, his body pressing against hers as she moulded to him, feeling all of him.

Lips smacking, tongues tasting, it went on and on and then ended all too soon. Huffing and puffing they tried to catch their breath.

'I did *really* want to kiss you,' he said as he brushed his thumb across her bottom lip.

'Duly noted.' She smiled.

'I'll see you next week.' He rested his hand on her car, pressed another kiss to her lips before pushing off and walking away.

Alice watched him disappear behind the Xtreme building before attempting to open her door. Fingers pressed against her lips as she tried to make sense of what had happened. Her eyes darted to the centre console where her rings rested.

*What have I done?*

With a shaky hand she managed to insert her key and start the car but she didn't leave the car park for another five minutes, her mind raging with all the noise again.

As she drew closer to home the noise only intensified. It took everything she had not to pivot and go back to find Jamie.

# 12

## Jamie — 2014

ALICE WAS A BREATH OF FRESH AIR. SHE SEEMED SO SERENE, so real compared to some of the other women at the gym. She had the beauty and grace of someone much older.

He found himself whistling at work, knowing that Alice was signed in for the yoga class today.

That kiss had left him wanting . . . so much more. The fact that he'd kissed her like that after meeting her so briefly . . . well, he couldn't explain it. She was intoxicating. She didn't say much, her eyes did most of the talking. Without a word she'd raised the hairs on the back of his neck. He'd never had such an instant attraction to a woman before.

'Someone's happy,' said Erica as he passed the reception desk.

'It's been a beautiful afternoon. And we get to knock off soon,' he replied, giving her a wink.

She rolled her eyes.

He liked Erica. She loved to tease him, and she told really

bad jokes. And she'd only just started dating Shianne, another gorgeous young woman on staff, so she was always chipper lately.

Jamie had never had trouble finding a girlfriend. There had been plenty, especially when they found out both his brothers were professional AFL players. A few he'd met through his work at the gym, which at least gave them something in common, but it was all done outside the gym – no mixing business with pleasure. His boss was a stickler for the rules, and Tony had taught Jamie everything he knew. Tony had trained him up when he noticed his potential, encouraged him to further his knowledge and education. He wasn't just a mentor, he was like a second dad, and it was because of Tony that Jamie was building a career that made him happy every day.

Jamie paced the yoga room, checking the water cooler was full and watching the front door.

'Are you joining in today, Jamie?'

'Yeah, Camryn. How's this timeslot working?' he asked.

Camryn was setting up her mat at the front of the room. She stood and put her hands on her hips. 'It's not, really. I thought it might work but I haven't had much interest. All the mums are busy sorting kids' meals, I think. Thanks for adding to the numbers.'

'No probs. It's better than cleaning equipment,' he said.

'Gee, thanks,' she replied with a laugh.

Four members and Jamie were sitting on their mats when Alice walked into the room.

'Afternoon,' she said with a sexy smile as she walked past him, yoga mat and water in hand.

He wasn't sure what he was expecting – some surprise or nervousness, but she was showing none of that. Poised perfection without a hair out of place. He liked the way she played things very cool, as if she was waiting for him to chase, which was new for him. Nothing like the batted eyelashes, touchy hand gestures and over-the-top flirting he was used to.

'Alice,' he said, giving her a nod. He couldn't help the automatic deep breath he sucked in as she passed. It was going to take all his concentration to get through Camryn's Ashtanga.

'All right,' said Camryn, drawing Jamie's attention away, 'if everyone's ready, let's get started.'

Jamie had often taken classes in his free time or to help with numbers, so he had no trouble getting through the poses. Right now was his favourite, as Alice bent over for the downward dog and then smiled at him between her legs.

It was a simple smile and yet it set his body on fire. It was the heat he could see in her eyes, the sizzle of energy between them.

He'd worked up quite a sweat when Camryn was finished with them, his concentration less than ideal. He would need a shower for sure.

Everyone filed out, mats and water bottles under arms. Erica was at the reception desk shutting down the computer when he approached.

'I'll lock up if you like, Erica,' he said, knowing full well that Alice was in the bathroom. 'I'm going to have a shower.'

Erica bent and picked up her handbag. 'You don't have to ask me twice.' She turned the computer screen off then skipped over and kissed him on the cheek. 'Thank you, you're a darling.'

'Are we the last ones here?' he asked.

'Yep, Matt and his client left two minutes ago. I'll see you tomorrow.'

'Will do.'

He quickly headed to the lockers as Erica walked out the front door. Alice was by her locker, collecting clothes and a towel for her shower.

'I'm going to have a shower too,' he said, forcing his voice to remain calm, casual, 'but seeing as we're the only ones here, do you mind if I lock the front door?'

'That's fine by me,' she said, her tongue darting out and brushing across her bottom lip as if remembering their kiss.

He didn't think twice, he closed the gap between them and kissed her. It was just a soft peck, but when he reluctantly pulled away, her eyes were shining like diamonds in the light.

'I'll just go lock up. Call me if you need a hand in there,' he said playfully.

He left without waiting for a reply and locked up the gym in record time. When he returned to the bathroom her shower was running, the steam rising above it, and all he could do was imagine her naked with soap running off her. He took his change of clothes, towel and soap from his locker, then headed for the shower next to hers. He ditched his clothes and cranked the water.

After a few minutes, her voice floated across.

'This is so good.'

'It always is after a solid workout,' he replied.

'I think I need my back scrubbed.'

Jamie sucked in a breath, processing her words as his body reacted.

'If you're sure . . .' God, he hoped she was sure.

'I'm sure,' came her reply.

Jamie swallowed as he turned off his shower. Soap was still running down his chest and he was now hard and throbbing.

He stepped out and found her door was unlocked. Had she been planning this, or hoping? He didn't care; he couldn't be any more turned on. The door of her shower gave way under his hand and in the steam her glistening body appeared, droplets running down her long back to her curvaceous hips and beyond.

She didn't turn when he approached, instead she raised her hands up to the water. Jamie stepped into the shower but kept enough distance so he didn't touch her.

Alice lifted her bottle of body wash and held it over her shoulder. He took it and squirted some into his hands before placing it on the floor and then started to lather up her back. His hands wanted to explore every part of her, but he gritted his teeth and concentrated on her back.

Her hands reached behind, finding his hips and pulling him closer into the water and against her. He snaked his hands around to her front, sliding up towards her chest. Two soft breasts with hard nipples filled his hands, making him unable to contain the moan that escaped his lips.

Alice leaned back, pushing her round backside against him as the hot soapy water ran to their feet.

'I think I'm clean,' she said, turning in his arms.

Her eyes ate him up, an eternity passed as he stood watching her explore. Until she reached his lips and their control crumbled.

Falling into each other they kissed with a released fever. Wet skin suctioned together, hot mouths and tongues, hands sliding. Jamie couldn't think, couldn't keep up with the pace. Alice tasted better than her sweet perfume.

A warm hand held him, guiding him to rest between her legs. Being so close to her apex made him ache so bad it almost hurt.

Jamie tore his lips away from hers. 'Alice . . .'

She smooshed a finger against his lips and shook her head. 'Hurry up and take me before I explode.'

Not needing to be told twice, he grabbed her backside and lifted her up, then gently leaned her against the shower wall before lowering her body down over him, burying him.

He threw back his head. 'Oh my God.' Light exploded behind his eyelids, like fireworks in techno colours.

Alice gripped his shoulders tightly, kissing his neck as spray from the shower kept them wet. Fingernails dug into his skin as she began to rock, grinding against him as he slid in and out. Her breasts pressed hard against his smooth chest, he felt her bite-sized nipples engrave a path along his skin.

'Yes, yes,' she started panting and riding him harder.

Jamie was burying himself, in and out at a frantic rate. The wall started creaking, water splattered everywhere and his feet were close to slipping. Hearing Alice's cries for more brought him undone as his sweet release came moments after she pulsed around him and quivered in his arms.

They stayed connected, up against the wall, as they heaved in deep breaths. Jamie's arms were tiring but he didn't want to let her go yet, not while her head was tucked into his neck and her breath against his skin.

Alice lifted her head, so he gently let her down. She stepped back into the shower and they slowly washed each other.

No words were spoken. They weren't needed.

He left once the soap was rinsed from his body, returning to his own shower cubicle to dry and dress in his jeans and T-shirt.

Alice emerged not long after, her wet locks brushing her shoulders.

'Do you want to go get a bite to eat?' he asked as she gathered her bag and locked her locker.

Jamie was standing beside her, his body still humming. The more he thought about what they'd done, with her close by smelling so sweet, he knew he'd be ready to go again very shortly.

Alice turned, reached up on tiptoe and kissed him.

'Thank you for a wonderful . . . shower,' she said giving him a wink as she dropped back on her heels. 'But I better be getting home.'

She took his hand and together they left the locker room, Jamie switching off lights as he went.

'So, at work is fine now?' Alice asked, the tease in her voice. 'Still "ever the professional"?'

Jamie smiled. 'I'm off duty and the place was locked, so yeah, at work is fine.'

Her laughter was beguiling, soft and sensual.

The key missed the lock twice before he managed to open the back door. He was still shaking slightly in the way he often did after a huge weights session.

At her car she turned to him. 'Thank you.'

'Can I get your number?' he managed to splutter out as she opened the door. A needy feeling struck him, he didn't want her to vanish into the night without some sort of contact.

Ignoring him she climbed into her car and started it. Then after a very long moment she wound down her window. Finally, her eyes turned to him. 'Maybe next time,' she said.

Jamie watched her drive away, excited and a little confused. Alice wasn't like the other girls. She didn't want to smother him, or pin him down; it was refreshing, even a little hot. He couldn't wait for her next appearance at the gym. He wasn't sure much could ever top what had just occurred, but he was suddenly desperate to find out.

# 13

## *Beth*

IT WAS NEARLY TIME TO MEET IN THE KITCHEN FOR LUNCH and Beth had only written half a page. She'd looked through all the writing Poppy had given her but nothing would work for what Jan was chasing. So, Beth had decided to just have a go.

Knuckles tapped at her door. 'How you going, Beth?' Jamie stuck his head in. 'Hope I haven't interrupted a good bit?'

Beth saved what she'd done and then closed the laptop. 'I doubt that. Not sure I'm cut out for writing an award-winning story, but hopefully it will do.' She shrugged. 'Jan didn't say how long it had to be, so I only did a snippet.'

'Same,' he added as they meandered along the passage. 'I think she wants us to write something from the heart, it doesn't have to be a whole story. It's impossible to write much in an hour, but we have the afternoon too. It doesn't give us much time to proofread it.'

Beth scoffed. 'Proofread, what's that?'

Jamie stopped, checked his watch then glanced up the stairs.

'Careful, Beth, people will start to talk,' he said in a stage whisper. 'They'll know you're an imposter,' he added, the corner of his lips curling.

Even though Jamie didn't know the full reason, a niggle of nervousness crept up her neck. He knew enough.

'Hey, have you seen Simone's Instagram page?' he asked, his brows furrowing.

'No. I don't actually get on Instagram much.'

'You ought to take a look. It's . . . interesting,' he said with a bemused look. 'Simone, are you coming? I want to get back and spend some more time on my piece.'

A blur of colour appeared, mostly fluoro green on black.

'Sorry, I got waylaid,' huffed Simone as she skipped down the stairs.

As they headed into the kitchen Beth said, 'I'll just be a tick.' Then she went to the bathroom. While she sat on the toilet she took out her phone to check out Simone's Instagram page.

Her profile photo was amazing, with the Alive logo below her immaculately made-up face. She had more than eight hundred posts and eighty thousand followers, and she followed a few hundred. Her bio stated: *Lose weight each week while eating your favourite foods. I went from one hundred and nine kilograms to a steady sixty-six kilograms. Believe. Achieve.*

There were a few photos of Jamie on here; Beth wondered if he'd seen them. Certainly gave the impression Jamie was all for these products. She clicked on a photo from their dinner last night.

*Zucchini noodle salad with herbs, cashews and corn. THE BOMB!*

*Raw zucchini noodles make a wonderful low-fat, low-joule and low-carb substitute for regular noodles, as well as providing vitamin C, potassium and folate. This is a quick, easy and delicious meal that's perfect for a weekday dinner.*

*Alive has changed my life and it will change yours.*

*Click website link in my profile.*

Beth's eyes glazed over when she saw all the hashtags.

She scrolled through more photos, mainly of other people's transformations and food, plus plenty of product photos. Beth couldn't help but wonder if Simone had taken a class on how to make a packet of shake powder look like a must-have pair of shoes. A few photos of Simone, before and after her weight loss, filled the screen. Beth had to study the photo, because it was hard to tell it was the same person. From hair colour, to make-up, fuller lips, fitness clothes and the weight loss – it was near impossible to think that both these women were Simone. Only the eyes and the small mole on her cheek gave it away.

Was this what Jamie wanted her to see?

Simone's page showed other people's weight-loss photos, using them to help sell her products. Some transformations were hard to believe, to the point that Beth started to feel a rising doubt. It was clear that Simone tweaked things to her advantage. Beth flicked back to the photo from their dinner. It didn't show the food she'd actually eaten last night – a bite of all the meat and pastry options, no salad at all. And the way she wrote about the salad could easily be interpreted as Simone having made it herself. Seemed like everyone at this retreat was not quite as they appeared.

*That includes me.*

Beth put her phone away and then finished up in the bathroom, washing her hands and checking her hair.

*Nothing will fix those split ends!* She rolled her eyes at her
reflection and left.

'Something smells great.'

'Simone's still taking photos,' he said, moving to the side
so she had more room to sit beside him. 'She's outside with
the pork sliders in the right light. And Alice isn't down yet.'

Beth saw Simone through the window wandering around
with her plate like she was trying to give an offering to the
Sun God. 'I had a quick look at her Instagram page,' she told
Jamie quietly.

'Hmm . . . I didn't approve those photos she put up of me,
by the way. Was a bit of a surprise.' He grunted and picked up
one of the four pork sliders on his plate which was tucked in
between some of the leafy walnut salad and spiced rice mix.
'Anyway, what did you think?' he asked through his mouthful.

'Well, she certainly has changed a lot.'

He nodded as if that was a given. 'She's had a bit of work done.'

Beth frowned. 'What do you mean?' She leaned closer to
him. 'More than her boobs?' she whispered.

'I'd say she's had her lips done, and botox, and hair
extensions.'

'How would you know that?'

He pulled a face. 'I've had a few high-maintenance girlfriends.
Don't judge me,' he said quickly when he saw Beth's mouth
open. 'I was young and clueless. I've seen the lengths women
can go to, striving for what they think is perfection. Took me
a while to realise that's not what I want in a girlfriend.'

'And what about Alice?' she blurted out, then clamped her lips closed. *Too late, Beth, you've already spilled the beans.*

'What about Alice?' he said clearing his throat.

'Do you two already know each other?'

He looked like he was thinking about his reply, working up a lie maybe? Would he deny knowing her? Did he wonder how much Beth had overheard at breakfast?

'Ah yeah, she used to come to my gym for classes.'

It was the truth, she could tell that much, and yet she had a feeling it wasn't the whole story. The more she learned about Jamie, the greater an enigma he became.

'You're full of surprises,' said Beth. 'You really notice things. I hadn't thought about any of that, looking at Simone. Probably because I'm not like that.' She waved at her own face. 'As you can tell. I wouldn't know one brand of make-up from another. The closest thing to a facial I get is when Hudson throws his breakfast at me and it congeals like a face mask. I had a baby not a boob job.' She glanced down at her decent-sized chest. 'Although a boob job would be way cheaper in the long run.'

A deep belly laugh erupted from Jamie and didn't stop until Simone eventually joined them.

'Did I miss something?' she asked, brushing her blonde tresses from her shoulders.

'Oh, nothing. I just don't think Beth realises how funny she is.'

'I've been told I'm funny at times,' said Simone. 'We could have a hoot doing a photo shoot together, you showing me some of your techniques and I could be trying to copy them. We could really make it quite fun.'

Jamie leaned back on the bench seat and crossed his arms. 'Have you written something for Jan?' he asked Simone.

Was that his subtle way of avoiding her question? Or was he just being a dick?

'Ugh, it's so hard. I tried,' she said with a shrug.

'Try writing a moment that really affected you,' said Beth. 'Something at school, maybe. An event that's always stayed with you. We all have them.' She picked at her nails, wondering why the hell she'd decided to open her mouth. She was no writer, but then again, she had the 'moments that affect you' in the bag.

'Did they tease you about your scars?' Simone asked openly.

Jamie shifted uncomfortably, but Beth wasn't offended. She was used to these kinds of questions, and the insensitivity that went with them. She'd be hard-pressed to find one that hadn't been asked over the years.

'Not really. I got these scars when I was nearly seventeen. Most of the kids at school were good about it because they knew how I got them. But I caught the train to school and sometimes people would stare, and some idiots would say awful stuff. You don't ever forget those moments, as much as you try,' she said honestly.

And as if she had summoned the image like pressing play on a movie, Beth could see the man with his missing tooth and tattooed arm. The way he stepped onto the train with a swagger, as if trying to convince the world he meant something. *You should wear a bag over your head.*

She blinked her memories away, and realised Jamie had moved his hand to cover hers. She looked at him and smiled; he gave a quick squeeze and withdrew his hand.

Simone had started to talk about how cruel people could be and how she was always picked on as a kid.

'My weight obviously,' she said nervously.

Even though Simone seemed open about her weight-loss journey, Beth could tell that parts of it still were difficult. She understood better than most that a wound might heal but it still left scars.

'But also the clothes I wore.' Simone glanced down at her top, as if she could still imagine her childhood wardrobe like it was yesterday.

'Pick one of those moments that stand out and try to write about it,' Jamie suggested gently. 'Use all those emotions you felt then and put them on the page. Try to make the reader understand what you went through.'

'You make it sound so easy, Jamie,' Simone said, switching back to her singsong voice.

Simone picked at her slider and a bit of the walnut salad. Mainly the nuts and pear.

'The salads are amazing,' said Beth. 'I hope Alice comes down soon or else I may not leave her any.'

'You and me both,' added Jamie.

'I don't really like salads,' said Simone. 'I know, I should but I grew up on meat and one veg. Lettuce was for rabbits, mum always said.'

'Do you have your shakes often?' Jamie asked. 'That's what you sell?'

Beth tried not to smile; she had a feeling they both already knew the answer to this one.

'Oh, when I need a quick meal I do,' she said flippantly. 'These sliders are good.'

Simone's painted nails clung to the little burger as she managed a bite, pork dropping out onto her plate. Her hair fell forward, and almost into the spilled food.

But before Beth could warn her, Simone flicked out a manicured finger and swiped up the pork and sucked it from her finger.

# 14

## Simone — 2008

AT THIRTEEN, SIMONE SAW HER DAD FOR THE FIRST TIME IN two years.

She was at the Carousel Shopping Centre with her old neighbour Mrs Satish. Mrs Satish lived alone except for her five cats and her dog Peppie. One day, when Simone was about twelve, Peppie dug a hole into their backyard. Simone had found him and played with him and fed him treats. She'd never had a pet before, and she loved his fluffy fur and wet tongue. But when she heard Mrs Satish frantically calling for Peppie, she took him home and explained where he had escaped to.

'Oh, my boy! Thank you, Simone.'

As a reward, Mrs Satish invited her in for some chocolate biscuits, and when Simone stepped in, she instantly loved the house, which was tidy and clean with lots of lace doilies and lace curtains and flowery chairs and carpets.

When Simone learned that Mrs Satish didn't have any family left except for her animals, she announced, 'I can be your family.'

'I would love that, dear. You can visit Peppie, the cats and me any time you like.'

And so, Mrs Satish had become Simone's best friend. At least twice a week Simone went over to help feed the cats and tidy up after them. Mrs Satish taught her how to make pancakes, scones and cups of tea. And they played card games sometimes. She hadn't been brave enough to tell Mrs Satish that she didn't have any other friends, or much family. Only her mum; her dad had disappeared into a merry-go-round of work all over the country.

One day, when Simone mentioned she'd never been far outside the suburb, Mrs Satish offered to take her to the shopping centre a little way down the freeway.

'But you'd have to check if it's okay with your mum.'

She'd raced home, found her mum reading in her bed, and begged her to let her go.

'That's fine, just be back to help with dinner.'

Simone had brushed her hair and put on her best jumper with her favourite long skirt; it was blue and green and swished in the breeze.

'My, you do look pretty in that skirt,' Mrs Satish said when she returned.

'Mum said I could go. I've never been to a big shopping centre before!'

Mrs Satish had grabbed her black handbag, locked up the house and tottered over to her little silver car.

'Are you okay to drive, Mrs Satish?'

'I'm not that old yet, dear,' she'd replied with a smile.

To thirteen-year-old Simone, Mrs Satish seemed old, with all those wrinkles on her face. She smelled like old-lady perfume and wore old-people blouses and pants. But her soft purple curls were so pretty, like the watercolours Simone used at school. Simone couldn't help but love her, no matter how old she was.

Simone had her nose pressed up against the window for most of the trip, watching all the new places and different shops whizz by. And then the shopping centre appeared – it was about ten times the size of her school.

'Wow,' was all Simone could say as they walked in.

'Yes, it's very big, so you'll have to help me remember where I parked the car, okay?'

Simone nodded, then moved closer to Mrs Satish's side, suddenly a little overwhelmed at the enormity of her surrounds.

'Would you like a hot chocolate?' Mrs Satish asked as they arrived at an island coffee stand.

'Oh yes, please, thank you.'

And while Mrs Satish was busy with the order, that's when Simone saw him.

At first she thought, *He looks like Dad*, because sometimes she saw him in men in the street and in shops. But the longer she stared at him, past the clean button-up shirt and dress jeans, the surer she became. The way he walked, favouring his left leg, the way his hair curled at his neck in a kind of mullet, his big hands.

Before she knew it she was walking towards him, her pace quickening as he drew closer and her heart pounding as if someone was beating her chest.

'Dad?' she called out when she was in his path. Only then did she register that he wasn't alone.

He had his arm around a thin woman with a cascade of sunlight-blonde hair and wearing a bright yellow dress. And on the other side of him was a girl, around Simone's age. She was everything Simone was not.

The man's steps faltered and he stopped a metre from her. 'Simone?' he asked.

The fact that he was unsure made her feel bad, acid-in-her-stomach bad. Was he unhappy to see her?

The woman beside him gasped and covered her mouth. The girl frowned and moved closer to his side. Her pretty yellow dress was similar to the woman's, like a matching mummy–daughter pair. Simone had the same matching tracksuit as her mum, but it wasn't anywhere near as cool as this girl and her mum.

'What are you doing here?' her dad asked.

Her chest unclenched as she breathed; finally he knew it was her. She wanted to jump into his arms but didn't because of the other two stuck to his sides.

'I . . . I'm with Mrs Satish,' she stuttered, looking around.

'Hello, Harry,' said Mrs Satish as she joined them, two takeaway cups in her hands. 'Here you go, dear.'

Simone thanked her as she took the hot chocolate.

'Fancy running into you here.'

Simone glanced at Mrs Satish, noting the funny tone in her voice and the way she was looking at the woman on Dad's arm.

'Why's that?' he asked, clearly curious.

'I thought you were off trying to find work.' Her tone changed. 'For the past two years.'

Simone nodded, feeling a rush of gratitude for Mrs Satish for saying what Simone had been feeling but unable to put into words.

Harry scoffed. 'Is that what she told you?'

'I can't say I didn't have my doubts. It didn't feel like the truth,' Mrs Satish admitted.

Harry sighed heavily and gestured to the woman beside him. 'This is Janet, my wife, and this is her daughter Shelly.'

Janet gave them a warm smile. 'Hi, lovely to meet you.'

Mrs Satish returned the smile, but it wasn't like the smiles she gave Simone. It didn't reach her eyes.

'Wife?' Simone echoed.

'I'm sorry, Chubalub. I thought your mum would have explained it all.' He turned to Janet, rolling his eyes. 'I guess that was too much to ask.'

Simone prickled at her nickname. It all felt wrong. Her dad was wrong. That woman was wrong. Simone wanted to scream. To run. But she couldn't run without her legs chafing and her lungs burning. So she stood there open-mouthed as tears prickled.

Her dad had ditched them for a new family.

'Chubalub, don't be like that. I didn't want to leave you, but I had no choice.'

He bent forward and went to reach out but then hesitated and eventually dropped his arm.

'I thought you were coming back,' she managed to whisper.

He could only shake his head. 'I have a new life now.'

One without Simone. One with a pretty wife and a pretty daughter. One where they all went shopping together at a huge

shopping centre. It was the life Simone dreamed of. Why didn't
he take her with him?

'It was nice to see you,' he said softly, his hand resting briefly
on her shoulder. 'And thank you, Mrs Satish. For looking out
for her.'

'She's a lovely girl. I don't know what I'd do without her,'
Mrs Satish replied, a sternness to her voice.

Harry nodded and shuffled awkwardly, then took his wife's
hand and they continued on their way. Only Shelly looked back,
wearing a stupid grin on her face as if she was walking away
with a fancy new pair of shoes that Simone could never own.

Her dad wasn't a pair of shoes. He would always be her
dad. And yet, he was walking away with them. Why was he
walking away?

She was not enough.

Tears rolled down her cheeks as she glanced up at Mrs
Satish, hoping she would explain why he'd left.

Pity, frustration, anger, sadness all seemed to be etched
into Mrs Satish's wrinkles. 'Come on, Simone. Let's do some
shopping. Drink your hot chocolate before it gets cold.'

Mrs Satish took her free hand and together they walked
through the busy shopping centre, away from Harry and his new
family. Simone didn't feel like looking at clothes or accessories
or any of the shops she'd always wanted to go into; nothing
was as exciting as she'd hoped it would be. She even knocked
back ice cream.

Mrs Satish kept sneaking glances at her, even on the drive
home. Simone knew she was concerned with how quiet she'd
been. Mrs Satish sometimes told Simone she was the fastest
talker she knew. But not today.

Simone would have talked to Mrs Satish, if only she could get the words out. So many thoughts going around, so many questions, so many feelings. She had no idea where to start.

'He got married,' she finally said as they pulled into Mrs Satish's driveway.

'Pardon, dear?'

Simone turned to Mrs Satish as she switched off the engine.

'Dad got remarried. I didn't even know they'd got divorced.'

'Me either.'

'Why didn't anyone tell me?'

Mrs Satish sighed heavily. 'I don't know. Pain affects people differently. Your mum maybe found it too hard.'

'But why hasn't Dad ever tried to see me? Even for my birthday.' A sudden thought struck Simone: what if her dad had sent cards and presents but her mum had found them first?

Simone looked down at her thick fingers, perched on her belly rolls. Was it simpler than that? Did he just prefer a pretty skinny wife and her perfect daughter? Did he just like his new family better than the one he had?

Why hadn't her mum tried harder to keep him? Simone knew she could lose weight, be a better cook. Maybe together they could try to clean the house so it looked nice like Mrs Satish's. Maybe then he'd want to come back to join their family.

But deep down she knew the truth.

'He's not coming back, is he?' she sobbed. As the tears flowed she blubbered more than she had when she was teased at school, more than when she'd fallen over and skinned her knee, more than when she couldn't buy the new jumper she really wanted. This was so much worse, and she didn't know if she'd ever be able to stop the tears.

Mrs Satish held out a flowery hanky, and when Simone took it and pressed it against her face, the old woman rested her bony hand on her shoulder, rubbing it gently.

Mrs Satish was her best friend.

# 15

## Beth

IT WAS AFTER TWO WHEN BETH JOINED THE OTHERS IN THE writing room, the last one to arrive. Not because she was busy working on her personal story but because she'd scrolled through all her photos and videos of Hudson then read some of the book before emailing her snippet to Jan. Also there was quite a bit of time spent toing and froing about whether she should email it or not.

Jan was already stationed at the front, wearing black trousers with a fluffy red scarf that matched her top and even brighter lipstick. Her big black glasses sat beside her on the table. She wore an air of self-importance, and Beth couldn't tell if she adopted this persona for her workshops or if this was Jan twenty-four seven. What went on inside Jan's mind while she ran the workshop? What did she think about the people around the table? Beth wished she could pick her apart. How could this old woman do what she did?

'Thank you for sending through your works in progress,' Jan said as they took their seats. 'I'd like you to keep working on them over the weekend. I had a quick glance through those that came through and later I will send you all some notes so you can make them shine.'

It was like a frantic game of ping pong as eyeballs darted from face to face, trying to detect just how deep everyone had dug into their secrets. Beth had to admit she was a little excited to hear some of the pieces read out. Is that what drove Jan? Was she addicted to this feeling? Of knowing everyone's secrets?

'Now, this afternoon we will talk about the difference between showing and telling in writing. Jerry Cleaver said that showing a little is better than telling a lot. It's easy to write something like . . .' Jan turned and pressed the clicky thing in her hand, and a sentence appeared on the screen.

'*The little girl was scared*,' she read out. 'That's telling. Instead, find ways to *show* she was scared.'

Jan clicked through to the next screen. Beth had a feeling her clicky thing made her feel like Thor and his hammer.

'*In a huge shopping centre filled with people, the girl spins around and around, searching unfamiliar faces.* This is an example of how you can set the scene; you already know how a child might feel in that situation. Or if she says, "I want my mummy. Please help me find my mummy!" You hear her fear through her words.'

Beth scribbled notes as Jan continued. Everyone else was doing the same. Like them, Beth was swept up in Jan's words, inspired to write. Yet she knew why she was here, and she needed to focus on that reason . . . except she didn't know how to go about it. Where to start? It just seemed easier to copy the others for now and listen to Jan.

As she brought the session to an end, Jan said, 'I'd like to read out a section from one of your works in progress, then we can discuss what you liked, what it made you feel and if you think there's room for improvement after what we've learned on showing not telling.'

Jan picked up her reading glasses and cleared her throat.

'*Joy flowed through her like a rushing creek. It was more than the excitement of Christmas, more than falling passionately in love, more than anything she could imagine. It was raw and powerful.*

'*Was it a tiny hand or foot that pressed against her belly where she rested her hand? Did this growing little human know she was his mother? Could he hear in her voice the love she already felt for him? She often spoke to her child, imagined his features. Would he have her eyes? Her chin?*

'*Or maybe he would take after his father? Her mind clouded. A father he could never know.*

'*No matter how many times she did the calculations, the numbers didn't change, the dates didn't change. No amount of force, of wishing, of praying could change the fact that this child was not her husband's son.*'

Beth glanced around the room, meeting the eyes of the others as they did the same, all with one thought: *Who wrote this?*

It was written from a woman's point of view, so no one looked at Jamie, except Beth.

He was watching Alice with an intensity she'd not seen in him before. *Interesting.*

Alice was now focused on Jan, her pen drawing circles on the corner of her page unconsciously.

'Does anyone have any thoughts?' Jan asked.

No one replied.

'Well, it's always hard to be the first one to critique. I will start. Firstly, I enjoyed the twist at the end and it started with a lovely simile. "Flowed like a rushing creek", which really helps paint a picture. Plenty of rhetorical questions. But I think this could be extended to show some more emotion. We feel the mother's love at the beginning but what is going through her mind by the end?'

While Jan was pulling the sample apart, Beth was focused on Jamie's physical reaction to Alice. His body had gone rigid, like a tiger poised to pounce with muscles taut and ready. But when she glanced at Alice, she was like a smooth, still lake. Not even a ripple upon her perfect face.

Something was going on here, had been all along. But what had Beth missed? The piece had clearly changed something in Jamie. Alice's wedding rings sparkled under the bright lights highlighting every carat. What if they had . . .

*Had I guessed right from the beginning?*

Beth's mind raced ahead; she blinked rapidly, trying to slow her thoughts down and catch one long enough to pull it apart. An affair? A love child? Was she grasping at straws? Was she reading far too much into their looks and his reaction to this story?

Beth had a feeling everyone was only half listening to Jan. She didn't seem fazed, so dedicated was she to getting them to find their inner emotion and pour it out on the page – which made the hairs on the back of Beth's neck rise and prickle like an angry dog. Knowing what Jan did, it all made sense. She was grooming them, building them up to tear them down. But how was Beth supposed to prove this? How could Poppy leave this for her to bust open? A wave of nerves rushed through her and she gripped her chair and forced a few slow, quiet breaths.

'I want you all to complete this exercise,' said Jan as she handed out sheets. 'Then when you're done, go back to your moment in time if you haven't finished it.'

Moments in time.

That's what Jan was calling their deepest, darkest secrets. She wanted them to pour their pain out onto the pages, where it would not stay secret.

But Beth would not give her what she wanted. She would not write about her most painful moment in time, especially because it was also Poppy's. Besides, Jan already knew all about it.

A blur of red whooshed past and Beth realised that Jan had left the room. Class dismissed.

No one spoke as, heads down, they stood and walked out, minds full of new information. Or obsessing over who had a child to a lover rather than a husband.

Back in her room, Beth checked in with Poppy.

'You need to see what's on her computer,' said Poppy. 'I think she has to have something on there.'

'I don't think she's going to have a folder called "People's secrets I've stolen",' said Beth with a sigh. 'It's not going to be that simple.'

'Maybe not, but surely she has to leave her room at some point? Can you get someone to help you, be a lookout?'

'They're aspiring writers, Poppy, not trained spies.'

Poppy grunted.

'Look, I'll do what I can, but I can't make any promises. How's Hudson?'

'Changing the subject?' Poppy shot down the phone, then sighed. 'Yeah, he's great. Love this kid.'

Beth could hear him making sounds in the background. She could picture his red cheeks and the drool oozing from his lips as he tried to talk around whatever he'd found to shove in his mouth and rub against his gums. Her heart felt so heavy, she wanted to hold him so badly; to place her nose against his soft curls and breathe in the scent of him. Even to feel the tug on her hair as he twisted his little fingers into it as if the strands were his own comfort blanket. Poppy sent through some more photos after they finished the call, but not even the images of her son helped Beth relax. She felt agitated. Stress from missing Hudson and knowing she should find a way to expose Jan. It overwhelmed her like standing on the Sydney Harbour Bridge with a fear of heights and knowing you should look down. Beth didn't want to look down. She started pacing. Four steps to the wall, four steps back to the door. Four steps out, four steps back.

The book on her bed suddenly seemed like a much better idea, and it might also allow her to do some recon on Jan.

*Recon.*

Beth sighed in exasperation. She would make a terrible spy.

Taking the book, she headed outside and feigned nonchalance as she wandered towards Jan's cottage.

Around the corner of the house she nearly tripped over a leg. Jamie was slouched in a wicker chair and beside him a thin curtain fluttered out from his room through a glass sliding door.

'Oh, you got the better room,' she said with a smirk.

Jamie stared into his lap. She thought for a minute he might be sleeping but his eyes were like the glass eyes on a doll.

'Hey, are you okay?'

'Mmm.'

She knelt beside the chair, her hand clutching the arm rest to keep her balance, as she looked up into his cloudy face.

'Jamie?'

Beth gave his knee a squeeze. Finally, he directed his eyes to hers. They were swimming with confusion. His lips parted, but no words came out.

'Something happen?' she asked softly.

Long eyelashes fluttered with each blink, his gaze so intense she wanted to look away.

'It's difficult with Alice, you know.' His head hung down, his chin almost to his chest. His eyes followed.

Beth frowned. 'Um . . . no, not really.' But even as she spoke the words, an image sprang into her mind. Jamie and Alice. Her belly jolted as she felt the satisfaction of guessing correctly, her thoughts racing as she tried to figure out what to say next.

'A few years ago we . . . we had an affair.' The words fell from his lips in a whisper.

Beth nodded, aiming for a neutral expression. 'Must make things a bit awkward?'

His head snapped up. 'I didn't know,' he said quickly. 'I didn't know she was married. I swear,' he said. 'I don't make a habit of seducing married women, if that's what you're thinking.'

She squeezed his knee again. 'It's not. It's okay.'

'It's not okay,' he said a little forcefully. It was laced with shame. 'It wasn't my finest hour. And I think . . .' His words died away.

*And I think ... what? You're still in love with her?*

Beth mentally groaned. This long weekend was about Jan and Poppy, not other people's drama.

'We all have things we're not proud of, but that's life. You have to move on and try to be better.'

'Don't worry, I've been trying to be a better person for years now, but sometimes the regret and shame is not that easy to shake,' he replied with a faint smile. He pointed to the book. 'Off to read?'

She smiled quickly. 'Yeah, I'm done with writing for now. I need a break.'

Poppy's words came back to her. *Can you get someone to help you, be a lookout?*

If she was going to creep around in the dark with anyone, Jamie would be the preferred option. Beth withdrew her hand as she chased away her wayward thoughts. Strictly platonic, of course. His muscles might come in handy to karate-chop Jan should things go wrong, worst-case scenario.

'Me too,' said Jamie. 'I can't get my thoughts straight.'

Clouds swirled across his eyes but he blinked them away. Beth felt for him. 'Want to join me on a little stroll around the house? I was going to have a sneaky look at Jan's cottage,' she admitted. Not the whole truth, but anything to help take his mind off his problems.

'Sure, why not? But I don't want to take you away from finishing the book.'

'I've got all night to read.'

Together they set off towards the back of the house, following the verandah. Butterflies took flight, making Beth feel skittish as they approached the walkway to Jan's cottage, but having Jamie by her side helped to quell the fear.

'So, what are your thoughts so far?' he asked. 'On the book,' he clarified.

'I can see why it's a bestseller,' she admitted honestly.

His smile in response was stunning.

*Oh dear.* Beth could only return his smile, she couldn't help it. He made her want to smile, even though she knew it distorted her scars. Warning bells went off – *ignore the tingles of delight, ignore that feeling, ignore him altogether.* And yet he didn't turn away like the others. He didn't wince from the sight. And he didn't focus on the way it pulled the skin across her face. If anything, he seemed to beam brighter, his eyes sparkling as if he knew it was a genuine smile.

*Oh dear, indeed.*

# 16

## *Jamie*

THANK GOD FOR BETH. IF SHE HADN'T COME PAST AND shaken him from his thoughts he might still be stuck there, frozen in time.

'Let's sit here,' said Beth, reaching the cushioned two-seater that sat back against the house.

The chair was small, or at least he was taking up more than his half, but Beth didn't seem to mind. She no longer seemed as wary of him, and she hadn't made him feel like a complete cad when he confessed his involvement with Alice.

He'd never had a woman look at him the way Beth did. Everyone else focused on the outside, but Beth seemed to look past all that. Her gaze was piercing. It made him wonder about Hudson's father, what kind of man he was, or had been. The itch to know was driving him crazy. What kind of father would leave his own son, anyway?

*Shit.*

Alice appeared in his head again.

'I can't believe I told you about Alice,' he mumbled. 'Sorry.'

'Don't be. We all have things in our closet,' she said.

Beth turned away and he got the vibe she hadn't meant to say those words, implying she had her own secrets. What would someone like Beth have to hide? She was a puzzle. Especially after she'd hinted she wasn't really at the retreat to write, so why was she here?

'I can't imagine you'd have anything in your closet you'd want to hide,' he said, daring her to say otherwise.

Her eyebrows shot up. 'Really? Have you seen my face?'

Jamie waved that away. 'There's nothing wrong with your face. You're beautiful. Those scars only make you unique.'

Beth's baby blues stared at him in confusion; she even squirmed, seeming uncomfortable. He suddenly wished he could take them back. He'd overstepped an unknown line.

'Sorry, my head's a mess. Seeing Alice . . . it's thrown me, you know? The affair . . . I hate calling it that because at the time I thought she was single, but I have to call it for what it was – *an affair*. It was six years ago, Beth,' he added in a whisper, watching her carefully. Wondering if she could put the pieces together and he wouldn't have to explain the scariest thing troubling him. 'Did Alice mention to you how old her children were?'

Silence passed while the only sound was the beating of wings as a bird flitted through a nearby bush. He could tell he'd thrown her with his question.

'Um, yeah. Her daughter was eight and her son was nearly seven.'

*Nearly seven. That would fit too perfectly to ignore.*

Should he share his concerns with Beth? This stranger? Jamie realised he had no one else to talk to, and right now his head felt like a thousand ropes tangled together. He needed someone, and Beth had the eyes of his mother – not the colour, but the gentle, nurturing way that made him want to tell her all his troubles. She sat leaning towards him as if she was indeed waiting for him to unburden.

'That story Jan read out in class, the one about the mother and her baby – a baby boy that doesn't belong to the husband . . .'

Beth nodded, her face remaining impassive.

'I think Alice wrote it. Her son is nearly seven; it fits the timeline of our affair . . . Do you think I'm crazy for thinking he could be mine?'

She looked neither shocked or appalled. Had she already guessed what he'd been about to say? She remained silent, which only made him ramble on.

'I can't help wondering if Alice came here to tell me, or this retreat is just a strange coincidence. Maybe seeing me has brought her deepest secret to the forefront and she decided to write about it.'

'I can see why you'd think that, Jamie,' Beth said softly. 'That's a lot to try and take in, and a lot of assumptions. Are you going to talk to Alice, ask her?'

He rubbed his face, digging his fingers into his eyes. 'Argh, I don't know. My head is spinning.' What if he was a dad? Had an instant child? What would that mean? Would Alice let him see him? Would she deny it just so it wouldn't disrupt the boy's life? Did her husband even know?

'Jamie?' Beth's concerned voice was like an echo in a deep dark tunnel.

It wasn't until he felt her hand on his back, rubbing gently, that he pulled his hands away and faced her.

'I have so many thoughts. I don't want to jump the gun, but I can't help thinking of the future or the fact I could be a dad already. It's mind-blowing.'

What messed him up was all the years he'd missed. Six precious years of watching his son grow. His first steps, his first laugh, his first smile. He would never be able to see them. He felt like he'd been robbed, he felt the loss immensely. The more he thought about it, the more his chest tightened, each breath harder than the last.

'You can't get too carried away until you know the facts.' A pause. 'Jamie?'

Beth leaned down so he was forced to meet her eyes. Only now he realised her hand was on his thigh, squeezing gently.

'Until you have the truth you need to stop tormenting yourself. This could all be for nothing.'

He knew she was right, yet his gut was churning, almost screaming at him that his suspicions were correct. It made sense. 'I know, but did you see Alice while that was being read out? She had her head down, didn't look at anyone other than Jan. She wouldn't look my way.' He had tried to catch her eye to see if he could read her thoughts but she'd shielded them, which only made him think he was onto something. 'And the way she reacted when we first ran into each other. There was fear, panic. What if she's scared that I'll find out and want to see him?'

'Whoa, slow the train down. Deep breaths,' Beth ordered. 'No jumping ahead of yourself, remember?' Cornflower eyes bored into his. 'Do you hear me? Just take a breath and step back.' Her lips pressed together. 'You need a distraction.'

He was quite happy with Beth being his distraction. Already he felt his panic fade away and his brain slowed until it was just Beth's freckles he was focused on.

After a moment, Jan appeared out the front of her cottage, a folder under one arm and her phone in her other hand.

The door beside them opened and Simone poked her head out. 'We have a one-hour session? Where do we do that?' she asked Jan, not even seeing Jamie and Beth on the seat against the wall.

Jan stopped near Simone, sunglasses firmly in place. 'Yes we do, in the function room,' she confirmed briskly and gestured for Simone to get moving.

Beth froze beside him to the point he thought she'd stopped breathing. He frowned, wondering why she was so tense.

They didn't utter a word as Jan and Simone headed inside the house. The door shut with a loud metallic clang. Jan had made no effort to acknowledge them. Jamie found her rather imperious, and she had a strut and stare to match.

'This is my chance,' Beth murmured before grabbing his hand and jumping up. 'Come on. I need your help.'

'What?'

Beth pulled him along towards the cottage, throwing glances back over her shoulder. 'We're going to do some snooping,' she whispered.

'What?' he repeated, feeling like he'd missed a whole conversation. Beth was dragging him towards Jan's cottage door. If this was her way of getting his mind off Alice and being a father, well, it was working. This was madness.

'Just help me, please?'

Wild eyes begged him as her fingers clutched the door handle. It clicked open, and he found himself following Beth inside.

# 17

## Beth

IT WAS DO OR DIE. WELL, MAYBE NOT LITERALLY, BUT BETH felt she might die if her heart pounded any faster. Could Jamie hear it?

Beth shut the door behind them softly and realised she was still holding Jamie's hand. The warmth left as she let go. 'I'm sorry to drag you into this but I need an accomplice. Quick, we need to find her office.'

The cottage had a small open-plan lounge, dining and kitchen area, and off to one side was the bedroom. No computers or files were lying about. Beth stepped towards the bedroom as Jamie spoke up.

'Um . . . Beth? Going to tell me why I'm trespassing? You win, my mind is clear. No more kid talk.'

'Shh, keep your voice down.' Beth shot her finger to her lips and glanced around wildly. 'You know how I'm not here to write . . . well, this is why.'

'I'm not following,' he said, even though he followed her into the bedroom and shut the door.

By the wardrobe Beth spotted a desk, set up with a laptop, printer and neat stacks of folders and papers. She rushed towards it and started to rifle through the papers. Tingles exploded around her body making her fingers slip and her breathing heavy.

A warm palm pressed against her back. 'Beth?'

*Shit.* Jamie was still waiting for an answer.

She spoke quickly and quietly. 'I think . . . no, we know, Jan's a fraud and I'm here to find some sort of proof.'

'A *fraud?*'

'Look,' she said leaning against his shoulder so she could get whispered words closer to his ear. 'My sister Poppy did Jan's retreat two years ago and then Jan's new book came out with Poppy's biggest secret in it, splashed all over the pages, practically word for word. Poppy is pissed off, like, *really* pissed off. That's her secret, her pain. And Jan stole it.'

There was a pause as he thought through her words.

'Anyway,' Beth continued, 'she wants me to, I don't know, find proof that Jan is using her retreats to steal people's secrets for her books.'

Beth wasn't sure if he would understand. Hell, she didn't want to do it either. She'd told Poppy to forget about it, no one would know it was her secret in the book. No one could put the pieces together. But Poppy was not willing to let Jan get away with it.

'That's outrageous,' Jamie finally murmured.

He believed her. Without any details, he straight-up believed her. Beth took a moment to process it while her heart swelled with gratitude.

'My sister's been to hell, and this is the first thing that has given her a purpose, so I have to see it through.'

He opened his mouth to reply when a metal clang sounded in the distance and they both froze, eyes wide.

'The door!' Beth said realising. 'Shit, hide.'

Beth put down the pages she hadn't yet read and turned to the bed. Jamie had the same idea and bent down to get under it but cursed instead.

'There's no room.' He pointed while getting back up. 'The wardrobe.'

Beth reefed open the door and eyed the space under the hanging clothes . . . it would be tight. She pushed the thoughts of being squished into a confined space with Jamie from her mind, replacing them with police sirens and jail time instead. 'We can't get caught,' she whispered.

Jan's high heels clicked along the path before they stopped and the door handle to the cottage rattled.

Without deliberating further Jamie threw himself into the bottom of the wardrobe and Beth half climbed and half fell in on top of him. It was narrow and the only place left was to sit on top of Jamie. Her legs nestled between his as she pulled the door closed as far as she could without jamming her finger. Just a tiny sliver of light crept through as she leaned back.

They stilled and strained to hear Jan. That's when Beth noticed the rise and fall of Jamie's chest against her back, his breath fluttering past her ear and his strong arms around her waist. When had he put them there, she wondered, though there was nowhere else for them to go that wouldn't pop the door back open. *Oh Lord!*

The click-clack of Jan's heels drew closer then went quiet as she stepped onto the carpet in the bedroom. Beth held her breath as Jamie tensed. It was hard enough to breathe without feeling like they were yelling out, *We're hiding in the wardrobe!* The scent that was weaving its way up through her nose didn't help. She tried not to think how close they were, but the more she tried the more the contours of his body pressed in; she felt every hitch of his breath and the way his fingers gripped her waist.

*Oh dear.*

A door closed, and a fan came on in the ensuite bathroom.

'Jesus, Beth,' Jamie huffed against her ear. 'What are we doing?'

'Hiding,' she whispered back, grateful for the noisy bathroom fan. 'I thought it was obvious.'

'Not funny.'

Beth moved a little, trying to find a spot where she wouldn't feel like a lead elephant on Jamie.

His strong fingers dug into her hips until she settled.

'So, if I have this right . . .' He paused. 'Poppy killed your mother?'

Jamie's words were so soft, they barely reached her ears.

She swallowed. 'Yes.' It still hurt to hear the words. They'd been a hidden truth for so long.

'And you were the sister with scars that ruined your beauty.'

Beth almost snorted. 'I'm not sure I was ever a beauty, Poppy embellished that bit.' No amount of begging or pleading to get Poppy to understand that she didn't care about her scars, that she didn't hold any resentment towards her sister, could stop Poppy from punishing herself.

'You're still a beauty, even with your scars.'

Beth caught her lip between her teeth, her tongue flicking across the ridges of her scar. Had he just said that? Twice now he'd paid her compliments. No man had ever looked at her the way Jamie did. It was like he didn't see them, and yet Beth knew they were still there; she felt the pull of her skin with each facial expression.

'Jesus, will you stop moving,' he growled. His hands were again clenched at her sides trying to hold her still.

'I'm sorry,' she hissed back. 'I'm trying not to crush you.'

He chuckled. 'You won't crush me. That should be the least of your worries.'

His voice hitched slightly, and the penny finally dropped. More like the penny pushed its way into her back.

Beth froze. 'What. Why?' She was confused. Her body on the other hand was thrilled with this realisation. Her lower belly suddenly felt like molten liquid.

'Hey, I can't control it. What did you expect? We're crammed together in a dark wardrobe, sweet apple perfume everywhere and you're rubbing up against me. It's been a while since I've been this close to a woman,' he murmured.

Jamie's lips were so close they brushed against her earlobe, sending jolts of fire scorching down her legs. She tilted her head, making out his jawline in the faint sliver of light. His breath caressed her face and she became aware of her palm pressed against his muscled pecs. When had she moved her hand? Must have been when she twisted around to talk to him; she was almost sideways along his body and her face was far too close to his lips.

Either Beth had forgotten how to breathe, or there was no oxygen left in the wardrobe. Was she about to pass out? She couldn't think, her body was taking over, reacting before she had time to put a lid on it. There was mutiny aboard the good ship Beth; her common sense had walked the plank.

'Beth?'

'Hmm?' It was all the reply she could muster.

'May I kiss you?'

Beth wasn't sure if she gave him an answer or he just didn't wait for one. Warm lips brushed against hers. A hand left her waist, finding her cheek as he brushed his thumb across her jaw then pressed a proper kiss to her lips.

His breath mixed with hers, lips crushed together, soft, intoxicating. The building momentum, the heat, the need. She parted her lips and let him taste and explore. His tongue brushed across her scar and it was thrilling, as if he was saying, *I see all of you.* He didn't pull away or stop, but kept kissing her until she lost all sense of where they were.

Her fingers ran over his arms – she couldn't explore much more of him in this awkward position. If they were on that bed rather than stuck in a wardrobe . . .

The thought brought her back to the present as she tore her lips away from his, trying not to sound like she'd just run a marathon.

At that moment she heard the toilet flush, water running and then the door opening and closing. Their lips were just centimetres apart, she could feel his heat and his soft breath. Beth's heart was racing, but was it from the kiss or the fear of being caught?

They didn't dare move as Jan's muffled steps came so close. Jamie was rigid against her, all of him. It sent a shiver down her spine thinking about it.

*Get a grip, Beth!*

A drawer on the desk was opened and closed and then Jan headed back outside. The bedroom door shut. Click clack. Then the main door to the cottage closed. Click clack.

'Thank God, let's go.'

But Jamie didn't let her go, he held her to him. 'Wait, before you open that door.'

Beth rolled over fully onto him, not worried about making a noise. She melted against him, causing heat to flare from her centre. His lips claimed hers. No asking this time. His hand on her back held her tightly to him while his lean legs closed in, clamping her into position.

Bright light poured in as the door was flung open by a stray knee. They lay awkwardly, centimetres apart, breathing and trying to read each other. Jamie's eyes dropped to her lips and she realised if she didn't make a move, they might never leave the wardrobe cocoon. She started to crawl off him.

'Damn, you taste good.'

Beth glanced back at him, wondering if she'd heard him right. The cheeky grin on his face certainly implied it.

She jabbed out a hand and pulled him up.

'Let's see what we can find and get the hell out of here.'

Jamie tried to sort the wardrobe back to how it had been. 'Oh my God, there's a night gown in here with puppies on it and some fluffy slippers.'

He was bent over, straightening said pink fluffy slippers. It didn't go with Jan's portrayed image at all. 'Weird.'

Beth shook her head, trying to get some perspective back as she started searching through the pages on the desk. Lots of notes. A yellow folder held some printed sheets and Beth recognised the piece that had been read out earlier. Try as she might there was no way of connccting it to Alice. No accidental name or clues left behind.

'What, is that our stuff?'

She nodded. 'I don't want to know what they say. If I read them, I'll be no better than Jan.'

He put his hand on hers and closed the cover on the folder. 'Then let's not. Look for older retreats. Try her computer.'

Beth wiggled the mouse and hoped that Jan didn't have any screen locks. It went straight to her desktop and she breathed a sigh of relief.

'Look these files are labelled "Story ideas" and they have dates. Do you think they're dates from other retreats?'

Jamie held up his phone and took a photo. 'One way to find out. We can look up previous ones and match them to these.'

'Good thinking,' she said, noting his use of *we*.

'Email them to yourself so we can compare them to Jan's other books, then delete them from her sent box.'

Beth stared at him.

'I read a lot of books, and you can pick up a lot from TV shows,' he said with a smirk.

'I'm thinking I picked the right accomplice,' she said. 'You do it, you'll be a lot quicker than me.' She tried hard not to glance at his butt as he bent over to email the files to himself.

'I've done three folders, looks like most only have five or six attachments. All stories. This could be it.'

'Poppy said they emailed them to Jan and then she handed them back to each one in an envelope with her comments, that way it all was private and confidential. Only Jan knew.'

Jamie shuddered and Beth suddenly wondered what his secret was. Had he written about Alice? For a moment she stared at the folder with their stories. Would she be tempted if Jamie wasn't here? She wondered if Jan found it addictive, reading everyone's secrets.

Beth paused again, ears straining. When she couldn't hear a thing, she checked her watch. 'Can you see anything else that might help?'

'Um. Maybe,' he said strangely.

He took more photos of the computer screen with his phone and then tried to put everything back to normal, deleting the sent emails once the last one went.

'Are you going to share?' she said, pulling on his arm.

'When we get out of here, yep.'

Jamie latched onto her hand, pulling her towards the bedroom door. He checked the coast was clear before they ran to the front door. Beth opened it slowly until she could check the verandah was empty, then they bolted out and back to the seat.

'Let's go back to my room,' he said.

Nodding, she picked up the book and tried to follow Jamie in slow measured steps.

'I can't believe we did that,' she murmured as they rounded the corner.

'I know,' he whispered back. 'You made me do naughty things.'

But the grin on his face said he was thinking about what happened in the wardrobe, not the breaking and entering.

# 18

## *Alice*

THE CLICK OF THE KEYBOARD WAS BECOMING HER CALMING mantra. Because when Alice was working the keys it meant she was pouring out all the things she wanted to say and share. Things she was still unable to put a voice to. Yet Jan had read them out.

She stared at the leather-bound journal beside her on the desk. Her life was in those pages. Her secret-keeper. Her most intimate thoughts and memories, scribbled in coloured inks, sometimes smeared with tears. Now she needed to find the strength to put them down in her memoir. Like Jan had said, a great book needed emotion and the ability to reach out to the reader. Alice wasn't sure if hers would be what anyone would want to read, but she knew she had to write it.

Her eyes began to feel gritty, staring at her journal for so long while her mind ran wild. With a sigh she pushed her chair back and went to the bathroom. A splash of water on her skin would help. While drying her face she heard something; she realised it was sobs coming from Simone's room.

The door was ajar.

'Simone? Are you okay?'

When no reply came, she opened it and spotted Simone on her bed, a cushion hugged to her chest and mascara streaks across her face.

Alice grabbed the box of tissues from the bathroom and went and sat on Simone's bed.

'Here.'

'Thanks,' she sniffed, grabbing a handful of tissues and smothering her face.

'Did you just have your session with Jan?' she asked softly.

Simone nodded, her blonde locks falling forward. As she pushed them back Alice noticed the extensions near her roots behind her ears.

'That bad?'

Simone smiled through her tears. 'No, not really. It just got a bit much, you know?' The tissues were balled up in her fists and she used them to pat her eyes again. 'I must look a right mess,' she sighed.

Alice touched her arm. 'You're fine. Do you want to talk about it? Jan can move quite quickly through all the information.'

Simone's bottom lip quivered. 'It's so much to take in and I'm not sure if I have any skill at writing. How am I going to do this? I'm so stressed. Being an online sensation is hard work and I don't like it. And now they want a book about it.' She threw up her arms.

Alice had a feeling this was about more than fear of writing a book.

'They'll help you. Once you get the first draft done, their editors will go through it and help you make it better.'

'Are you sure?'

'I have some friends through a writing group who assure me that's where the real book takes shape.' Alice paused. 'Or is something else bothering you?'

Simone looked like one of her kids when they'd done something they knew she wasn't going to like – big eyes and an expression that would melt ice.

'There's stuff I'd rather not write about, you know?'

Alice shifted on the bed. 'I understand. I'm writing my memoir, which I hope to get published one day, and that's about everything I've done, about the good and the bad.'

Simone frowned. 'Bad?'

She seemed doubtful, as if she didn't believe Alice could have done anything bad. But there were difference versions of bad: drug dealer bad; 'left your kid in a hot car' bad; rude to someone bad. She'd noticed Jamie was particularly good at the last one. If Simone had picked up on his rudeness, she hadn't shown it. Alice hadn't thought Jamie would be that sort. Then again, had she ever really known him?

Alice nodded. 'No one's perfect. We all make mistakes, we all stuff up. It's how we go forward that matters. I'm writing to clear the air, I guess you could say. I'm hoping my journey through murky waters might help others. Plus, I think it's helpful to write down the deep things, the stuff that's hardest to talk about. You should try it.'

Simone looked sceptical.

'It won't be easy, but the truth can also be freeing.' That's what Alice was working towards. 'Baby steps, Simone.

Sometimes I just write a memory that pops up in the moment, then I work on it and expand on it until it's ready to shuffle into my book.' And it never got easier. Each memory filled her with shame, horror and fear, but it was so much easier to deal with it once it was on the page. It couldn't hurt her, it was just words on a page.

'Well,' said Simone, with a slightly more hopeful tone, 'I *have* been doing a little bit. Snippets from when I was little and how I think my dad leaving affected me.'

'How old were you when he left?' Alice asked carefully. She didn't want to push the issue, but her gut told her Simone needed an ear, even someone who talked as much as she did.

'I was about eleven when he left. I didn't know why he'd left; Mum said he was off finding work. I don't think she could bring herself to say he'd left her. Instead he was off getting married and starting a new family.'

Alice sat quietly, giving Simone time.

'Dad had to run around after Mum a lot. When he left, it was up to me. I just feel like I didn't have a great childhood.' Simone's jaw tightened.

'Have you ever thought about getting counselling?'

'No, I had enough of that at school. Instead of just treating the bullies they wanted me to talk to a counsellor.' Simone snorted. 'How backwards is that? Then in high school they wanted to medicate me, but I'd heard how antidepressants can make you gain weight, and I didn't need that either.'

'But a counsellor would also just be there to listen, without judgement, to all your concerns and it wouldn't get back to your huge following.'

Simone's nose wiggled and her lips pressed together as she considered it. 'I guess I could try, if you think it would help.'

'It might help you decide what you want to write about in your book. I know talking with my counsellor has helped.'

'You have a counsellor?'

Alice nodded.

'But why?' Simone frowned. 'Sorry, I don't mean to pry, it just seems to me like you have everything together.'

Alice didn't feel like going into details. 'Looks can be deceiving, Simone. We all like to put on brave faces and pretend everything is alright when inside we are a ball of twisted emotions.'

'Yeah, totally. That person on my Instagram isn't me. Not the real me in here.' She touched her chest.

'That's the downside to social media, it can make it easy to pretend.'

'Don't I know it,' Simone mumbled. She dropped the ball of tissues on the drawers by her bed. 'I really appreciate you talking with me. Maybe a counsellor can help me find a happier path.'

Alice gave her hand a squeeze. 'If you're not happy, it starts with you. You need to make the changes. Sometimes facing the hardest things in life is the most worthwhile or rewarding.' She stood up and glanced at her watch. 'It's nearly time for dinner. You want to come down with me?'

'I bet I look awful.' Simone dragged herself off the bed. 'Thanks, Alice. I don't . . . I don't have many friends.'

'I've lost a few friends over the years and what it taught me is that the ones who stick around through everything are the real ones. You need to be comfortable being you, not what you think others want you to be. And it's never too late to make new friends,' she said with a smile. 'Come and get me when you're ready to head down.'

Alice returned to her desk, her mind now even more busy than before she'd taken a break.

She knew that memories were something she couldn't bury, no matter how hard she tried. At random moments they would emerge as clear as day, dragging her back down through history whether she wanted to go there or not. Her therapist Rhonda was teaching Alice to accept the past, that it couldn't be changed and she couldn't punish herself for it.

It seemed like ages ago since she'd had the last panic attack, brought on by one of her memories, but she nearly came close yesterday when she first saw Jamie. Talk about confronting! It was easier to forget that part as she went about her regular life, but not now when he was here, face to face. Opening her journal, she started to write about the feelings that clambered over her.

Shame. Embarrassment. Regret.

Jamie didn't deserve how she'd treated him. She'd left him with no explanation, but she owed him one now. First, she needed to explain it to herself.

# 19

## Alice — 2014

'ALICE, TIME TO GET UP. I'M LATE FOR WORK AND MIA NEEDS a change.'

Dale nudged her and pulled the corner of the cover down.

'I made you a coffee, and Mia's had breakfast,' he said as he kissed her forehead.

'I'm up,' she mumbled, though she felt anything but ready. She hadn't slept at all, her mind ticking like a clock all night. Sometimes it built up into a mild kind of panic attack – heart racing, skin slick. As if on a boat, she seemed to roll through the waves, sometimes calm and the next minute a full-on storm.

Alice was so tired. People kept reminding her that having a baby was hard, the hardest thing she would ever do. She'd thought she was prepared for it – in theory – but she'd had no idea it would be this difficult.

'Don't forget you have the gym today,' said Dale.

Alice sat bolt upright. *Gym day.*

Gym day was the only day that Alice seemed to look forward to. The day she could leave this life behind and pretend she had a different one. One where she wasn't a disappointment.

'I've fed Mia, she's playing happily in her playpen, so you've got a few minutes,' he added as he left the bedroom.

Alice strained her ears, heard the front door close and the car pull away. The house remained silent. No screaming Mia. Surely, she had time for a shower? Throwing back the covers, she got out of bed, and showered. Her quick shower had ended up much longer and it had taken a while to decide on her outfit, but she hadn't heard Mia in all that time. Her ears strained again for cries as she headed downstairs. A sick heartburn feeling rose up her throat.

Mia was, as Dale said, in her playpen with toys around her. Only she was fast asleep on her back. *Thank God.*

A guilt-tinged relief flooded through her. She wished she could be a better mum for Mia. Why couldn't she get it together? Everyone at her mothers' group seemed well adjusted. *It will get better*, her mum kept telling her, but Mia was nearly eight months old. When was it going to get better?

On the table sat the coffee Dale had made her. She tipped the cold liquid down the sink and got her bag ready for the gym, even though she didn't have to leave for another half hour or so.

Alice stood over her daughter, expecting to feel love, but instead an awful dread rushed through her, a feeling that something bad was going to happen. Sarah would be here soon to babysit. Sarah was better with Mia than Alice could ever be. Another failure rubbed in her face.

She couldn't smell Mia, so she decided her number one could wait for a change, especially as she was sleeping. Was it too much to hope she'd sleep until Sarah arrived?

Alice stepped back and sank down onto the edge of the couch. She was still perched there staring into space when Sarah arrived. Time had been sucked away as if she'd been in a void, stuck between dimensions.

'Oh, she's so gorgeous when she's asleep,' said Sarah, going straight to Mia. 'That hair and those lips.'

Alice stood, running her hands down her leggings as she tried to rouse her mind. 'She needs a change, but I didn't want to wake her.'

'That's fine, I can sort it when she's awake. Have you got everything you need?'

*My bag.* Alice grabbed it from the kitchen along with the car keys. She was meeting Jamie this morning before he started work.

'Enjoy your day,' Sarah called out after her.

Sarah used to babysit for two hours, but it had grown to a full day here and there. Alice had told Dale she needed some time, and he'd agreed. Dale had been a little concerned, always asking if she was okay, but she'd fobbed him off saying some time with her friends would help. But Alice had lost interest in her friends and had started ditching mothers' group as well. It was almost a full-time job trying to stop their parents from coming around all the time. Alice just wanted everyone to go away. To give her the space to be a person again, not just a mother.

Jamie gave her that. With Jamie she wasn't a terrible mother and wife and friend . . . the list could go on. She lay awake most nights thinking about it.

'Hey, finally. Ready?'

Jamie was waiting at the car park of the gym for her and opened her car door.

'Up to your apartment?' she asked, stepping into his arms and feeling the rush of adrenaline. She welcomed that feeling. At least it was something, a change from the emptiness she felt in her other life, her real life.

'Come on, let's go get a coffee first.' Jamie pulled away, threaded his fingers through hers and started to lead her to the coffee shop down the road from the gym.

Alice didn't want conversation. That would mean more lies. Alice didn't want coffee in public. That could mean being spotted. Alice wanted to strip Jamie naked and be taken to a place that wasn't on this earth.

Last week was the first time she'd gone to his apartment, above the gym, only because there were late classes still on. Other times they'd worked it so they were alone at the gym, more shower sex. Sex in his office, sex against the wall of the locker room. It was hot, fast and intense.

His place had been different. At his place and on his bed he'd wanted to take his time. Not that that was a bad thing. It was just a little too personal. Jamie wanted this to be a relationship. Alice did not. Jamie wanted to know more about her, started asking far too many questions. She refused to answer; luckily, he thought she was just being mysterious.

'While you know nothing about me the sex will always be like this,' she'd informed him. Keeping him distracted was the key, and she was all over that.

'Jamie, I already had a coffee. Can we give it a miss?' She tried to flutter her eyelashes through a heated gaze.

He slowed and then stopped.

*That's it, let's go work up a sweat.*

But instead of heading back he just stood there, head cocked.

'What?' she asked at the same time as his grip tightened.

He pulled her hand up to his face like he was going to kiss her fingers and then stared at the rings. The rings she'd forgotten to take off in her hurry to get out to the car this morning.

*Oh shit.*

'Alice?'

It was all he said, only her name. But the way he said it twisted the knife in further. Just another wound to add to the self-inflicted ones.

*I'm a horrible person.*

'Is this why you've been so coy? So mysterious?'

Mouth tightly closed, she said nothing. Could only stare at him for ruining her last chance to feel something.

He flung her hand away as if it were a red-hot coal and scowled. 'Here I was thinking you were teasing me, trying to keep things interesting, but you were really hiding the fact that you're married?' He pushed his fingers into his hair. 'Jesus, Alice.'

'It's okay. We don't have to stop.'

'No. No. *No.*' He stormed off back towards the gym then stopped, spinning around to face her again. 'I won't be a home-wrecker, Alice. I hate that you did this to me. You used me.'

'Please, Jamie, I need you,' she said, running after him.

'Why? You have a husband. And don't try to tell me you're separated.'

He stopped suddenly, his chest heaving.

'Are you separated?' he asked gently.

Alice wished she could lie, but nothing came out. Instead she pressed her palm against his chest. 'Please, Jamie . . .'

Please . . . what? What could she say? *I need you to feel alive. Without you I'm just a ghost.*

His eyes were blazing heat, his body rigid and cold.

'I'm sorry,' was all she could muster.

'It's a bit late for that.' He wrenched her hand from his chest. 'How long were you going to string me along? Was I just some bit of meat to help you through a slump in your marriage?'

Each word was aimed at her heart and she knew she deserved every one of them. She was a crappy person. Not fit to be a wife. Not fit to be a mother.

Jamie strode off to the gym, disappearing inside.

Cars drove past as she stood on the footpath, not even able to conjure up tears. She was a shell of a person. Just a shell with nothing inside but a blackness that went on forever.

No point going to her class now. It was the last thing she felt like doing. Alice numbly got back in her car and drove to a nearby park, not wanting to go home either.

On the green grass, families played, dads pushing prams, mums laughing as they chatted and bounced babies on their hips. Watching them was beyond painful. Alice didn't want to be here anymore. Not the park. Not anywhere. She didn't feel like living anymore. Her bed, she just wanted to lie in her bed and try to sleep, she was so tired.

Somehow Alice ended up back home. She didn't remember the drive. Or telling Sarah she didn't feel well and was going to lie down.

'Alice, how are you feeling?'

Alice tried to focus on Sarah's young bright face as she stood at the doorway to her bedroom. It took long moments for her to get her brain to register what Sarah was saying.

'I really have to go now. Do you want me to call Dale or your mum and see if they can watch Mia while you're unwell?'

With a faked smile she tried to sit up, but her body wouldn't respond. It was as though she was duct-taped to her bed.

'Oh, it's okay, Sarah. I'm feeling better. Thank you.'

The last thing she needed was her mum fussing around or disrupting Dale at work.

'If you're sure. I'd happily stay but I have another job at two.'

Sarah glanced at her watch and Alice noticed it was afternoon already. But she hadn't slept at all. How had the time evaporated so quickly?

'I understand. I'll see you next time.'

*Just leave already.*

Thankfully, Sarah disappeared. Alice dragged herself from her bed, still in her gym leggings and singlet. She put on a jacket and headed downstairs.

It was well past lunch, but she wasn't hungry. The thought of preparing food made her feel sick.

Mia was starting to stir, her whimpers affecting Alice like nails down a chalk board. She knew crying came next. Loud needy crying. Could she tape her mouth? Maybe wear ear plugs?

*No . . . no . . . no.*

Why couldn't she be a better mum? Mia deserved better.

People had told her about postnatal depression, she'd read about it before Mia was born but she didn't realise it could last for this long or morph into this feeling of nothingness.

Alice couldn't take it anymore. As the whimpering grew louder she had to leave. Had to get out. Had to find air. She couldn't breathe, couldn't think.

Opening the front door, she walked out into the sunshine and across the road to the park not far from their house, Mia's cries disappearing along with the prickling sensation down her spine. A little bench seat appeared, and Alice sat and stared at everything and nothing. The joggers and pram-pushers may as well have been invisible as they passed; the dogs on leads, kids on skateboards with school bags, they whizzed by in a blur and yet Alice sat, like a stone at the bottom of a river.

She couldn't keep feeling like this. Couldn't keep going.

'Alice? Oh God, there you are.'

Slowly she lifted her eyes to find Dale standing in front of her. Mia was in his arms, face red and wet.

'What are you doing home?' she wondered aloud. Was it that late already?

'Nadia called me because Mia had been crying for ages and she was concerned. I asked her to go over and she found the door open and Mia distraught. I came straight home.'

His face was strange, his eyes dark and accusing, as if he wanted to be angry and yet was holding himself back to try to understand what was going on. Which was funny, because Alice didn't even know herself.

'I think I need help,' she whispered. 'I can't keep going like this.'

Dale sat down on the bench, swinging Mia onto his lap.

'Like extra home help?' he asked. 'Or is it more than that?'

Alice shook her head. 'I feel so empty. Something's wrong with me.'

He scooped up her lifeless hands. 'It's okay, honey.'

His eyes were cloudy with confusion, but she couldn't explain what she'd done. She could sense his despair, and see the way he held Mia so tightly with so much love, but Alice couldn't feel any of it. She was emotionless. Vacant. Could Dale see that now? Alice turned, staring back out at the park with unseeing eyes.

'Jesus, Alice,' he whispered.

She tilted her head to Dale. He should hate her, had every right.

'I didn't mean to abandon Mia, I just . . . I don't know.' Her shoulders started to shake yet no tears came.

Dale put his arm around her and pulled her in close. 'I thought you were having a hard time, but I didn't realise how much. I'm sorry.'

In that moment, the tiniest bit of hope flared like burning a candle with hardly any wick.

# 20

## Simone — 2015

'MUM, DID YOU PAY THE POWER BILL?'

Simone stuck her head into the lounge room. Cecilia sat on the couch watching the midday movie.

'No, my knee was playing up yesterday,' she said, stretching out to rub it. 'Can you do it, please?'

At age eighteen Simone could roll her eyes with the best of them. Cecilia seemed to have aches and pains when it suited her and yet she could find the TV remote or get to the fridge just fine when she was home alone.

'Mum, I don't get paid until Thursday. I spent all my money on food and rent.'

*And the new top from Target.*

Simone tugged on the bottom of her green work shirt. It was embarrassing that Woolworths had had to give her a man's shirt because the women's sizes weren't big enough. It wasn't a different style, but all the staff knew. The cut was a little

different, enough to make her feel awkward when she caught
them staring at her.

'Don't you have any money left? Give me your card and
I'll get some out at the ATM on my way to work,' she said,
palm out expectantly as she eyed off the eBay page open on
Cecilia's old laptop.

'I don't think I have enough in the bank. Have to wait for
pay day,' Cecilia replied.

Simone knew she meant dole day. But Cecilia liked to
pretend. Just like she still pretended Harry was off looking
for work.

'Oh well, if they cut off the power, there'll be no TV,' Simone
said snarkily and went back to the kitchen to sort out her lunch.

The rubbish bin was overflowing, Coke cans and food
wrappers spilling onto the floor like lava from an erupting
volcano. If Simone waited for her mum to tidy it up, the mess
would stay there forever.

'Take the rubbish out, Simmo, my legs and back hurt too
much.'

*Ugh.*

Kicking an empty can, Simone decided the rubbish could
wait. Punish her mum a little. Only she knew her mum didn't
care; she'd just keep throwing her rubbish beside the bin. Some
days Simone could see why her dad left.

She packed her lunchbox with a chicken wrap leftover from
last night, some snacks and a can of soft drink, and headed for
the door. Piles of empty boxes and packaging lined the hallway
and she had to shift them to open the door. *Bloody Mum and
bloody eBay!* If there was a way to stop her mum from getting

online and buying stuff off eBay, she'd do it. Maybe letting the power bill slide would be a good thing.

Simone used to walk to work before she'd got her licence, but now with her P plates she drove her mum's car. It's not like she ever drove it anymore. She couldn't even get in it.

First she went next door to Mrs Satish's old house and picked some Mr Lincoln roses from the bushes that lined the street edge near the low white picket fence. Life wasn't the same without Mrs Satish nearby. A young family had bought her home and they never seemed to notice the missing flowers. Four perfect blooms would do. She placed them carefully on the passenger seat.

The small car was a tight fit for Simone, but it was worth the freedom it gave her. It was practically hers now; she paid the registration and bought the fuel. With an hour before she was due at work she took the familiar route to Willow's Rest.

With roses clutched tightly she headed inside the building and waved to the woman at reception.

'Hi, Regina.'

'Morning, Simone.'

Regina's face didn't hold its usual bright smile, and straight-away Simone knew that today wasn't a good day. She knocked then pushed open the door to room number eight and smiled upon seeing Mrs Satish's face.

'Good morning, Mrs Satish. How are you today?' she said. 'I brought your favourites.'

Mrs Satish was sitting in her armchair, knitted blanket over her knees. The TV was on but the volume was down. She turned from the window and smiled.

'Oh, those are lovely. Thank you, dear.'

Simone visited as often as possible, but it wasn't the same as having her next door. And since going into the home two years ago, Mrs Satish had deteriorated. Simone's nose prickled, tears threatening. It always did when she thought Mrs Satish didn't recognise her. It hurt to be forgotten by the only person who seemed to care about her.

Simone waddled over, knelt by her chair and held the roses out for Mrs Satish to smell and touch.

'My favourites, Mr Lincoln.'

'Yes, that's right.' Simone held her frail hand and wanted to hug her tightly and cry her eyes out.

'What's wrong, Simone? You look sad today.'

Simone beamed as her tears fell. 'I'm so happy to see you. I miss you so much.'

'But I'm right here, dear.'

Mrs Satish squeezed her hand back, still strong for such a wisp of a person. One robust breeze would blow her away like a feather.

Regina had been wrong, today was a good day.

'Would you like to play a game of cards? I have a little time.'

'Sounds wonderful. Do I know how to play cards?' she asked.

Simone laughed. 'Oh, yes. Even when you don't think you do, you still manage to win.'

A glass vase sat empty on the TV cabinet, so Simone filled it with water and arranged the flowers, putting them on display where Mrs Satish could easily see them. Under the TV, in a drawer, she collected the cards and they played a few rounds of Fish.

'Knock, Knock. Sorry to interrupt but it's time for the doctor's visit,' said Regina, leaning against the door. 'She always looks happy when you're here,' she added.

Simone blinked rapidly, feeling the emotion swell.

'Okay, I best head off to work. I'll be back soon. Next time I'm sure I'll win,' she said, bending to give Mrs Satish a kiss on her papery cheek.

'You can try,' she said with a grin.

Gone were her purple curls, replaced with white strands of silk. And if Simone had thought she was wrinkly when she was little, it was nothing compared to the woman shrinking inside her skin now. Her face was gaunt, her eye sockets seemed too big for her eyes and her bones jutted out.

And Simone loved her more than ever.

'I'll see you tomorrow.'

Regina moved out of the doorway so Simone could pass.

'Hi, Mr Holmes, how are you? Are you okay?' Simone went to help the old man who had dropped his hanky and was trying to bend over to pick it up, his walking stick wobbling precariously.

'Here, I'll get it,' she said scooping it up and then helping him to regain his balance.

'Thank you, Simone. Are you here to play cards?' he asked hopefully.

'Not today, sorry. I have work. But the weekend is in two more days. I'll see you all then.' She patted his shoulder gently and waved goodbye.

With her hands in her pockets, Simone headed back to the car and on to work. Visiting Mrs Satish was the highlight of her day and also the most depressing part. Why did life have to change? She used to think that Mrs Satish would always live next door. But that was a child's dream.

'Hi Simone, looks like it's you and me on the deli section today.'

Tina was putting on a hairnet over her short bob, the tattoo of a bird on her wrist moving as if it were in flight. Simone liked Tina. She never looked at her as if she were something she'd trod in.

'That's cool.' Then she frowned. 'You look different, Tina.' Her hair was the same, it wasn't that. But overall, she seemed slimmer maybe. 'Have you lost weight?'

Tina beamed. 'Yes, I have. Can you tell?' She pressed her palms down her black jeans. 'I've just fitted into a size fourteen jeans. I feel great.'

'Congrats,' said Simone while trying to curb the powerful thrum of jealousy.

When Mrs Satish had taken a turn for the worse and the doctors wanted to put her in residential care, Simone had been so scared she'd decided to try to lose some weight for her own health. It was so hard. The hardest thing she'd ever tried to do, and after all that effort she'd lost just a kilo. She'd tried to eat less and go for walks but it was tricky with no help – in fact, her mum seemed determined to sabotage her, waving packets of Tim Tams in her face after she got back from a walk, or cooking her favourite pasta dish when she'd told her it was a fasting day.

*You're big boned, Simmy. Not eating won't fix that.*

'Thank you,' Tina said. 'I've joined the Alive program. They have these shakes.' She opened her bag and showed Simone the packet. 'They have all the goodies in them, and I use it as a meal replacement. It's so easy to prepare, which makes it easier to stick to. If you ever want to try one, let me know. This one's chocolate and it's divine.'

'Alive? Never heard of it.'

Tina gave her a rundown of the company and the products as they headed to the deli section to start work. 'They're jam-packed with nutrients and minerals and active enzymes for your digestion. Oh, and it satisfies cravings, so you feel fuller longer.'

'I'm not sure I can afford it.' Simone shrugged. It did sound good, though. She'd love to be able to lose some weight so she could help Mrs Satish more. And to not puff like a freight train on the walk to the deli section from the staff room. Her knees ached and she didn't want to end up like her mum, stuck in a chair all day. Simone wanted so much more. She wanted to be able to flit around like a butterfly, hopping from one place to the next with ease and without pain. She wanted to wear pretty clothes and to have people see her like Mrs Satish did. The only clothes she could find were shaped like a tent in plain dark colours.

'You don't have to. With the products I sell it pays for what I use. If you're keen, I can help you set up and build your own Alive business. You can use social media, if you know how, and as it grows you make more money.'

'Um, well, I'm on Facebook and Instagram, but no one follows me.' But Simone liked the idea of earning more money. And losing weight. This Alive program sounded too good to be true.

'You'd be surprised at how many people want to lose weight and feel better. I sell the Alive products to friends and family and you could do it too. Build up your own members. It'll grow itself when you start posting all the results you get. I have loads of shakes at home; I'll give some to you and you can see if you like them, and we can go from there. Are you keen?'

Tina was so excited, it was hard not to get swept up. And it must work, because she was looking amazing and Simone wanted that so badly.

'Hey Jed,' Tina said as they passed a young man stocking the shelf not far from them.

Jed was the staff hottie. Tall, handsome and athletic, with the cutest smile. Simone couldn't help but have a little crush. The only problem was that Jed didn't even know she existed.

'Hey Tina,' he said, throwing her a smile that would melt any heart.

Jed's eyes followed a customer, a thin pretty petite blonde.

'I'll do it,' Simone said suddenly.

'Pardon?'

She turned to Tina, who was getting some ham ready to slice. 'I'll try these shakes.'

Tina clapped her hands. 'Yes! It will be so great, Simone. You won't regret it.'

Simone's skin tingled with the prospect of a transformation. From a boring fat caterpillar to a thin bright butterfly.

Then Jed would see her. Everyone would see her.

# 21

## *Beth*

JAMIE HURRIED HER INTO HIS ROOM AND CLOSED THE sliding door behind him, then strode across to check the other door was closed properly.

Beth started to feel like a deer stuck in a lion enclosure, no exits, nowhere to run. What was he planning? Her pulse jumped at her wayward thoughts; she couldn't deny her attraction to him. She could pretend all she wanted but her body was screaming it loud and clear. She wanted to kiss him again.

And then she thought of Alice's son.

*Even more reason to keep your distance.*

'Let's see what we got,' he said, crossing to his desk to open his laptop.

*Damn.*

It was hard not to be a little disappointed, especially when his kisses still lingered on her lips. Maybe now they were back out in the daylight he'd realised his mistake? Just like Hudson's father.

'They've all come through.'

Beth went and knelt alongside his chair. Below Jan's emails she could see others in Jamie's inbox, all from other women.

Kelly. Sandra. Claire.

One from Susan had 'OMG! I love it' in the subject heading. Just what had he sent that was so amazing? Surely not a dick pic? Beth pushed the thought from her mind.

'I'll start looking for previous retreat dates,' she said, pulling out her phone. She needed to keep focused. 'Okay, I know the one Poppy went to was on the second of July – is that on there?'

'Yep. This one.' He opened it and looked through the folder contents. 'Look, Beth.'

Jamie was pointing to the screen. Beth gasped as she started to read the page. 'That's Poppy's! She gave me her copy of it. It's on the thumb drive in my room.'

'So, we know Jan kept a copy of her work when she said she doesn't. That's a blatant lie.'

Jamie went quiet as he read through Poppy's work.

'Wow, this is pretty heavy. No wonder Jan picked it. Poppy's a great writer. I can see why Jan didn't change much because it's so well written. That's what got her caught – she hardly changed anything.'

'Yeah, I know. Poppy loves writing, it's all she's ever wanted to do. That's what makes this so much worse. That is Poppy's trauma – it should be her sharing it with the world when she's ready, not Jan.'

'I couldn't agree more.' Jamie stopped reading and turned to Beth. 'How are you going?'

'Huh?'

He watched her a moment before he said gently, 'It's your trauma too.'

His words hit home with such force it was as though he'd punched her. Her mouth gaped for a moment.

'I . . . I'm okay. It was a long time ago.' She shrugged. 'I try not to think about it too much. I guess I buried myself in my studies and helping my dad.'

Beth sat back on the floor. Jamie pushed his chair aside and sat beside her.

'So, you're doing better than Poppy?'

'Well, it's different for me.' Beth didn't have to live with the burden of feeling responsible for their mother's death. Not only that, Poppy knew how lonely their dad was – he'd lost a wife, and Beth a mum. 'Poppy feels a lot of guilt.'

'Do you want to tell me your version of it?' Jamie asked quietly. She sighed.

'If you're up to it,' he added, 'but don't feel like you have to.'

No one had listened to her side of it, or maybe she just didn't really want to burden others with it. Either way it wasn't something she'd talked about in many, many years. And yet that night came back with such clarity.

'We'd been out for dinner, celebrating my sixteenth birthday at a fancy new restaurant. We all had wine with dinner; well, I was allowed a quick sip, but the others had more. Poppy did mention she couldn't drink much because she was driving, but I saw her have more than one. She had her own car, so we'd all come together with her.' Beth smiled as she picked at the grey carpet. 'I remember Mum was teasing Dad about how his footy team wouldn't make the finals. She told him I'd do a better job of coaching them. If anything, Dad seemed proud at that. I remember him looking at me with this twinkle in his eye, and he told Mum she was probably right and that I'd be the first woman to coach an AFL team.'

'You're that good?' Jamie asked with a grin.

Beth rolled her eyes and continued her story. 'Anyway, after dinner it was bucketing down. We walked as fast as we could through the rain and piled into the car. Dad and I were in the back, Mum was in the front with Poppy. It was a shit night, so dark and wet. We were all talking and laughing, and then suddenly the car veered off the road. Just like that. It was so quick – one minute we were chatting, the next we were . . .' Beth closed her eyes, she could almost taste the blood in her mouth.

Jamie sat quietly beside her. She stared at the carpet as she plucked at it.

'When I came to, I could smell blood. It was everywhere. I felt the . . . wetness on my face and my hands, through my shirt. Glass was in my hair and all over my lap. I remember Dad screaming my name and then crying when he saw that I was moving. Then he was leaning in between the seats to check on Mum. The car was literally wrapped around a tree; there was no getting out from the passenger side.' Beth felt the panic rise, the hopelessness, the fear in everyone's voices.

'Poppy was screaming and calling out to Mum. I remember Dad trying to see if she was okay and telling us the ambulance was on its way. I think I was in and out of consciousness. My cuts were bleeding badly and my face was starting to swell. It took a while for some of that night to come back to me. I remember snippets: Dad holding my hand crying, ambos asking me questions and trying to patch me up, getting put on a trolley. I remember seeing Poppy on the side of the road, sitting in the mud and rain rocking back and forth. It's so patchy, even now I only get tiny bits. I do remember lying on that trolley in the misty rain and staring back at the car wreck, seeing Mum still in her seat.'

Beth paused. The last image of her mum was burned into her brain. It was like she was asleep, head slumped to the side, hair over her face. And the rescuers had dropped their sense of urgency.

'All I wanted to do was to scream at everyone to get Mum out, but I couldn't talk, no words would come. I couldn't understand why no one was helping my mum.' She swallowed the lump that constricted her throat. 'I . . . I didn't find out Mum had died until I was in the hospital and Dad was able to come and tell me. I feel like I missed so much; the rest of the crash is just what Dad has told me.'

She looked at Jamie, wondering how far to go, how much to trust him. But then the words came out. 'Dad told the police he was driving that night. But he wasn't. He didn't want Poppy to be interrogated by the police, especially because she'd had a couple of drinks. They were well out of the car when help arrived, so no one could dispute it. Dad didn't think she'd blow over the limit; there was a possibility, but he didn't want to take the risk. He took the brunt of it all, answered all the questions, took care of Poppy. Meanwhile he'd lost the love of his life. Luckily, Dad didn't blow over either but was very, very close.

'Poppy was a mess. The car had aquaplaned on a pool of water and shot us off the road; it wasn't her fault. Maybe a more skilled driver could have prevented it, reacted better . . .' Beth paused, trying to gather her thoughts. 'I don't blame Poppy, but she still blames herself. She hasn't been behind the wheel since. That's why it was such a huge effort for her to attend Jan's retreat. Almost a little breakthrough. And then this happens.'

Jamie caressed her hand. 'I can't imagine what you've all been through, especially Poppy. And to live with the secret that she was driving, not your dad.'

'We're a strong family, but everyone has scars, not just me. There isn't a day that goes by that I don't wish that crash had never happened.'

'You were lucky, considering . . .' He brushed his thumb gently across the white scar along her left hand, almost under her wrist.

Not many noticed that one. Not when the ones on her face took all the attention.

'I know,' she whispered. 'Don't think I haven't thought about that. A lot. I was lucky my head didn't split open. I mean, it nearly did. I had some skull fractures, brain swelling, so many stitches . . . I was a real Frankenstein. I'm sure the kids at school called me that behind my back.'

Jamie shook his head slowly. 'You are one tough nut, Beth. You've been to hell and back and yet, here you are. To me you seem happy.'

'Yeah, I am,' she said, and she felt relief sweep through her at the truth of her words. 'I still have Dad and Poppy, and now Hudson. I enjoy my work. I feel very lucky.'

Now he was looking at her strangely.

'What?' she asked.

The corner of his lips curled up. 'You've got guts. *And* you're a little scary – breaking and entering.'

She smiled. 'What can I say, I do what I can for those I love.'

It hadn't escaped her notice that he was still holding her hand and Beth couldn't bring herself to remove it. 'So, any ideas on what to do about Jan? It's not like we can take this to the cops.'

'No. But we can keep looking, see if we can find any more matches with retreat stories and her other books.'

'And then?' Beth prompted.

'And then I say we bring it up with her tomorrow in our session. We have a right to know. Who's to say she won't try to use one of ours in her next one? We have to put a stop to it.'

Beth suddenly grew nervous at the thought of confronting Jan. But with Jamie at her side maybe it wouldn't be so scary.

'Do we tell the others?' Jamie asked.

She nodded as he stood up and helped her stand. 'Yes, I think so. That way they won't feel blindsided.'

He took his laptop and sat on the bed, patting the space beside him. Beth sat, and his arm and leg pressed against hers. It was so hard to think, being this close to him, even harder to forget that kiss. Especially when they were sitting on his bed.

'We can tell Alice and Simone after dinner,' she added to fill the silence.

'All right, let's go through the other retreat stories.'

Jamie brought them up on the screen and Beth leaned over to skim read them.

'This one. It sounds familiar. Beth, can you search for her book *The Tiniest Thread* and read out the blurb?'

Searching through Jan's books on her phone, she found it.

'No, it's not that one,' he said when she'd read out the blurb.

'But maybe this one?' she said, reading another, and Jamie sat up, triumphant.

'That's the one. It's about a woman who was sexually abused by a close family member.'

'Oh, that's horrible. And is that . . .' Beth pointed to his laptop, 'the real story that someone wrote at a retreat?'

'Yeah, it's pretty rough. Gut-wrenching. Jan obviously uses the ones that pack the most emotional punch. Being a renowned bestseller, she knows what her audience wants. Kind of ironic when that's what she's teaching us.'

'Why can't she come up with her own ideas? Isn't that what being an author is about?'

'I've always thought so. Maybe she got to a point where she ran out of new ideas. It doesn't excuse what she's done though. She's taking advantage of people who are paying money to attend her workshops. It's blatant plagiarism, and it's just so . . . wrong.'

'I can't believe she just steals other people's work and publishes it as her own. I can't wait to see the look on her face when we bring this up.' Though it made Beth feel a little queasy thinking about it. 'I'm so glad I've got you to help with that. I'm shitting bricks just thinking about it.'

Jamie's eyebrow rose, his lips holding back a smile. The air sizzled, and Beth felt like the oxygen had disappeared from the room.

But that's what had landed her in trouble last time, with Hudson's father.

Jamie breathed out, his breath caressing her face and setting it alight with tingles. She brushed her tongue across her lips, his eyes watching every second of it.

Words echoed down the hallway. 'Dinner is here!'

He closed his laptop and stood looking down at her, holding out his hand with a smile. 'Shall we?'

Beth swallowed. Saved by the dinner bell.

*How disappointing.*

# 22

## Beth – 2011

WHITE BANDAGES CUT OFF HER PERIPHERAL VISION. STRANGE chemical smells invaded her nose. Sharp beeps – some regular, some intermittent – meant that sleep was a constant illusion. The sense of isolation, of loneliness, lying day after day in this white sterile room, did nothing to soothe Beth.

It was as far from homely as she could imagine. She was certainly a long way from her old self, the one who had colour, life, a face and a mother. This Beth was a mess. Her family was shattered worse than her face. A few scars were nothing compared to the shockwaves that had opened an abyss of heartache that could never be fixed. This was her new life.

It was monotonous. It was dull. It was excruciating.

Family came to see her between visits from kind nurses who dressed her wounds and tried to get her to eat. Her aunt and uncles and cousins, of course. Some were chatty and talked about everything under the sun with extra-bright voices. Others simply held her hands and cried.

Beth preferred the first approach. She didn't need reminders that her mum was gone forever. Even if some mornings she woke up and thought she could smell her perfume, as if she were hovering by her door, telling her to get up for school. In those moments Beth could swear she heard her mother's voice.

'Rise and shine, sleepy head,' she would singsong as she did most mornings. Beth could picture her hand on the doorknob, smiling and wearing her favourite dangly blue earrings Poppy had made her in jewellery class.

Then slowly, the sterile scent of disinfectant would crawl up Beth's nose. The harshness of the sheets would rake against her skin, and a chill from a feeling of space and emptiness would engulf her, cruelly reminding her she was a world away from the fluffy rugs, endless decorative pillows, thick curtains and soft toys from her toddler days that made her room at home glow with warmth.

It was then that reality would hit, over and over every morning like groundhog day. Except there was no chance to repeat these days to fix them. Life wasn't a movie.

The bandages felt strange under her fingers, rough and lumpy. Beth would always have a reminder – she had only to touch her face or look in a mirror.

Did she want to look in a mirror? Yesterday, when they were changing her dressings, she'd asked the nurse.

'You could, honey, but you won't like what you see,' she said gently but firmly. 'How about you give it another week and by then it will be much better. It's still trying to heal.'

*And we're not sure you will cope.* Beth heard her unspoken words and didn't fight the nurse on it. Mainly because she was scared she was right. Beth didn't want to know how bad it was.

A tear slipped down into her bandages; it was like having a constant tissue – she had no need to wipe her eyes. Beth thought about how her dad was coping at home surrounded by her mum's presence in every tiny detail, from the wall hangings to her scent in her room, to the way she'd arranged her cactus plants on the kitchen table. There was nothing she hadn't touched.

And Poppy.

Beth had been in hospital for what seemed like ages now, the hours and days blurring like one big mass of nothing. No beginning, no end. Her dad visited daily, and that's how she knew another day had flitted by. She glanced at the clock in the room. The skinny black hand ticked through the seconds. How many rotations went by before her door opened? She wasn't sure, she'd lost count.

'Hey, sweetie,' said her dad.

He appeared through the door and Beth strained to see past him, hoping for those glass-framed eyes of her sister. Every time she was disappointed.

'Sorry, love, she's not ready.'

Beth slunk down into her bed. 'Did you tell her I want to see her?'

Tom's crutches thwacked as he hobbled to the chair and skidded it closer to her bed before sitting down. He shook off the crutches and his big rough hands scooped up hers. He'd lost weight, leaving his eyes sunken and his whole face gaunt, hollow and wrinkled. He seemed suddenly old and frail. And having his hip pop out during the crash made him hobble like a nursing-home resident. He wasn't even supposed to be walking, but nothing would stop her dad. It made Beth want to cry more, seeing him suffer like this, but she bit back her tears so he wouldn't feel worse. Besides, if he sobbed any more he'd probably shrivel up completely.

'Yes, I told her, but she's not doing very well. Aunty June is taking her to a psych today; she thinks it will help her to talk to a professional.' He paused, staring at Beth's hand against his. 'Poppy won't come out of her room. I think the thought of seeing you hurt like this is too much for her. The guilt is crushing her, no matter what I say, no matter how many times I tell her it's not her fault.'

'I know, Dad. I can't even imagine . . .' Beth whispered.

She'd tried to imagine it, being the one driving, looking over to see their mum motionless in the passenger seat – but it hurt too much. It had caused her to cry for hours, to the point the nurse gave her something to help her sleep.

Tom hung his head.

'Will she get through this?' Beth asked.

Shoulders, once so big and strong they could carry footballers around on them, shrugged like a weak old woman's. 'I wish I knew, Bethy. We're all hanging on by a thread. I'm trying to help her. I think if she could come and see you it would help. It helps me,' he said, tears shining through his shaky smile. 'I cling to the fact I still have both my girls. If I'd lost you as well . . .'

His Adam's apple bounced like a yoyo and tears fell from the corners of his eyes, rolling down the deep lines in his face.

Her idol, her hero. He could fix cars and manage a room full of burly men and still be as gentle as a butterfly. To see him break down squeezed her heart until it bled out her eyes.

'I'm sorry,' he sniffled. 'I know I need to be strong.'

'Dad, it's okay. I know you miss Mum.' Beth reached over and caressed his face but neither of them could stop the tears. The harsh reality was too raw. 'I miss her too. It's okay to be sad.'

It was probably better for him to be sad here than to let Poppy see the extent of his devastation.

A nurse came in later to see the room resembling an exploded cloud with all the scrunched-up tissues scattered across her bed.

'Time to change the bandages,' the nurse said and moved to unclip them.

The interruption had been a relief, something for them to focus on other than their grief.

'How's the team going?' Beth asked her dad, as the room went in and out of focus as the bandage was unwound from her throbbing head.

Tom sniffed loudly and collected the tissues to put in the nearby bin. 'They keep calling to check up on us. I feel like every hour I'm opening the door to one of the lads, holding flowers or food, offering to take out our rubbish and do some housework. They all loved your mum, and you especially. Their little mascot.' He grinned as he sat back down. 'I've refused to tell them where you are, so you can get some rest. They all bloody want to come and see for themselves that you're okay.'

'That's nice. Maybe they should visit before the bandages come off for good,' said Beth.

She'd had her eye on Turner, the small forward who looked a bit like Richmond Tigers' new gun, Dusty Martin. She'd told her dad that Dusty was going to be one to watch in the coming years. As for Turner, he had great tackle pressure and clean possession of ground balls and he rarely fumbled – unless he was talking to Beth. Which she liked. But would he like her now?

Her fingers went up to her face but the nurse brushed them away like a spider web.

'Don't touch, you might get them infected,' she warned.

'So do you want them to visit now?' Tom asked.

'I don't know. Wouldn't it be better to see me as a mummy than Frankenstein's monster?'

Fixated on her dad's face, she watched for any reaction as the nurse peeled the last of the bandage away.

'You can't see much,' he said. 'There's still gauze bits over the stitches.'

'You'll look like a sexy Edward Scissorhands,' said the nurse. 'Some people love scars,' she added with a wink.

Beth loved her optimism. Or was that a learned thing from working in hospitals and having to cheer up patients who felt like their world had fallen apart?

'Have you been a nurse long?' Beth asked. She looked to be about her mum's age.

'Fifteen years, love.'

*Well, that explains it.*

'I've seen sick ten-year-olds, who've spent most of their lives in a hospital bed, smile and laugh even in the face of death.' The nurse bent down to eye level. 'Many have passed away, hardly a life lived. I think you need to be brave, be thankful that you're alive, and remember that those who love you won't see the scars.'

It was the truth and yet Beth knew it was easier said than done.

'Yeah, that's right,' her dad reinforced, giving the nurse a grateful smile.

'No boy is going to look at me now though,' she whispered, not wanting her dad to hear her true fears, the ones she once would have confided to her mum.

'The right one will,' said the nurse as she took out a fresh bandage and began her mummification ritual again.

Beth pushed it from her mind. Getting out of the hospital was her first priority. Poppy couldn't avoid her then. Dad kept telling her to be patient, but Beth knew that if she could just hold her sister as tightly as their mum had, it would help. Poppy needed to know her sister was there for her. That there was no animosity.

Tom cleared his throat and pulled at his shirt collar as if it were a noose. 'Your mum's funeral's been set for next week, love.' His voice trembled over the words.

Beth nodded, unable to formulate a reply. She would be there, hopefully out of hospital by then.

'How's your hip, Mr Walton?' asked the nurse. 'I don't know how you're even getting around on it. You shouldn't be bearing weight.' She shook her head and tsked.

'He's tough as old boot leather,' said Beth. That's what Mum always said.'

'Tough or not, you'll be doing damage by not letting it heal. You'll need physio for a long time – maybe for the rest of your life.'

At first, Beth hadn't realised that her dad had been in pain from the crash; he'd been so strong helping his daughters, getting them out and moving around the vehicle. It wasn't until she really thought about it that she recalled him hobbling. She'd overheard the nurses say the shock from the crash had masked some of the pain, allowing him to get around, but it had only made his injury worse. It was amazing what you could pick up when they thought you were asleep. Her face was sliced to shreds but her ears were fine.

'Please, Dad, take it easy.'

Tom smiled sadly. 'Don't worry, I have a wheelchair at home. It's only when I come to the hospital I use the crutches, but no weight goes on that hip at all, I swear.'

Beth couldn't find the words to tell her dad just how much she needed him to be okay. And how she needed Poppy to be okay and for their life to get back to normal as soon as possible.

She needed her home, her room, and her mother's things around her.

She needed her mum.

# 23

## *Jamie*

'WOULD ANYONE LIKE A GLASS OF CHAMPAGNE? OR SOME red?' asked Alice, reaching to get a glass down from the cupboard.

Jamie moved to the kitchen as they cleared away their dinner plates. 'I'd love a red, thanks.'

Beth and Simone shook their heads. They were in a lively discussion about some nursing home they were both familiar with.

Jamie paused, uncertain whether to take advantage of this moment alone with Alice. He didn't like the idea of cornering her in the kitchen, but he'd stewed over it enough through dinner and couldn't stand it anymore.

'So, how have you been these last few years?' It was a stupid question, but he didn't really know where else to start. 'So you've got kids, right?'

The wine glugged into the glass as she smiled. 'Yes, they keep me pretty busy.'

His heart was racing. He wanted to ask about her about them but was it too soon? Would it be too obvious?

But she spoke first.

'I'm sorry, you know. About what I did back then.' Alice met his eyes and held out a glass for him. 'I was in a crappy place and I used you to escape it. It was wrong.'

While her apology sank in, he sipped the red.

'I don't expect you to forgive me, but I'm sorry for my deception. I . . . I ended up seeing a psychologist, who helped me. I knew what I was doing was wrong, but I was suffering from postnatal depression. It wasn't until we had that fight that I ended up getting help.'

'So that's why you never came back?' It was all making more sense. 'I mean, I didn't expect you to. I didn't give you any room to explain.'

'Don't worry, it was for the best. I was using the thrill of being with you to actually feel alive,' she lowered her voice, glancing at the others who were still deep in conversation. 'I was in such a dark place, I felt numb except when . . .'

She didn't finish. Her cheeks flushed pink as she turned away.

Jamie didn't know what to say to that. He'd heard about postnatal depression but he'd never known anyone who'd suffered from it. He never would have guessed it about Alice; there were no obvious signs.

'I didn't set out to find someone,' she went on. 'You just happened to be there, and you were – still are – extremely attractive, and . . .' Again, she couldn't finish.

'We connected?' he offered.

She nodded. They both knew what it had been like. That undeniable pull between them. Hot and wild. The kind that was fast to fizzle out.

'But you're going okay now?' he asked.

Her wide smile had warmth now. This was the Alice he remembered.

'Yes, thank you for asking.'

Her elegant wrist flitted and then dropped, as if she wanted to touch him but realised it might not be the right thing.

'When I had my second child, Abe, we were extra cautious and prepared. That's why I'm here – I want to write about my journey through postnatal depression. If I'd read some books about that, instead of all the standard baby books that overloaded me with all the things I was supposed to do to be a perfect mum, maybe things could have been different. Maybe I would have realised sooner what I was going through.'

'Wow, that's a wonderful thing to do, Alice. And no doubt very hard?' he said, trying to offer support when really he just wanted to ask about Abe. *Abe.* When was he born? What colour were his eyes? But how could he ask any of that?

'You got that right.' She gave a nervous laugh. 'Jan's right about digging deep. That's what I have to do with this book.'

He opened his mouth to say more about Jan, but now wasn't the time. 'So, your kids are good? They take after you?'

'A little.' Alice reached for her phone. 'Do you want to see?' she asked, holding her phone out uncertainly.

'Yeah, I'd love to.' *More than you'd ever know.* He managed not to pounce on her phone.

Jamie watched her every move, trying to judge what she was thinking. Was she worried about showing him? Did she think he'd notice a resemblance? Or did she hope he would?

'This is Mia, she's eight.' Alice swiped across the photos. 'And this is Abe.'

He noted she didn't mention his age. Zeroing in on the photo of her boy, Jamie took in the light wisps of hair, like angel wings, and the soft blue eyes. Alice had green eyes.

*Mine are blue.*

'Good-looking kids.'

Alice swiped again to another one of Mia and he silently cursed. If that was his son, he wanted to see all the photos. He wanted to study them, put them alongside his own baby photos and hunt for similarities.

'Anyway, they're good kids, considering how easily they can stir up trouble.' The thin phone slipped back into her trousers, away from his prying eyes.

*Damn it.*

He gulped down more wine as his mind raced. Should he ask her now? Should he ask to see more photos? Hell, did her husband even know about their affair?

Jamie knew he had to think more about this, had to figure out how he might want it all to work out. Did he want to pursue this seriously? What would that involve? A paternity test? Was he even in a position to demand that from Alice? And if he was his father . . . then what? Visitation rights? Would that disrupt Abe's life? Confuse the poor kid?

'Jamie, are you all right?'

Beth had appeared by his side and was tapping his arm. Alice was putting the wine back and Simone had headed into the lounge room.

'Is there something wrong with your wine?' Beth asked.

Jamie realised he was just staring at his glass, lost in thought. He held it out to her, finally snapping out of it but unable to find any words.

She took a sip. 'Tastes great,' she said with a nod.

Jamie stared at his glass, then at Beth's lips. Then back to where her lips had been on the glass. It reminded him of the wardrobe kiss all over again. He felt a spark between them, was sure she felt it too, and yet she was keeping a wall up. He wondered why she didn't seem to trust him. Was it because of her accident, or because of Hudson? Hudson's father?

'Come on,' said Beth, 'let's get this thing over with. Alice, Simone, would you mind coming into the lounge room? There's something we all need to discuss.'

He shook his head clear as Beth led the way into the lounge room. Simone and Alice sat together on the couch, seemingly getting along.

'Is this going to be juicy?' asked Simone.

She was cocooned in a big pink hoodie, a few sizes too big, and had relaxed back into the couch with her legs crossed at the ankles. It was the first time she had looked – well, like herself. He couldn't put his finger on the right word, but she seemed at ease. Maybe she was getting used to them? He made a mental note to check her Instagram as well, see what else she might have put up without his consent.

Beth sat on the small coffee table, so she was directly in front of Alice. Jamie followed suit.

'A cone of silence would help,' he said.

'I'll get one sorted next time, Max.'

Jamie automatically smiled. 'You're the best, 99.' He couldn't help it.

'What are you two going on about?' said Simone.

Beth and Jamie grinned at each other. Simone shook her head. Alice glanced at her watch.

Jamie couldn't afford to let his mind wander off. It was beginning to be a full-time job any time he was near Beth . . . when she smiled, the way her hair fell forward and the scent of her shampoo wafted. *Get it together.*

'Okay,' he slapped his hands together. Then glanced around to double-check Jan wasn't hiding in the wings.

Beth jumped up and ran to the lesson room. 'All clear,' she murmured as she made her way back.

'Right, we need to tell you something we've discovered about Jan and her retreats. We plan to approach her in tomorrow's lesson and ask her why she's stealing people's secrets for her novels.' He kept his voice low.

'Pardon?' Alice was first to respond. 'Whose secrets?'

'Ours. Everyone's,' Beth clarified. 'My sister did this retreat two years ago. Jan had them write down their secrets, emotions, memories – just like she has with us.'

'So? She uses a set guideline. There's nothing wrong with that. Just like a teacher uses a lesson plan every year,' said Alice.

Beth's fingers gripped together on her lap, faint white lines like spiderwebs speckled across them.

'Only, Jan used my sister's work and put it in her latest book. Nearly word for word.'

Alice's mouth dropped open. Simone glanced at them all as if hoping someone would explain what it all meant.

'Beth came here to try to get solid proof – and we found it earlier today.' Jamie grimaced. 'Not by the most honest of means, but we needed something we could confront her with. It's plagiarism and it's completely wrong.'

'And now we're telling you both so you don't feel out of the loop tomorrow,' Beth finished.

'Wow. I don't know what to say,' said Alice.

Simone frowned. 'Do you think she'd use one of ours?'

Beth shrugged. 'Maybe, if she thought it would make a good enough story. We found out she's keeping copies of all our work.'

'Did you read them?' Simone burst out.

'No,' Jamie said quickly. 'We didn't. Not our group. But we found folders from other retreats and matched some stories up to Jan's other novels. She's been doing this for a while now.'

'Oh my God. That's awful,' said Alice. 'Your poor sister, to read a book and find her words in it.'

It was as if Alice had found her own work spread around without her knowing, her face was so pale. Jamie wondered if she was thinking about her son? Or did she have other secrets to hide? Even Simone looked sickly, her forehead shiny. What secrets did she have that she didn't want others to know?

*And they are all probably wondering what yours is!*

'How dare she tell us to write from the heart and she can't even do it herself,' spat Simone. 'She can't steal my secret. What are you going to say to her?'

Beth cleared her throat. 'Well, um, we plan to tell her we know and see what she has to say for herself.'

Her voice was calm, which was amazing because Jamie had a fair idea how much she was churned up.

'And make sure she doesn't keep doing it,' added Simone. 'Or we'll tell the whole world. I have *thousands* of followers,' she added. 'She wouldn't want that.'

'So, are you guys okay if we expose this tomorrow – before or after our session?' Jamie asked.

'I'd like to say after, so I can get more out of the lesson, but then again I'm not sure I'll be able to concentrate, knowing what I now know,' said Alice.

Her eyes briefly met Jamie's and then darted away. Was she giving him a hint?

'She's not just plagiarising other people's work,' he said strongly. 'She's abusing their personal stories for her own gain.'

'Okay, I say you do it at the start,' said Simone.

'Me too,' added Beth. She shrugged when he glanced at her. 'I want it over and done with. I'm struggling to relax.'

'More time for you to finish that book,' he said with a smirk, trying to ease the turmoil he saw in her eyes.

Beth smiled, but it wasn't a full one. And yet he could tell she appreciated his attempt.

'I'm on board with whatever you decide,' said Alice. 'I feel like I should read all Jan's books now, just to . . . I don't know, see if I can tell. Do you know how many books she's stolen stories for?'

'Beth and I only managed to check three files, so we know that's definitely her three most recent books. Maybe there are more, or maybe that was it. She's published eight books, so who knows? Her first one went crazy on the bestseller list, and the next few did really well too. I'll do some more research tonight, see what else I can learn about her.'

He took in Beth's profile and wondered if she might join him. *Not now you told her about your affair with Alice and a possible son!* She probably wanted to steer well clear of him.

Immediately an image appeared in his mind: Beth in his arms in the wardrobe. He could still feel her fingers through his hair and on his arms, remember her sweet taste on his tongue.

The opposite of slow.

*Damn.*

'Jamie?'

'What?' *Shit.* 'Sorry, I missed that.'

Beth's brows knitted together. 'Alice asked if we had any ideas on how we're going to broach the subject.'

Jamie swallowed. He wished he knew.

# 24

## *Beth*

'I DON'T KNOW, POPPY, ALL THE FILES ARE ON JAMIE'S computer.' Beth paced her room as she relayed everything they had found to her sister.

'Jamie, the hot guy you still haven't sent me a photo of yet?'

Oh why did she have to mention him to Poppy? She couldn't afford to think of Jamie like that. She had Hudson to think about. Two more nights and she could hold him again. He was the man in her life.

'Poppy!'

'It's okay. I googled his gym and found a very sexy image of him. Those muscles. How can you bear it, sis? He's so handsome.'

Beth bit her lip. So far she wasn't bearing it well at all. She was struggling to *not* think about Jamie.

*Or those kisses.*

There was no way Beth would tell Poppy about that.

She gritted her teeth and tried to focus on the conversation. 'How's Hudson? Is he missing me?'

'Terribly. He's in the corner sobbing, he won't eat, he's pining for you.'

'Really?' Panic rose for half a second, before Poppy's deadpan tone gave her away.

'No. But did the idea make you feel better?' said Poppy.

'Not really,' Beth laughed. She didn't want Hudson to be unhappy. But it'd be nice if he missed her, just a little.

'He *is* missing you, but I'm keeping him busy. And Dad's about to take him down to the footy oval to watch the Lions train. Dad said since you're not here, he'll have to start training up the next best assistant coach.'

Beth laughed. 'Well, he'll love that.' Then she sighed. 'I'm going to go and finish this book. I'll call you tomorrow around lunchtime and tell you how the confrontation went.'

'Maybe you could record it. Or better yet, call me and let me listen to the whole thing.'

Poppy was sounding desperate and a little nervous. She wasn't the only one.

'I can't make any promises. It'll take all my effort to keep my breakfast down,' Beth said honestly.

'I love you, sis.'

'Love you too, Poppy.'

Beth put down her phone and picked up the book. Flopping onto the bed, she snuggled her feet under the blanket draped over the end. Paper crinkled as she flicked towards the end and found her page.

An hour later, she burst into Jamie's room. 'I hate you!' she spat.

Jamie was at his desk, typing. He lowered his laptop lid and stared at her.

'Are you crying?' He stood up suddenly, nearly knocking his chair over.

Beth threw the book on the bed. It bounced off and landed on the floor. 'It's your fault,' she sniffed, suddenly feeling very vulnerable and silly. She'd never let any man see her crying except her dad. And yet she'd gone straight to Jamie. *Strange*.

He grinned. 'Did you like it?'

His eager expression melted her concerns. 'It was amazing, and so gut-wrenching. I haven't sobbed like that since Hudson was born. I loved it.' It made her realise why Poppy loved writing so much and how you could immerse into someone else's life, forgetting your own.

Jamie's face lit up, dimples appearing on each cheek and those blue eyes dancing. 'I was hoping you would.'

'Is she a close friend?' Beth asked.

'Who?'

'The author. Your friend?' Jamie had seemed so invested in Beth's opinion, maybe the author was a potential love interest?

'Oh, um, yeah,' he replied, his eyes darting around the room, anywhere but at her.

Beth looked at him, his sudden discomfort. She picked the book up and went to the acknowledgements.

*Thank you to my parents and my brothers. To the fabulous publishing team, Kelly, Sandra, Claire, and especially Susan for believing in me.*

Something was playing around in her mind, a thought that was trying to make itself clear. 'Your friend didn't mention you?' She looked back at the page again. Those names rang a bell.

'She personally gave me a copy of the book,' Jamie said unconvincingly. 'I think that's close enough.'

Beth re-read the acknowledgements, then glanced up at Jamie. He looked sheepish.

'Did you write this book?'

His lashes fluttered as he blinked, his mouth open. Then his face and neck started to turn a shade of pink.

Beth hadn't meant to blurt that out, she wasn't even convinced herself, but his reaction confirmed it.

'Oh my God, you really did!'

He put his finger to his lips. 'Shh.'

'What? Why don't you want people to know?' Beth glanced at the book in awe. 'You really wrote this?'

He gave the tiniest nod.

'Wow, you should be bloody proud.' She stared back at him. 'I can't believe you wrote it.' Her mind was spinning, trying to fit the image of Jamie and a successful author into the same person. *Wow.*

'That's amazing.'

He still hadn't spoken.

Beth frowned. 'Why are you using a woman's name though?'

Jamie turned, thrust his hands into his hair and paced the room. He closed the door and eventually came back to sit on the bed. Beth sat down beside him and waited.

'Both my brothers are professional footy players.'

'So?''

'I grew up in the footy world. Everything was about being a bloke's bloke. Writing a novel doesn't really fit in that world.'

'Maybe.' Beth nodded. 'But what about your mum? Is she creative?'

Jamie tilted his head. 'Yes, she is actually. She wrote a lot of poetry.' His smile broadened. 'She used to read her poems to me before bed. My brothers liked it too, but they'd never admit it.'

'Whereas you wanted to please her?'

'Not only that. I guess I wanted her to know I did love them. I loved her reading them, and other stories to me at night. My brothers always got the attention from dad, being older and better at footy. But Mum was all mine, you know?'

'Yeah, I think I do. So, I take it you haven't told her, then?' A pause. 'Is this your big secret? Does anyone else know?'

His elbows went to his knees as he clamped his hands together and leaned forward. 'No,' he mumbled. 'Just you and my publishing team.'

'Far out. Don't you think your mum would be proud? That she'd want to know?'

He shrugged. 'I think she'd be proud,' he said, giving her a bleak smile. 'But I'm not sure how Dad and my brothers would take it. It's not ... well, if it was a crime thriller or a biography, I'd find it easier to tell them.'

'Jamie, it's a bestseller! It's freaking awesome. It shouldn't matter what genre it is. I think it's incredible that a man could write something so juicy and full of emotion. I never would have picked it.'

'I'm not sure how they'll react. I'm not sure how any of my friends will react either. I never set out to write a book ... well, I did, but not for the purpose of being published. I was just pouring out all the hurt and pain from Letisha leaving me.'

'Wow, she must have really done a number on you,' Beth said sympathetically.

He flung back on the bed and rested his palms on his chest. Beth twisted to see his face.

'Be glad you dodged a bullet. And look what came from it – a writing career,' she said, slapping his leg playfully.

To avoid gazing at him like a love-struck teenager, she lay down beside him and stared at the ceiling. She didn't want to be attracted to Jamie. Men as good-looking as him tended to be arrogant and untrustworthy. *And hurtful.* Beth had been burnt before . . . and yet no amount of history could stop her body from reacting to his closeness. *To those kisses.*

*It's just a weekend thing, all will be back to normal by Monday!*

'I guess I haven't looked at it like that,' he said, his voice quiet now that they were close. 'At the time I was lost in my own agony. Now I see that I'm much better off. I didn't see Letisha for who she was, I was too busy trying to create my dream of a home, wife and children. I thought she was the missing part of the puzzle, when really she wasn't even a contender.' He paused. 'When I think of a life partner, of the mother of my kids, a version of my mum comes to mind. Homely, sweet, caring. Letisha didn't tick any of those boxes. I was a stepping stone, something to win, like a prize. She didn't know me or understand me at all. If I'm being truthful, I didn't understand her either. Funny how back then I couldn't see it.'

'Don't be too hard on yourself. It's easy to be swept up in something we think we want.'

'I *am* thankful, because she's the reason I'm now published. I finished writing it and one night I got a bit drunk, when my brother – or his team, I should say – won the grand final. I guess I always felt lost in their shadows.'

'It'd be hard not to. Both playing AFL, getting all the attention.'

'Anyway, I wanted some of that attention for myself, and so I emailed my manuscript off to a publisher. Totally regretted it the next day when I realised, but it was too late. Then weeks later, I got an email telling me they loved it, and the rest is history.'

They were both staring at the ceiling as they spoke, in hushed whispers in case the others were asleep – or might overhear them.

'Then you made up a fake name?'

'It's my mum's maiden name. I gave her the first book I received when it was printed. I said the woman had her name, so I was inspired to get it for her.'

'That's sweet. Did she love it?'

'Yeah, she did,' he said.

Without looking at him she knew he was smiling.

'You should tell her.' And Beth meant it. Her mum came straight to mind. Gentle eyes, warm smile, the little creases around her mouth from laughing so much. Some days it was hard to remember those things and it broke her heart.

'I did think about it. It could be our secret. But Mum doesn't keep secrets from Dad. So, I haven't.'

Beth rolled onto her side, Jamie tilted his head to look at her.

'One thing I've learned from our accident,' she said, swallowing, 'is that life is short. There are so many things I wish I could have told my mum. I didn't get to tell her about my ninety-nine per cent score on my Year Twelve maths exam. Or about my first real boyfriend. She didn't get to help me pick out my ball dress or take a million photos.' Beth found it harder to get the words out as tears prickled. 'She'll never meet Hudson. I always thought my mum would be there to help me through the birth of my kids. To hold them and spoil them. Kids need grandparents. And scared little girls want their mums.' A tear slipped down her cheek, but she ignored it.

Jamie curled his hand around hers with as much warmth as his concerned expression.

'Let your mum be proud of you while she can,' Beth said. 'It's a special moment. Imagine if she was gone tomorrow . . .'

He wiggled his nose and sniffed a little. 'You sure you're not a writer?' he said, his voice gravelly. 'You can help me with my next book.'

'Ha,' she said, flicking away a tear. 'I'm not so sure about that, but I'd love to read it.'

'Well, that's if I can write it,' he said. 'That's why I'm here, at the retreat. The first book poured out of me, but now they want another one and I'm lost. I thought Jan might be able to help,' he said with a strained laugh.

'Well, if anything, this Jan ordeal might inspire some ideas.'

'Ha, maybe.'

Silence filled the air as they sifted through their thoughts. Beth tried hard to ignore the heat of his body and his earthy scent. *Or the fact you're in a man's room . . . alone.*

Jamie cleared his throat. 'That kiss . . .' he started, but didn't finish.

'Which one?' she teased.

'Oh, you are . . . a lot of fun.' He grinned. 'And my undoing.' He laced his fingers through hers. 'Look, I know we hardly know each other, but I feel like I've known you my whole life.'

She smiled. *I feel the same.* But she couldn't bring herself to say the words, as if that meant giving away a piece of her. *Hudson needs all of me.*

'I don't want to rush into anything,' said Jamie, 'and ruin what I think could be something pretty darn good. I know you have Hudson to think of, and I . . .' He glanced back at the ceiling as if it held the answers.

Beth tugged his hand until he was looking at her again.

'You need to find out about Abe?' she said, filling in the blanks.

'I want to spend more time with you, Beth. I like how I feel and who I am around you.'

A tingle raced across her skin and she felt drunk on his words. No one had ever spoken to her like that. But it was a dangerous mix. She couldn't offer Jamie anything at this moment. Nothing that jeopardised Hudson and their life. A bit of fun over a weekend was one thing, a relationship with someone she hardly knew was another.

'You realise I'm a scarred single mother who lives with her dad and baby?'

He grinned. 'I'd love to meet both those important men in your life.'

A gazillion fireflies took flight inside her, buzzing around with their lights.

'What?' he asked, watching her expression.

'It's just, this is the last place I would expect to find someone, you know. Let alone someone like you.'

'What do you mean? Someone like me?'

'Are you fishing for compliments, Jamie? I'm the one who needs them more than you.'

'I need reassuring just as much as anyone. I know you probably don't see yourself the way I do, but your strength, your sweetness, your humour, your sass – it all shines through your scars. It makes you unique, and someone I can't seem to get enough of.'

'Don't go using up all your fancy author words on me,' she said wryly, but in truth she'd loved every syllable, every word. 'Tell me more about your family. What's your dad like?'

Beth had to get them back onto safe ground. She should leave, go back to her room, but lying beside Jamie was intoxicating. Jamie might say all the nice things, but did she really know him at all? She wanted to be cautious. And yet he made her feel alive.

# 25

## Simone — 2017

SINCE DROPPING THREE DRESS SIZES, SIMONE FELT AMAZING. Getting into her car was easier, even walking was easier, but she was still a while off her goal weight. If her mum had noticed the change, she didn't mention it. If anything she seemed grumpier than ever. Simone had offered her an Alive shake several times, suggesting it might help her shift a little weight off her joints. That had not gone down well. So now they pretty much kept to themselves.

Simone had an image of how she wanted to look, and it took the shape of a thin girl in a yellow dress, hanging off her dad's arm. That memory had always stuck, like superglue to skin.

One day, when Simone looked like that girl, her dad would come back. Or if he didn't, she would seek him out. They'd renew their relationship, because he'd see this new version of his daughter and be so impressed. So proud.

Her phone rang as she made her way to her car after work, the afternoon light starting to fade to grey.

'Hello, Simone? It's Regina from Willow's Rest . . .'

Simone barely heard the rest as her footsteps faltered and her knees wobbled, threatening to give way. Her hand thumped onto a nearby car as she gripped on for dear life.

'Are you still there? Simone? Please say something?'

Regina's worried voice gave her something to focus on.

'I . . . I'll be right there.'

*Don't cry. Don't cry.*

Simone blinked madly as she tried to focus, tried to remember where her car was parked. She needed to get to the nursing home. Tears streamed down her cheeks as she climbed behind the wheel. How she got through the afternoon traffic she would never know, she just remembered the relief she felt as she pulled into the car park at the nursing home.

The lump in her throat was growing by the second as she rushed into Willow's Rest as if in a dream.

'Can I see her?' she managed to ask the new girl at the reception. She'd only been working the past month and yet the girl was familiar with Simone.

'Yes.'

Her face remained impassive, she wasn't yet fond of all the residents the way Regina and the other nurses and carers were. And Simone. Simone knew a little about everyone here. Mr Tomblinson, with his thirty grandchildren and missing leg, loved to tell the ever-changing story of its demise. Mr Eckle loved to flirt and tell really bad dad jokes. Mr and Mrs Smith still loved each other seventy years after marriage, probably because they were both deaf. And the forgetful Mrs Beecham who always seemed to know when Simone was visiting Mrs Satish and popped in to say hello. They all craved company and Simone loved how their faces lit up when she arrived. Nowhere else was she received so warmly as she was here.

She found her way to Mrs Satish's room and pushed open the door.

Mrs Satish lay in her bed. Small and peaceful, like a child sleeping. Again, the lump surged up Simone's throat, constricting her breathing. Her whole face felt as if it was going to burst like a broken water main, and yet she still hadn't done the hardest bit.

Step by step she moved closer to the most important woman in her life.

'Hey, Mrs Satish. I'm here now,' she said, voice cracking.

The white sheet was tucked under the old woman's chin, exposing only her withered face and soft hair. Simone stroked the soft white strands, as if lulling a baby to sleep. Only Mrs Satish was already asleep.

Tears flowed down her cheeks in a torrent. She felt under the sheet for Mrs Satish's frail hand and held it for a moment.

'You'll be able to look after all your cats now. And Peppie will be so happy to see you,' she blubbered through the tears. 'I love you.'

Grief swallowed her whole. Falling back into the vinyl chair by the bed, she sobbed, her body shaking as she curled into herself. She knew this day was coming, but it still hurt to let go. Mrs Satish hadn't recognised her these past ten months, but Simone knew her, and that's what mattered.

'She's in a better place now. A place I wish I was, too.'

Simone looked up to see Mr Eckle by the door, his eyes flicking longingly over his friend's peaceful face.

'She was a good egg, that one. We'll miss her.' He shuffled in with his walking stick and put his hand on Simone's shoulder. 'Don't cry too much, missy, she wouldn't have wanted that.'

She nodded, feeling like a lost child. The sense of aloneness washed through her like ice water. White knuckles and numb toes, she felt frozen.

'Aren't you sad?' she asked, glancing up at his dry face.

'I am. But I've said goodbye to so many friends and family over the years, I think I've got no tears left. Besides, I don't have long to wait to see them all again,' he muttered with a hopeful shrug.

'I don't know what to do now that she's gone,' Simone mumbled, feeling a sudden need to just stay here with her old friends. They were her kindred spirits.

'Well, I hope you'll come back to visit us. If you don't come, who will we play cards with? Who will sneak in Beryl's favourite biscuits? Who will bring Gordie things like that fidget spinner? No one else cares.'

'People care. They just get busy,' she said sadly, knowing all too well that her visits to Mrs Satish had grown further apart. It had got harder to see her so unresponsive, so helpless.

She felt for these elderly men and women, stuck in Willow's Rest, waiting out their days while others went about their lives. Too old to live alone outside the walls and still aware enough to resent their imprisonment.

'I'll still visit, if you want me to,' she told him and was rewarded with a wonky smile.

'You're a good lass, Simone. Heart of gold.' He hobbled back towards the door. 'I'll leave you to your goodbye.'

Gripping the chair, she pushed herself up and bent over Mrs Satish, and for the last time she pressed a kiss to her forehead. 'Thank you for looking after me,' she whispered. 'Thank you for loving me.'

Fresh tears fell as she headed for the door. There was nothing else she could do.

The funeral was quiet, and life afterwards felt empty. She visited her friends at Willow's Rest in the weeks after Mrs Satish's death, and the first few times she walked into Mrs Satish's old room by mistake, only to stare at the new man who'd taken up residence. Bill invited her to come in and chat. He didn't like his new home one bit. Talking with him helped, and yet it didn't. Seeing Mrs Satish's belongings gone, replaced by unfamiliar family photos and football scarves, made it even harder to remember her, sitting in this room by the window.

'What's up with you!' her mum had said loudly over the TV in the lounge room. 'You're all sulky.'

'Mum,' Simone scoffed. 'I told you, Mrs Satish passed away.'

'Yeah, wasn't that a few weeks ago though?'

Later that evening, sitting at her desk, Simone pulled her laptop closer. She hadn't told her mum that Mrs Satish had left her some money – not much, but enough to buy a new car. It felt like Mrs Satish had given her the possibility of a new life, a little hand up, even from the grave. This car would be Simone's new set of wings.

So, instead of checking her Instagram page, Simone searched for something new. Bugs – Volkswagen Beetles – of all colours and prices overwhelmed the screen. It was such a hard choice, but she and Mrs Satish had talked often about how they both loved the Beetle. As she scrolled, she felt the confines of her jeans squeezing like a python. Cursing, she got up and peeled them off, grabbing handfuls of her belly and wobbling it in despair. How many years was this going to take? At her current rate, another four to get to where she wanted. Maybe more. At least she was starting to make some money selling the Alive shakes. Her Instagram profile was growing; people seemed to love hearing about her progress. It was terrifying but also a little exhilarating.

Pulling on a pair of tracksuit pants, she sat back at her desk and checked her Instagram and Facebook accounts. Some of the comments filled her with pride, others warmed her heart. Some days she felt like this was her only source of happiness. People seemed to like her, to want to hear what she had to say. She finally felt like she had a voice.

Then something caught her eye: 'Gastric Sleeve'.

Just a harmless ad, but she'd seen ones like it before. Like mice, they sat in the back corners, nibbling away. She clicked and read more, about clients who'd had it done, their journeys, how quickly they'd lost the weight. Because Simone had already lost a bit, she would qualify for surgery. Hours ticked by as she drank in all she could find, taking notes as her excitement grew.

*I could do this!*

And the cost wasn't prohibitive. She'd been putting a little away to save for a new car, but now with the money from Mrs Satish, she didn't need it.

*I really, really want this.*

She couldn't deny the desire to be at that goal weight. It would change everything. It would change her life. Glancing at her pin board above her desk, she took in the magazine images of women she aspired to be like. The outfits she longed to wear – mostly yellow dresses, all designer, with expensive accessories. Images of tattoos she'd like to get one day. A Mr Lincoln rose for Mrs Satish was first on the list.

Then to be able to find her dad and feel amazing. To have people want to talk to her, be her friend. To have a boyfriend as handsome as Jed. If she could just be her goal weight and have the things she'd always wanted, people would finally see her.

She wouldn't have to be alone anymore.

# 26

## Jamie — 2017

THE SUN BEAT DOWN AND BOUNCED OFF THE WALLS AND pavement like the inside of an oven. Jamie swung his arms to help cool himself. He felt so restricted in the tight button-up shirt Letisha had insisted he wear. The dark clingy fabric didn't help.

He wasn't usually bothered that Letisha chose his clothes for him; she was the fashion expert, after all, and he was happy to comply. They'd met friends for breakfast in the city centre before she'd run off for a lunch date with another friend. Which had left Jamie wandering the streets.

He squinted as the sun hit a sign ahead, lighting up the sparkling letters: Rosendorff Diamonds. He found himself gravitating to the display window. Big diamonds sat on thin bands of gold, silver and platinum. He'd been thinking about proposing to Letisha more and more lately. They'd been together for more than a year and he wasn't getting any younger. He wanted a family. He wanted to be able to play footy with his kids while he was still young.

Letisha had moved in three months ago and things were going well. She had enough make-up, products and clothes to supply all of Perth, but that was a small price to pay.

Nothing about Letisha was out of place. She never left the house without a full face of make-up, her hair straightened, her outfit perfect. It was like she put on a different woman to go out in public. It was also why he loved living with her: he got to see her straight after her shower, in all her raw, naked beauty. That's when he could see her holding their child.

'I don't want kids yet, Jay,' she said one night after he'd mentioned the future.

Letisha was three years younger than him, so he understood her reservation, but it would be a few years before kids would come into the picture. Get engaged, get married, and then have kids. That gave her two to three years. He could probably wait longer knowing it was all going to happen eventually.

The door chimed as he stepped inside.

'Excuse me, what do you have in engagement rings?'

Twenty minutes later he bounced back through the door with a smile that almost hurt. He'd refused their bag, not wanting to advertise his purchase, and instead insisted on carrying the little black box.

'Hey, Jamie.'

'Nicole,' he said, a little rattled to be caught out.

Letisha's petite friend stood before him with her face full of freckles and a warm smile. He'd just had breakfast with her and the others not long ago.

'What were you doing in there?' she asked before her eyes dropped to the box. 'Oh, Jamie.' Her face fell.

'Don't tell her, Nicole. I have a big surprise planned. At first I thought about doing something big and public, but then I decided private might be better. What do you think?'

'Private,' Nicole burst out. 'Definitely private.' She put her hand on his arm. 'Can I have a look?'

'Sure.' He popped the lid on the box, revealing a huge diamond surrounded by smaller ones, all set in a gold ring. 'She likes gold.'

Yet Nicole's face suggested otherwise.

'You don't like it?'

Big green eyes turned up to him. 'Oh no, it's absolutely gorgeous, Jamie. Any woman would love to have this on her finger and you on her arm.'

She closed the lid on the box and stepped closer, eyes darting around before locking onto his.

'And because I think you're the nicest guy she's ever dated I feel I need to warn you that . . . I don't think Letisha wants to get married. Have you guys spoken about this at all?'

His shoulders relaxed. 'A bit. She doesn't want kids yet but that's understandable. But I'm ready, Nicole. I think she is too.'

Nicole squeezed his hands. 'Then you don't really know her at all. She can be selfish, Jamie, and if she feels trapped, she acts out.'

His belly flipped. 'What are you trying to say? That I shouldn't marry her?'

Nicole stepped back and glanced down the street. 'I know she's my friend, that's what makes me qualified to say this, Jamie. And I really like you. Maybe you should ask Letisha where she's been all this time – the truth – before you ask her a big question like that. I'm sorry, Jamie.' With that, she turned down the street at a brisk walk.

'Nicole, wait,' he called, but it was no use; she was almost running into a crowd of people.

*What the hell?*

As he headed back to his car, her words played over and over in his mind. What did she mean by 'ask Letisha where she's been all this time'? Did she mean today, or their whole relationship? Was she leading a double life? Did she have another boyfriend?

He drove home in a daze, then pulled up in his driveway and sat outside his house. It was a small house with a big backyard. Even when he'd bought this place a few years back he'd done so with kids in mind. Letisha had complained how small the house was but he liked the closeness, it felt like his parents' home. He'd upgraded the kitchen and was working his way through the whole house as he had the money. It was in a great area and close to schools and a park with a big lake. It had been a great buy. He'd always believed that Letisha would come around.

A rap on his car window made him jump. A man was standing there, waiting expectantly.

Jamie got out of his car. 'Can I help you?'

'I hope so. I have a truck full of roses,' he said, gesturing down the driveway.

A big white refrigerated truck sat behind his car. When had that turned up? A flashback to the jewellers, calling to order ten dozen roses, made him sigh.

'Oh, wow, that was quick. Let me open the door.'

For the next ten minutes they transported bouquets of roses and bags of coloured petals from the truck.

'Good luck, mate.' The delivery guy shook his hand vigorously.

At least he was more excited than Nicole had been. Jamie couldn't get her concerned expression from his mind. It didn't help his nerves at all.

But he didn't want to think about her words now, couldn't think about them. With the house smelling sweetly, he started decorating. Candles were arranged up the entry walkway and petals scattered. Letisha would have to walk through them to get to him. He'd hold out a red rose for her and then drop to one knee.

He glanced at his watch – she was due home in twenty minutes.

Jamie showered, smothered himself in her favourite cologne and dressed in the designer jeans and black button-up shirt Letisha had recently bought for him. He lit the candles, which had taken a while as he was breathing so hard he kept blowing them out and he nearly burnt his fingers because his hands were shaking. Then he discovered he'd disturbed the arrangement of petals and trodden on a few, squashing them.

*Damn it*. Quickly he scooped up the squished petals and resorted them. He checked his watch, let out a deep sigh and stood at the end of the hallway. And waited.

A car door slammed shut and he snapped his legs together, then relaxed them apart. Then he put weight on one and then the other, trying out various poses. Keys in the door jangled and his heart pounded into his throat.

The box! He was only holding the rose. He spun around and picked up the ring box from the side table and got back into position as the door swung open.

'Jamie, I'm . . . What's all this?' Letisha said as she took in the candles and roses.

He smiled, pushing his nerves down as her eyes came to rest on him. 'Hey, baby. Welcome home.'

Her face blushed pink as she stepped towards him, planting her high heels in the gaps between the petals.

'Um . . . what's going on? Is it our anniversary?' Her eyes bulged. 'Shit, honey, did I forget it?'

He held out the rose for her. Letisha took it but didn't smell it, just held it awkwardly to her chest. Her gold top shimmered against her smooth tanned skin. It had double straps at the shoulders but one was broken. He hadn't noticed that at breakfast.

'You know I love you,' he said, the box digging into his hand as he gripped it tightly.

'I know, babe,' she said automatically.

Her plump lips looked swollen. Had she been and had them botoxed again? 'I like your lips the way they are, you don't have to get them botoxed,' he said, reaching out to touch them but she jerked away.

'I haven't,' she snapped.

'Then why . . .' His voice faded even as he got down on one knee, his body doing one thing while his mind tried to process the rest. Images merged with Nicole's words. 'Where were you today?' he asked, when he meant to say, *Will you marry me?*

Letisha tilted her head, blonde waves shimmering like a waterfall.

'I was . . . I was with a friend,' she stammered. 'Jamie, what are you doing down there?'

He stood up and frowned. 'What friend? Have I met this one?'

'No, I don't think so. Just a work colleague. What's in the box? Did you get me something for our anniversary?' she said, her voice faltering slightly.

But he didn't fall for her switch. 'Was it a guy or girl?'

She blinked rapidly. He was making her nervous. She never got nervous.

'Um, a guy. Can I have a look, or do I have to wait?'

Jamie stepped towards her. She thought he was moving in for a hug and opened her arms, but when he started to sniff her hair and skin she jumped back as if electrocuted.

'What are you doing?'

Suddenly it all came together. Too much to wave away as nothing. He felt his face flush. 'You smell like him,' he accused.

When he'd kissed her goodbye at the cafe she'd smelled of her favourite perfume, but now it was different: musky, spicy, male.

'We were sitting side by side chatting,' she said and reached out for the box.

He let her take it, wanting to see her reaction. But the words he'd been so keen to say to her had disappeared. A dry acid taste filled his mouth instead.

A gasp. 'Oh, oh no.'

Just what every bloke wants to hear when a girl sees an engagement ring. Right then, he knew Nicole was right. She'd been trying to warn him, but he was too stupid, too blind to see it. Had been for a long time.

'Are you proposing?' she whispered. 'I'm not ready.'

Brows knitted together as she backed away from him a step.

'I know,' he croaked. 'But what I don't know is, how long you've been having an affair.'

Letisha snapped the box closed, its echo ringing through the hallway. Candlelight flickered as if it also felt the vibration.

'W-what?' she stammered.

'How long have you been seeing this guy? Is it just him, or are there others?' He'd been a fool.

'I . . .' She shoved the box back at him as if it were full of snakes. 'I don't know what you mean.'

'Don't lie to me, Letisha. I deserve the truth.'

She licked her lips and stared at him a few moments before finally nodding. 'Only one, only recently.' She put up her hand. 'You were getting so clingy. I felt suffocated.'

'You could have told me,' he muttered.

An eyebrow arched up. 'Would you have listened? Did you even hear me when I said I didn't want kids or marriage yet?'

'So your answer was to go screw the next bloke that came along?'

Her mouth fell open and then her eyes narrowed to pinpoints. 'Fuck you, Jamie.'

Letisha pushed the rose into his chest and headed back out the door. It slammed like a demolition ball and shook the house.

It happened fast, so fast it didn't feel real. It was like his anger, disappointment, despair and heartache were still catching up. Jamie dropped to the floor and sat on the petals, his chest constricting as if someone was squeezing all the oxygen from his lungs.

None of that had gone to plan. Not one bit.

# 27

## *Beth*

BETH BLINKED AGAINST THE LIGHT FILTERING THROUGH HER hair like a threadbare curtain. She moved her head slowly, dragging it onto a pillow. Furry teeth from forgetting to brush, and a dry mouth. Was this a hangover? It sure felt like one.

A Jamie hangover.

Beth tilted her head and saw Jamie sleeping beside her. She flung her arm over her eyes. *Damn I thought that was a dream. A very good dream.* A smile touched her lips but she forced it away, still debating if being in his bed was a good idea or a very silly one.

Golden sun-kissed skin and tousled hair made morning Jamie almost more divine than last night's. He was lying on his belly, bare back exposed, lean muscles perfect in the soft light.

*What am I doing?*

This was a nice way to spend a long weekend but what happened tomorrow when she went back to her real life, to her son? Jamie was just a distraction. An attraction. Nothing real.

As far as she could tell, Beth had two options: one – caress that body and wake him, or two – sneak out of the bed and pretend it never happened.

Right now, option two seemed the most sensible, even if option one was screaming *pick me, pick me!*

Already she was making the shimmy towards the edge of the bed. Having a baby made her a master at the stealth exit. Clothes were collected with nimble fingers and the door opened and closed without a sound. Beth was hedging her bets that Simone and Alice were still upstairs in bed asleep. The sun wasn't up yet, just the hues projected over the horizon through the windows. She shut her own door, dropped her clothes and jumped into her cold bed. Her mind went straight back to the heat from Jamie's body.

Last night, it had been enough just to lie beside him and listen to the sound of his voice and his breath. He'd seemed content just to talk with her, to run his thumb across the back of her palm in rhythmic motions.

But then they'd lain on their sides, studying each other and learning each line, curve and shadow. Somehow, they'd inched closer until his breath caressed her face. Jamie reached out a finger, shifted her fringe and traced the scar through her eyebrow before moving to the one along her lips. He didn't say anything and neither did Beth for what felt like the longest time. It was just their rhythmic breathing as they'd studied each other, silently appraising, silently asking for permission, silently scared. *Maybe that was just her.*

It wasn't until Beth's hand had reached for him, touching his waist as she brushed her tongue along her lower lip, that any real action happened. Like ice on hot rocks, they'd melted together in a mess of arms and lips and hands. Frantic was one word that came to mind. Sizzle was another.

Beth felt her face burn with the images, of the desire starting to build again. They were supposed to have figured out a way to tackle Jan and instead had peeled off each other's clothes, tongues tasting flesh, behind the ears, below the belly, inside the thighs. She could still smell Jamie's sexy scent upon her skin. *Oh my God, what have I done!*

Hot liquid swirled in her lower apex as she remembered the way he'd feasted upon her, his lips and tongue treating her body as a temple, worshipping every curve, every line, every scar. That was not something she'd ever thought possible.

*Or that sex could be that amazing!*

Adrien had certainly not been skilled or exceptional; the only lasting impression he'd left was Hudson. And there had only been two bumbling teenagers before her accident, and one very short-term boyfriend after, so her experience was as limited as her expectations. Jamie had opened her eyes – no, he'd blown her mind open, and it scared her. Would she ever experience anything like that again?

Earthy wood-smoke filled the air, as if each movement released his scent from her skin, and her nipples hardened at the memory of his hot mouth. His hard body against hers. The way it all fit together so . . . heavenly.

*Now you are going too far. It was just sex.*

But it was sex like Beth had never had before. And she knew it was going to mess with her head. How was she going to face him this morning? Pretend it never happened? That was the preferred option, seeing as they both had enough drama in their lives to write ten soap operas.

If she could wash Jamie off she might have half a chance at thinking straight.

Throwing the covers back, she staggered out and put on some clothes and headed to the bathroom for a shower. She made the water boiling hot, to the point the extractor fan couldn't keep up, turning the room white with steam.

Forty minutes later, Beth joined Alice and Jamie in the kitchen by the coffee machine. Jamie handed her a coffee he'd just made, but he seemed preoccupied and wouldn't meet her gaze when she thanked him. Her spine stiffened . . . was this it? Had he finally realised his mistake? The coffee was the last of his kindness? She'd made the right decision to leave his bed this morning to avoid the awkwardness. He clearly was regretting it and pretending it didn't happen.

'Morning. D-day,' said Alice, gritting her teeth. 'How are you feeling?'

'Nervous,' said Beth, before taking a gulp of her coffee.

Jamie didn't even reply, he just stared into his own coffee and looked grumpy. Unless he was like this in the mornings before coffee kicked in? More than likely regretting sleeping with some single mother who looked like Wolverine's punching bag. Beth hated how her doubt could come back so quickly when she'd worked so bloody hard to be proud of who she was, scars and all. It didn't take much for people to knock the wind from your sails.

Her stomach churned.

Alice's fingers brushed over her arm briefly. 'You'll be all right. We'll be there to back you up.'

Alice's phone rang as Jamie asked if she'd like a coffee. She nodded and took the FaceTime call.

'Hi Mummy,' kids' voices rang out. 'Happy birthday!'

Alice held her phone in front of her. Beth could see two kids trying to get their heads in the frame to blow her kisses.

'Oh, it's your birthday. Happy birthday,' said Beth.

'Happy birthday, Alice,' added Jamie.

She gave them a smile before focusing back on her kids. 'Thanks, my darlings. That means the world, and thank you for your kisses.'

Jamie's arms had gone rigid, the tension clearly building in him. He finished making the coffee and put the cup down jerkily before leaning in, trying to get a look at Alice's kids. Beth couldn't blame him, even she was trying to catch a glimpse of Abe to see if he was a mini Jamie. Would seeing Abe confirm it for Jamie? He must be in so much turmoil.

Jamie was practically leaning over Beth to see Alice's phone. Alice tilted her phone and walked around the breakfast bar for some privacy.

Jamie's eyes never left Alice. Beth didn't like the awkward sensation that slithered through her like an electric eel.

'You okay?' she asked softly.

Something deep and painful washed through his eyes, his face full of confusion.

'Not really.' He let out a sigh and returned to making the coffee as Alice hung up.

'Oh, Jamie, are you our barista today? Can I put an order in, please?'

Simone skipped into the kitchen wearing jeans with frayed patches up the legs and a bright yellow fitted top. Her silky straight hair still carried a hot melted scent.

'Simone?' Jamie said gruffly, which made Beth frown. 'Can I have a word, please?'

Beth used the same tone on Hudson when he was naughty.

Simone froze like a scolded child. Beth figured she knew what was coming, or at least had an idea.

Jamie guided her to the sitting area but Beth could still see them and make out his angry words. Maybe because she'd moved to the end of the kitchen, closer to them. *A little snoopy, Beth.* She knew it but couldn't bring herself to shift.

'I noticed a post on your Instagram page this morning – of me and my business – and it implied we supported *your* business.' He stepped towards her, pointer finger out. 'I don't recall giving you permission to post any such thing, or my photo, nor do I recall saying I support your products.'

Simone's face flooded red. Her mouth opened but no words came out.

'To say I'm pissed off is an understatement. It's not ethical, Simone. Not even close. I let the first few slide but now it's beyond a joke.'

Alice and Beth shared a glance, not game to speak and interrupt Jamie's head of steam. Alice whispered a goodbye to her kids and quickly hung up.

'I'll take it down,' Simone stuttered and fumbled with her phone.

Jamie crossed his arms. Beth thought Simone was about to cry.

'I thought you'd have a better understanding of what you can and can't post. I expect it all to be taken down NOW.'

His voice rattled through the room like a roaring bear. Simone squeaked and took off up the stairs at a run.

'Oh dear,' said Alice.

Jamie dropped his shoulders and headed back towards them.

Beth felt her stomach flip and pressed her hand against it. There was enough drama unfolding here to write a few books. And they hadn't even dealt with Jan yet.

*Ugh!*

'You went hard on her,' Alice said.

'I wanted to make a point, Alice, so she wouldn't be inclined to do it again.' He glanced at Beth. 'Do you think I was too harsh?'

'Um, probably not,' she mumbled. He did have a point. If he'd been nice about it, would it have stopped her from doing it again? Was this something Simone did often? Is that how she built up her followers?

'So, do you know what you're going to say to Jan?' asked Alice, clearly changing topic.

'Um, no,' replied Beth, resisting the urge to glance at Jamie while heat flooded her cheeks. He was the reason they'd never formulated a plan last night. She felt totally unprepared.

'Ah, yeah, we didn't really come to any great conclusion.' Jamie rubbed the back of his neck.

Alice was watching them closely, or was that her imagination? Were they acting weird enough to rouse suspicion? Beth was no good at this.

'Quite frankly, I'm too nervous to even think about it,' said Beth. 'I guess I'll just wait for the right moment and then bring it all up.'

A flash of silver through the kitchen window caught her eye. Jan was on her way, folders clasped in her arms, her walk purposeful.

'Oh, it's nearly time,' she whispered, gut clenching as sweat started to gather on her neck. Her phone dinged with text messages from Poppy.

*You got this!*

*Good luck!*

*I love you!*

Every fibre in her body screamed at her to run, but she managed to make herself enter the meeting room, her laptop clenched to her chest, and take her seat. It helped that Jamie put his warm hand against the small of her back and guided her to her chair. Did he know she was close to bailing? The one thing that kept her moving was the support from the others. She wasn't alone, their constant winks and nervous smiles gave her comfort. Except for Simone; she hadn't returned.

'Breathe, Beth,' Jamie whispered against her ear as he sat down beside her.

'Should we check on Simone?' she asked Alice.

'I don't know,' she replied.

Beth didn't really need Simone here to help, but they were all invested in this. Jan could share all their secrets. Maybe Simone might realise and make an appearance. Or if she was upstairs crying her eyes out, she might not. *Oh dear.*

'Good morning,' said Jan as she slid her big black sunglasses to the top of her head. 'I hope you've all been busy working on your projects.' She gave a pointed glance at Simone's empty chair.

'Will she be long? I'd really like to get started promptly,' Jan said with a huff.

'I'll go see,' said Alice, standing up and rushing out the door.

While she was gone, Jan rustled through some papers, sighing heavily while glancing at the door intermittently. Jamie shrugged, he didn't seem that concerned about Simone's absence.

Alice soon returned with Simone in tow; clearly she'd been crying. Jamie squirmed awkwardly in his chair while Simone took her seat and faced the front, cutting them all from her line of sight. She sank down low into her chair; any lower and she would have been under the table. Which to Beth seemed like the better place to be right now.

Now that they were all here, how was Beth going to start this? Her head was such a mess she could hardly follow what Jan was saying.

'So, we've covered emotion, and touched on showing not telling. I recommend buying these great craft books to further your learning, as two days isn't enough to cover everything in depth.'

Jan displayed a list of books and authors on the screen, but they just blurred into a mash of words for Beth.

'You will write badly first, there is no such thing as perfect right away. No one writes a book in one draft. I can't stress how important it is to let your work be bad to start with, and that sometimes mistakes can lead to new possibilities, ones you'd never thought of before.'

Jan's words were fine wisps of smoke that thinned and disappeared into nothing. Beth couldn't grasp any of it.

'Would anyone like to read out what they've written so far?' Jan asked a moment later.

Jamie kicked Beth's foot under the table. She sat up straighter and put her hand up.

'Yes, Beth.' Jan beamed, glossy red lips curling.

Beth hadn't planned to share anything, but she had Poppy's story on her laptop. She quickly found it, cleared her throat and began to read about the most awful night of her life.

If she found the words familiar, Jan didn't stop her. Instead she let her finish it. All of it. Beth's voice was strong as she read; tears that didn't fall caught in her eyes. Everyone around the table was watching Jan.

Beth stopped reading, and locked her eyes on the small woman at the front. Her lips were pencil-thin, face tight and jaw clenched. Beth felt a wave of victory. She had rattled Jan's cage.

*Yes, I know what you did.*

'Very good,' she muttered. 'Anyone else?' she asked while fiddling with the screen remote.

'Is that all?' Beth scoffed. She couldn't believe Jan's nerve, pretending nothing had changed. There was no way she didn't recognise that piece.

'That sounds so familiar,' said Alice with mock innocence. 'Has that ever been published?'

Beth pressed her lips together to stop the sly grin that threatened. She was grateful the group was on her side and she wasn't alone.

She turned to Jan. 'I wouldn't have thought so. My sister actually wrote it. About a very personal and private moment in her life. What do you think, Jan? Has it been published?'

'I'm not sure what you mean,' Jan said, clearly picking up on the accusing tone but quickly changing tack. 'Jamie, did you want to read something?'

Her distraction tactic didn't work. Tension hovered over them like tear gas.

Beth stared at Jan for what felt like minutes before she spoke. 'Does the name Poppy Walton ring a bell?'

Jan shook her head, her hair moving with her like a white helmet. Her lips twitched.

'Well, it should. Because Poppy, my sister, attended one of your retreats two years ago. And she handed in this exact story. The story you said you returned to her, along with all the other participants'. But the funny thing is, when I read your latest book, I was hit with a feeling of deja vu.'

'That's a serious accusation,' said Jan, her voice stern, but there was panic in her eyes. She remained still, as if frozen in time, but her eyes bounced around the room, maybe looking for an escape, maybe for an ally.

Yet she had not said a word to dispute the claim.

'That was my story too,' Beth said, feeling her voice grow deep and strong, coming from a dark pit in her stomach where all the hurt and pain resided. 'That's how I got these scars. That was my mum who died, and you had no right to use any of it.' The room blurred around her, it was only Jan she could see clearly. Locked in her sights.

'Have you got anything to say?' she prompted.

'There is no such thing as an original story,' Jan began.

'It's word for bloody word!' Beth cut in. 'Would you like me to show you?'

Beside her, Jamie started to read. Beth spun around to find him with a copy of Jan's book, reciting the section that was an exact replica of Poppy's work. Her brows shot up, impressed that he'd thought ahead.

He paused for a beat after he finished, letting each word sink in.

'A bit too close for my liking,' he said.

Alice clicked her tongue. 'Plagiarism is not a good look on a bestselling author.'

Jan hadn't blinked, hadn't moved, hadn't even twitched a muscle. She was staring at the back wall but Beth would bet her mind was racing. No doubt working out how to dig her way out of this mess.

'Are you going to try to dispute it when the evidence is right there?' Beth shifted in her seat. 'The worst thing is, this isn't an isolated incident, is it, Jan?'

Jan remained very tight-lipped. Her arms hung limp by her side, but Beth could see the tension in her clenched fingers.

'We did a bit of digging, and it turns out other stories from your retreats have been used in your other books. Did you think we wouldn't work it out?'

'What do you want?' Jan croaked. Her usual commanding presence was fading away, leaving her more a frail old woman by the second.

'I want what's right,' said Beth. 'I want you to own up to the fact you've been using other people's stories for your personal gain. I want you to admit that you used Poppy's story. I want you to fix this.' Even though the words gave her a sense of power, she still felt acid churn in her stomach.

'Are you after money?' Jan asked. 'How much?'

Beth's mouth fell open. This woman was a piece of work.

'Money?' shot Alice. 'You are so immoral, it's disgusting. How do you live with yourself?'

Jan had the decency to flinch. Maybe the old duck wasn't solid stone after all. She slowly tugged off the bright scarf around her neck, as if she felt it constricting, like a noose.

'I'm sorry, but I'm assuming you're bringing this up because you would like compensation?'

Alice's jaw dropped. Beth mouthed the word *compensation*. Jamie's chair groaned. Simone hadn't moved since she'd joined them. Beth was worried Jamie had really affected her.

As if Beth's thoughts woke her up, Simone spoke. 'You know, I have thousands of followers who'd love to hear all about this.' She held up her phone as if ready to broadcast the whole sordid lot.

'I could tell the world *your* big lie, Simone,' said Jan calmly. 'So I wouldn't be too hasty if I were you.'

Beth had expected some venom from Jan, but to see it in action sent a chill down her spine. Like a tiger snake cornered with no place to go, her only option was to strike.

Simone's face went pale as she glanced at everyone. 'I didn't lie, I just didn't tell the whole truth . . .' Her words fell away when she got to Jamie. Hanging her head, she went back to her original position of facing the front of the room, face flushed red like a rose.

Jan's eyes narrowed. 'You all have secrets.'

Beth looked around the table. Jan was right, they were all hiding something from each other, from their family, from themselves. They did have secrets. At least Beth's was out in the open now, well, besides the sleeping with Jamie bit. She turned to him, wondering if now was the time he'd ask Alice about Abe. He was watching Alice, but his lips remained pressed firmly together. Was he scared of her answer? Would he want to be an instant father?

'Whatever Simone might have done, it can't be as bad as what you've been up to,' Alice cut in. 'Using your retreats – taking our money – to steal people's memories to use as story fodder. Why can't you use your own ideas?'

Jan shuddered and looked blankly at the floor. 'I don't have any.'

Beth lifted her head in a confused jerk, then glanced at Jamie. 'What do you mean?' he asked.

But the moment had vanished in a heartbeat as Jan re-centred herself, which left Beth wondering if she'd imagined it.

Jan rushed out a breath. 'Look, what do you want me to do? Write a public apology? Talk to your sister? Surely, we can work something out?' She planted her feet and waited.

Beth glanced at the others. They hadn't discussed this far along. Not even with Poppy. What would Poppy want? Public humiliation? Money? Revenge? None of those things were Poppy. She'd want justice, and Jan stopped. The others in the room wore blank uncertain faces, no one having any thoughts on her punishment.

Just then, there was the sound of a car pulling up outside, then doors slamming. Excited kids' voices floated in.

'Mummy?"

Alice sat up. 'Mia?' She listened again and then bolted from her seat and out the door.

Jamie got up so quickly his chair threatened to topple backwards, before he followed Alice.

'What's going on?' asked Simone, her brow creasing as she stared after them.

Beth knew. She shot up, not wanting to miss any action.

'You, stay here. We have lots more to talk about,' she said threateningly to Jan before rushing off after Jamie. What kind of shitstorm was about to arrive?

# 28

## *Jamie*

HE DIDN'T THINK. HE JUST ACTED.

Alice's kids were here. That meant his son was here. Abe. Jamie had to see him, just to know if there was any chance.

He found Alice outside, two little beings clinging to her sides like Velcro. It painted a pretty picture – mother and children with green glittering leaves in the background as the morning sun flitted through, giving everything a golden glow.

It was a vision of the future he wanted. But if Abe was his, it wouldn't look like this. Abe would never consider him his father. And at the moment the boy had everything he needed. And yet, Jamie couldn't walk away.

'We've come to surprise you for your birthday, Mummy,' said Mia. 'But Daddy said we had to be quick because you're very busy.'

'Aw, that is so lovely of you.'

Jamie was about to speak when Beth stepped beside him. 'Jamie, maybe now's not the best time?'

He knew she was there but her words didn't reach his ears. He was fixated, his heart racing.

'Jamie?'

He turned to her. 'Look at him, he has my eyes,' he said under his breath.

'Dad has your present in the car,' said Mia, and then ran off around the corner to the parking area.

As the little girl disappeared, Jamie zeroed in on the boy standing with Alice. Golden skin and blue eyes. A sudden compulsion made him stride over and touch Abe on the shoulder. 'Hey, Abe.'

He was still clinging to his mum, head tilted back as he stared up at Jamie warily. But his tiny shoulder was warm under Jamie's hand. Could Abe feel a connection to him?

Alice was rubbing small circles on Abe's back while giving Jamie a strange look.

'Alice?' He kept his hand on Abe, his warmth seeping through while he silently begged her to speak the truth.

'Jamie?' Alice cocked her head, eyebrow raised.

'Were you ever going to tell me?'

'Tell you what?' She screwed up her face.

Had she lived with the lie for so long that it didn't even come to mind?

'About Abe?' He glanced down at the blond-haired boy.

Abe hugged his arms tighter around Alice's legs as if trying to inch away from Jamie. Not wanting to scare him, Jamie retracted his hand.

'He has my blue eyes,' he muttered.

Alice blinked for a moment then she exploded. 'Oh my God!'

'I have a right to know,' Jamie said.

'Surprise!'

A man came around the corner of the house carrying a huge bouquet of flowers, Mia bouncing along beside him. Abe ran over to him and clung to his leg.

Alice shot him a pleading look. 'Dale, give me a minute, please?' She turned to Jamie. 'Jamie, not now,' she said, her head shaking slightly.

'Come with me,' Beth said forcefully, then changed to a more upbeat tone as Dale drew closer. 'Let Alice have some family time.'

'Alice? Is everything all right?' Dale's voice was deep and concerned.

Tension was thick like morning fog, everyone was on edge, even the kids picked up on it. Mia's hand shot out to her dad's pants and held on. The flowers in his hands quivered.

'Jamie, no,' said Alice. 'It's not what you think.'

'What is it then?' She said she was open with her husband; they could sort this right now.

Dale handed her the flowers. 'Happy birthday, beautiful.' He kissed her cheek, but his eyes remained on Jamie. 'Who is he?' His eyes narrowed as he glanced between Jamie and his wife. Then he bent down to his kids. 'Mia, honey, take Abe and go grab the special box,' he said sweetly, giving her a conspiratorial wink.

'Oh yes, come on, Abe. We forgot the chocolates!'

Their excitement would have been cute any other day but Jamie was too focused on Alice. 'Are you going to tell him? Does he know?'

'Do I know what?' Dale barked. 'Who the hell are you and what did I just step into the middle of?'

'Dale, this is Jamie, the one I met at the gym six years ago,' Alice said warily.

Jamie saw the penny drop; he braced for a tongue lashing but was unprepared for the fist that came flying at his face.

Beth yelled out. 'Hey!'

Alice squealed, 'Dale, no!'

But it was too late, Jamie could feel the hot blood running down his chin, the throb in his lip.

'What the hell are you doing here?' Dale cursed.

'He came for the workshop, like me. Neither of us knew, it was a total surprise,' Alice tried to explain.

'Yeah, total surprise . . . like finding out about Abe,' Jamie asked, spitting out some blood.

Dale spun on him so quick he thought he was going to lay into him again. Jamie put his hands up in defence, even though he figured he deserved what was coming.

But Dale only hit him with words. 'Abe is all mine, not yours.'

A car door slammed and kids' voices grew louder. Jamie felt the venom in Dale's gaze, the hurt in Alice's.

Beth tugged on his arm. 'Inside, before the kids see you. You're a mess.'

Somehow Beth managed to push him inside and onto a chair near the kitchen. He didn't know if it was shock or defeat or just emptiness he felt, but he allowed Beth to take control.

'You idiot,' she said as she started cleaning his face with some paper towel. Her eyes were alive with adrenaline and yet he could see compassion. 'You really like confronting people, don't you?' she sighed.

'Not really.' It was true. Normally he was a laid-back guy, unless something meant a lot to him. 'But I was going insane, I needed to know.'

'Are you happy now?'

Her words were harsh but her tone gentle. He watched her brow crease as she worked on cleaning him up.

'You've split your lip bad,' she muttered.

He didn't really feel it. He felt numb. Dale said Abe wasn't his. That had hurt more than the punch.

Beth had paused and was watching him, those eyes dipping down into his soul. 'Are you okay?'

'I don't know.' It was the truth. 'Do you think her husband was telling the truth? Or that he just believes it to be true?'

Beth caressed his face. 'I don't know, Jamie, you'll have to ask Alice. If she ever wants to speak to you again.'

'Yeah, I know. She probably wants to kill me.'

'That look on her face said as much.' Beth grimaced.

He liked how close she was standing to him. He liked being able to see the freckles across her nose and the ripples in her blue eyes. His fingers danced at his sides, itching to brush the strands of hair back from her face.

'Jamie?' Beth warned. 'Don't look at me like that.'

Her face flushed and it warmed his body. It made the room come back into focus. He noticed Simone pop her head in before scurrying off again. Today had just been a balls-up from the get-go. Waking to find Beth had snuck from his bed, to seeing what Simone had posted on her Instagram, then Jan, and now Alice and Dale. What else could happen?

'Here, drink this.' Beth shoved a glass at him and sat down on the chair beside him. 'Are you going to be okay?'

'Gunna have to be. Will it need stitches?' He reached up and felt his swollen lip.

'No, I think you'll live.'

'Have you spoken with Poppy?' he asked.

Beth rolled her eyes. 'Not yet, been too busy saving your arse,' she teased.

Alice walked in, clasping a huge bouquet of white and blue flowers and a box covered with blue ribbon shoved under her arm. She pointed straight at Jamie. 'You and I need to talk.'

'Have your family gone already?' Beth asked.

'Ah, yes. They're off home again. Just came to drop off these,' she said.

'I can put them in a vase for you,' said Beth, getting up and throwing a firm look at Jamie as if to say, *be nice.*

Alice passed her the flowers. 'Thank you,' she said, before putting her chocolate box on the table and sitting beside Jamie.

Her emerald eyes pointed sharply at him. 'Want to explain what the hell just happened?'

*Not particularly.*

Beth was close by filling a vase, which he found reassuring. He gulped, feeling entirely out of his comfort zone.

'Alice, I need to know. Did you write that piece Jan read out?'

Her eyes darkened. 'I did.'

One question down, now for the most important one.

'Is Abe my son? Or is what Dale said true?'

# 29

## Alice

'WHAT IN THE HELL POSSESSED YOU TO THINK THAT ...'
Alice checked herself, lowering her voice. 'To think that Abe
was yours?' she finished in a whisper.

The scene he'd caused in front of Abe was bad enough;
but if the kids had witnessed Dale punching Jamie ... what a
nightmare. Beth had managed to drag Jamie away, which had
given her time to placate Dale. There were no secrets in their
family anymore. She would have told Dale about Jamie being
at the retreat – but when the time was right, not like that, not
with the kids close by and so much friction in the air.

'What the hell is going on, Alice?' Dale had demanded,
shaking his hand and flexing his fingers.

She'd stepped towards him, instinctively wanting to check
his knuckles for swelling, but he'd flinched away from her.
Even now that image still lingered.

The kids had returned, excitedly holding up the box of

chocolates together. Dale had plastered on a smile for their sake, but Alice could tell he was pissed off.

'Here, take a chocolate each.' Any tension the kids might have noticed disappeared the moment they could have a treat. 'Mia, would you like to head down that path over there and show Abe the pool? Don't go in, you can see it through the fence.'

The moment the kids disappeared Alice started to explain. 'Dale, please listen. I didn't know he was going to be here.'

He stared at her and she almost forgot how to breathe.

'I promised to never lie to you ever again – that is the truth. We were both shocked.'

'What made him think Abe was his? Did you tell him?'

Dale's words still echoed in her mind now. She hated this upheaval and resented Jamie for causing it. *Selfish arsehole.*

Alice explained as fast as she could before the kids returned. When she was finished, tears fresh in her eyes, Dale had merely pulled her to him and kissed her forehead. 'I'm sorry. I should have handled that better,' he said, holding her tightly.

Dale had been with her through the darkest times and they'd come out stronger. So much stronger. She'd confessed to having an affair, and the pain in his eyes was something Alice would spend the rest of her life trying to make up for. Dale, the sweet and forgiving man she loved, had understood she wasn't herself, and they'd never spoken about the affair again. At that point in their lives, trying to get Alice through her depression became their number one priority, along with raising Mia.

Her husband was her strength, her home, her passion. He'd given up so much to help care for her and together they'd embarked on a different, better version of their life, one in which their family was firmly at the centre.

Staring at Jamie now, Alice wanted to throttle him for the scene he'd caused. She would thank Beth later for dragging him away before things got any worse.

'His age fits,' said Jamie now.

Alice blinked. She'd lost her train of thought.

'Jan read out that story,' he went on, 'and the ending . . . it just all made sense.'

Alice frowned. She hadn't been happy when Jan had started reading it out. She figured no one would think it was hers anyway. But Jamie, well, she'd hoped he wouldn't put two and two together. 'Oh. I see.'

He gave a little shrug and a weak smile. His top lip had swollen to twice its original size, and was turning purple. Dale had really got him good.

'Well, I can see how that might make you think . . .' She faded off before sliding onto the chair beside him. 'Jamie, after our affair I did fall pregnant. I wrote that story about that moment in my life when I had no idea if Abe was yours or Dale's.' She gritted her teeth, watching his eyes widen. Quickly she put her hand up to slow where his mind was headed. 'It wasn't great timing,' she admitted as she leaned back.

Jamie sat, quietly listening. Beth stood by his side. Alice didn't care if she heard; Beth had been kind.

'I was making progress with my psychologist and being a better mum to Mia. And for the first time in a long time I felt like the old me. Then I found out I was pregnant. It was such a shock. But Dale was amazing. We went in prepared with

Abe and I was honest with him – I told him I didn't know who the father was.'

'That can't have been easy,' he said softly. The anguish in his eyes was real and she felt a strange comfort from it.

Alice shook her head. 'It wasn't. But Dale, after taking some time to think about it, decided it didn't matter. You have no idea how strong he is, to put his feelings aside and put me and the baby first.'

'So, are you saying you still don't know who Abe's father is?' Jamie's words were faint.

It hurt to look at him, to see the hope in his eyes and know she was about to smash it to bits. 'When Abe was born, he had webbed toes, it's a family trait on Dale's side. He knew as soon as he saw them that Abe was his.'

That moment in the birthing suite, Dale had whooped and cried. 'He's mine, Alice. He's bloody mine.' And then the tears of relief and joy. Alice had felt a huge weight lift from both their shoulders. She knew Dale would have loved him regardless, but still, his own son trumped all.

Alice didn't know if she should try to comfort Jamie somehow. In the end she did nothing, just let him have a moment to process. 'I'm sorry.'

His body sagged. 'It's not bad news, but I still feel a little disappointed. It's hard not to get excited at the prospect of being a dad.'

Alice smiled. 'Hey, you're still young and there's plenty of time left. Don't force it. It will happen. At least this way you still have a chance for a happy family?'

They stared at each other and Alice could tell he was picturing just that – a little family of his own.

He nodded, his eyes clearing. 'You're right. I'll be fine. Thanks for being honest with me, Alice . . . especially after the way I reacted.'

'It's the least I could do. I feel so bad about how I treated you back then, Jamie. I've been so close to writing you a letter, but I've always wimped out. Let sleeping dogs lie, you know?'

'I don't imagine having postnatal depression was a walk in the park, especially falling pregnant with Abe at that time.'

His concern was sweet. 'It felt so different with Abe. I was so worried I'd feel like I had with Mia, but it was much better. I wish I'd had that help the first time round.'

'And so you're writing a book about it all to help other women?'

That sexy smile of his lit up his face and Alice felt his approval warm her heart. 'Yes.'

'All of it?'

Alice knew what Jamie meant. Would she write about the affair?

'You know, I had this discussion with Dale. About if it would upset him if people knew what I'd done.'

'And?'

Alice smiled, remembering the day she was at the laptop writing and Dale came up behind her, rubbing her shoulders and kissing the top of her head.

'How's it going? Need a cuppa?'

'Okay, I guess.' She'd turned in the chair to face him. 'Do I tell it all?' she asked, taking his hands in hers. 'Or would you like me to leave some bits out?'

Dale had knelt down in front of her so they were both at eye level.

'Honey, it's your story.'

'I know, but it affects you too. I want your honest opinion.' It upset Alice to think about it, but it was the truth. She didn't want to hide it. All she could do was look forward and try to right some wrongs and help others not to go down her path.

'I think you should put it all in. It's what happened. That's how you felt and what you went through. It's a part of your journey.'

Dale's words had been the reassurance she'd needed. Alice repeated them to Jamie now.

'He sounds like a good guy. With a solid right hook.'

Beth made a small half-laugh as she stood by awkwardly.

'He is. And he's sorry about that.' Alice grimaced.

Jamie shrugged. 'It's forgotten already.'

She had a feeling Jamie was almost glad about it – he hadn't dodged the swing at all.

'And don't worry, I won't mention your name or the gym. If you like I can send it to you to check before I try to find a publisher.' Her heart was racing, talking about her book and having Jamie read it. Only Dale had read bits so far.

Jamie tilted his head, his eyebrows raised. 'Really? You'd let me read it?'

Alice blushed. 'The whole world is going to be able to read it soon – well, if I can find a publisher,' she said with a laugh. 'No one will probably want it, but Dale said we can self-publish.'

Jamie leaned towards her, his expression serious. 'Before you do, come to me first. I might be able to help. And I'd love to read it.'

'I'll email you the first half of the book, it has our section in there. You let me know if there's anything you don't like or is too revealing. It's a bit rough,' she warned. 'After what Jan's told us, I really need to go through it some more and get that emotion across.'

'First drafts are always rough. Finish it first and then go back. You'll be surprised what you pick up the second and third time around.'

'How do you know so much about writing?' she asked curiously.

Jamie waved his hand. 'Ah you know, just what my friend told me.'

'Hey guys,' said Beth, stepping towards them. 'So, I'm thinking it's time to speak to Jan. If you two are all sorted?'

'I guess we should. We did leave suddenly.'

Alice and Jamie stood at the same time and Jamie moved to stand beside Beth. Beth smiled, and Alice was struck by her beauty. She certainly glowed when Jamie was nearby, and vice versa. The more Alice thought about it, the more she recalled images of them smiling at their own secret jokes as if they had a language of their own.

'Yes, I'm curious to see how this pans out,' Alice agreed, following them into the meeting room. 'I'd hate for my work, or anyone's for that matter, to be used in such a way.'

'Um, where is everyone?' Beth spun around on the spot.

The room was empty. No Jan. No Simone.

# 30

## *Beth*

'WHERE THE HELL ARE THEY?' SAID JAMIE. 'DO YOU THINK Jan did a runner?'

'I'll look upstairs for Simone,' said Alice, walking off.

'Shall we check her cottage?' asked Beth. She didn't want to do it by herself, which was ridiculous considering she'd already broken in once before. *You weren't alone then either!*

Jamie pressed his hand against her lower back, shooting warmth along her skin. He seemed back to normal, his annoyance earlier gone. Or was that mainly directed at Simone? *Urgh, how do I tell the difference!*

'Yep, let's go. Might catch her packing for an escape.'

A brisk walk, as running would seem too desperate, to the cottage door made Beth's nerves flare again. This day just seemed to get worse.

'Hello? Jan?' Jamie called out, head poked inside the door.

They froze, straining to listen, but all Beth could hear was their breathing. The hairs on her arms bristled at Jamie's closeness. Last night's frolic came to the forefront of her mind, and she struggled to force it away. Jan was the focus right now, not Jamie.

'I don't think she's in there. Should I go search just in case?' Jamie asked.

Beth didn't really want to chance getting caught and giving Jan something to take to the police if she wanted. 'Let's see if her car's still here.'

Alice was already in the car park, standing by Simone's Beetle. 'I can't find Simone. Her room's empty, the house is empty. All our cars are here. Where else could she be?'

'Jan's not here either. Could they be together?' Beth wondered. That'd be weird. She cast her gaze around the place and her eyes came to rest on the shed-like structure nearby. She spun around to Jamie but he was already nodding.

'The pool house!'

'It's the only place we haven't looked,' said Alice.

They weaved their way to the paved path that led to the pool house. Unkempt branches slapped at Beth like long fingers snagging her hair. The owners had done a great job of making the pool house feel secluded, the shed blending into the surrounding bush with its eucalypt-green walls and roof.

Jamie reached the gate first and paused with his hand on the latch. Beth peered around his shoulder and blinked.

'What are they doing?' whispered Alice.

Jan and Simone sat on two sun lounges by the pool, three bottles of wine on the table between them and a glass in each hand.

Jamie unlatched the gate but Alice pushed through first, heading to Simone.

'Are you okay, Simone? We've been looking for you.'

'I am now,' she said, swirling the mouthful left in her glass. 'We thought we'd escape the fight club scene and try some of these wines.' Her eyes flitted to Jamie's split lip. She winced before turning away and finishing her wine.

'How did you end up here?' asked Beth.

'I came here to escape . . . everything,' she said, talking into her wineglass. 'Then Jan arrived with the wines as a bit of a peace offering. We've been talking.' Simone glanced at Jan. 'Another, Jan?'

'Don't mind if I do,' Jan said, reaching over to refill their glasses.

It seemed to Beth like a fair bit of talking had occurred.

'We thought you'd done a runner,' said Jamie.

Jan shrugged. 'What would be the point of that? If one must face the music, best do it with a glass or two.' She lifted up a bottle and wiggled it at them.

Legs crossed at the ankles, Jan looked like she was on holiday at a resort, resting back with a wine, shirt unbuttoned at the neck, sleeves rolled up and her glasses perched in her white bob. Was she not even anxious about their lynching party, or was that the reason for the wine? Beth licked her lips, maybe she was onto something.

'Well, don't just stand there, pull up a chair and grab a glass. There's plenty more in the pool bar,' Jan said, pointing to the left.

Beth gravitated towards the cabana with its fake thatched roof and natural wood bar. Inside there were rows of glasses above a mini fridge and ice-maker.

'Beth,' Jamie whispered behind her. 'What's the plan?'

'May as well have a few drinks. I think we all need it, don't you?' Beth glanced over at Jan. 'Maybe a few drinks might help get Jan talking.'

'Fair enough,' he agreed.

Jamie collected three glasses and gave one to Beth before they joined the others. Alice had already pulled up a spare lounger next to Simone, which left the wicker two-seater for them. Beth couldn't help feeling a little conspicuous sitting next to Jamie again. Had the others noticed?

'What wine are we drinking and what is the reason?' asked Alice.

'Voyager Estate from Margaret River, and I think the reason is pretty self-explanatory,' said Jan. 'We all could use a glass or two. And some time to let the dust settle.'

'It's not even lunchtime yet,' Beth muttered, but still held out her glass to Jan who had taken on the role of wine pourer.

'It's five o'clock somewhere,' Simone said, gazing into her red wine, her legs crossed under her and a large jumper over her knees. A messy bun held her hair up and her eyes were puffy and smudged black. She looked the most relaxed Beth had ever seen her, though she still seemed to be avoiding Jamie.

'Simone?' he tried to get her attention. 'Look, I'm not angry with you anymore. I've said my piece, it's time to move on.'

Her eyes were wide like full moons as she risked a glance in his direction. 'I'm so sorry, Jamie. It won't happen again. I feel awful.'

Beth believed it. Her heart went out to Simone.

Alice leaned towards Simone. 'We all have shit going on in our heads that make us do stupid stuff.'

*Touché.*

Alice had hit the nail on the head and Beth couldn't dispute it. She glanced at Jamie and knew he was having similar thoughts. None of them were perfect.

'It's okay, Alice,' said Simone. 'Just because I'm floundering doesn't mean I can use people for my own gain. Sorry, Jamie, it won't happen again. I just wish I knew how to get out of this rut.'

He took a sip of the wine and winced, touching his lip gingerly. 'You've just got to keep taking steps in the right direction, Simone. The past is the past, the future is what you make it. You choose how you want to go forward. Just don't do that shit again,' he finished with a smile.

Simone was looking at him, dumbstruck. Beth had the feeling she didn't have many friends or much guidance in her life. It was as if she'd been floating through life untethered, trying to find her way by herself in rough waters.

'Look at my past,' said Alice. 'I'm working on my future and I don't usually look back. Unless it's forced upon me.' She pulled a face and turned to Jamie.

Beth pretended not to notice their shared smile.

'Is this about Jamie's lip?' said Simone. 'I heard some yelling but . . . well, I was here chatting to two little cherubs before Jan arrived.'

Alice took a breath. 'My babies. I sent them for a walk while things got heated at the house.'

'Slight understatement,' added Beth. 'Alice's husband punched Jamie.'

'No way! What did you do?' Simone asked him.

Jamie opened his mouth, but no words formed.

'Jamie and I were together once,' Alice declared.

'Really? Did you know he'd be here?'

'No, it was a surprise. Anyway, Dale, my husband, decided to share his thoughts on the matter with Jamie's face.' Alice frowned. She leaned towards Simone again and dropped her voice. 'Um, Simone, what did Jan mean before? What she said to you earlier in class?'

Beth sat up, unable to hide her curiosity.

Simone stared at the pool. 'You mean about my "big lie"?'

Alice rested her hand on Simone's arm. 'You don't have to tell us. But we wouldn't say anything.'

'What happens at retreat, stays at retreat,' said Jamie.

Beth wondered if that meant their hook-up too? He turned to her, but she quickly looked away, afraid of what she might find written on his face.

'That's not what's worrying me,' said Simone. 'It's more that you won't like me once I tell you.'

Her voice was soft and childlike. In that moment Simone seemed like a small girl who just wanted to be liked.

'Simone, we all have things we aren't proud of,' said Alice. 'Like my affair with Jamie, but that's not the worst thing I've done. I left my baby girl once, all alone, and I can't take that back.'

'You left your baby?' Beth asked, confused.

Alice straightened in her chair, but the sorrow was evident in the deep furrows on her face. 'I had postnatal depression, but still I feel like that shouldn't be an excuse. I'm her mum, I . . . I'll probably never forgive myself for that day. Although I'm trying to.'

'Oh Alice, you must forgive yourself,' said Beth. 'Raising a child is hard work. I can't imagine how much harder it must be while suffering from postnatal depression' She reached out and touched Alice's arm.

'Thanks, Beth.' Her eyes were full of gratitude.

'I'm sorry, Alice,' Simone mumbled.

'I'm not after pity. I want you to understand we all have things we're not proud of. I don't think you should beat yourself up.'

Simone smiled half-heartedly. 'I was a big kid, growing up,' she began. 'Quite overweight. You've all probably seen my photos on Instagram, everyone has. And then a friend put me onto the Alive products and in two years I'd lost some weight and was feeling good.' Her fingers played with the bottom of her glass. 'Then our neighbour passed away. Mrs Satish was my best friend, the only person who really liked me for me. Not even my dad wanted me. He traded me in for a new pretty kid and a wife.' She looked up at them.

Beth frowned as she started to put the picture together.

'Without Mrs Satish, I had no one. I thought that if I could be like this,' she said gesturing to herself, 'that he'd want me. I'd go to see him and he'd be happy and we'd be a family again. But I didn't want to wait another two years to get to that point, so I went and had a sleeve gastrectomy done.'

*Wow, I can see why she'd want to keep that quiet.* Beth could see all the implications if that news came out, her Instagram, her book deal. She snuck a quick glance at the others who were probably thinking the same but remained expressionless as they listened, focused on Simone.

'But I didn't tell anyone. I was still using the Alive products, so I figured it was only a little lie. My Instagram following grew as I lost more weight. I kept changing myself until I was what I thought Dad would like, what everyone would like. Men started to notice me. Somehow my page became an addiction I needed to feed with new and better posts to get more likes. I knew it was wrong and yet I couldn't stop it. Now I have to write this book and feel more like a fraud than ever. I just want it all to stop.'

'This is why you were upset last night?' asked Alice.

Simone nodded.

'Why don't you write about it?' said Beth.

'Yes, maybe that could be your story to tell? The whole truth exposed on your terms,' added Jan.

Beth shot her a look. 'I hardly think you're one to talk about truth.'

Jan slunk back into a chair like a mouse hiding from a cat. Beth didn't know how she felt about Jan at the moment, but she'd prefer it if she remained quiet nonetheless.

'It's better people hear it from you than it getting out some other way,' said Jamie.

Simone took another sip of her wine. 'I've thought about it, but I'm scared of the fallout. My Instagram page is all I have, and yet I don't want it to be anymore. I'm still so lonely. None of those followers are my true friends and I'm still stuck at home with my mum.'

'You deserve a better life than your Instagram page, Simone,' Beth said softly. 'You deserve to be loved for who you are, with real people.'

'Mrs Satish's place was where I loved to be, and Willow's Rest.'

'So, Mrs Satish is the one in the nursing home you were talking about before?' asked Beth.

'Yeah.' Simone's face lit up. 'She was.'

'You should write about her too, and your dad,' said Beth. 'And maybe even your mum. It sounds like they all led you to who you are now.'

'Yes, I agree,' added Alice. 'This is what you should be writing. All of it.'

'There might be some backlash, but that's part and parcel when you're in the media, especially with your number of followers,' said Jamie. 'I think Alice is right. People will love to hear your whole story, and the reasons behind it.'

'Did you ever go and see your dad?' Beth asked curiously.

Simone shook her head. 'I haven't. The more I think about it, the more I'm scared he won't want me. I don't know what's worse – living without knowing or actually knowing. What if he never wanted me all along? What do I have then? A big fat nothing.'

Beth felt Simone's anguish and her fear, but she also heard the life and passion that came into her voice when she spoke about Mrs Satish and the others at the nursing home. They were definitely her people.

'Thank you all for not hating me.'

Beth shot Simone a reassuring smile. 'Hate's a strong word. The trolls will get over it. And as for your dad, I think you need to ask yourself if you even want him back in your life after all these years. You need to work out what you want, Simone.'

'I'm going to move out of home,' she declared. 'That's what I really want. That's why I said yes to this book, to the money. I want to be free.'

# 31

## Jamie

JAMIE GLANCED AT BETH, A LOOK THAT SAID SO MUCH WITH so little. He cleared his throat. 'Beth made me realise that I shouldn't be afraid to speak up and be proud of what I've achieved. No one can take that away from me, or from you, Simone.'

Heat rose into Beth's cheeks, and it wasn't from the midday sun. Now everyone was looking at her, yet it was Jamie's eyes that held her attention.

'You should be proud, Jamie. I mean, look at your body, it's a temple,' Simone swooned.

He appreciated the compliment, but he knew it was time to set the record straight. He needed to find his voice, like Alice, like Simone. And staring at Beth right now filled him with a desire to tell the world. Already he saw the spark of pride in her eyes. A slight tilt of her head, a nod of approval. Strange how a simple gesture made him feel so strong and sure.

'Thanks, Simone, but I was referring to my book. The one I had published, I mean.'

Alice slapped his forearm. 'What do you mean? You've published a book?'

He nodded.

Her eyes narrowed. 'For real? Why didn't you say so? What have you written?' Alice turned to Jan. 'Did you know?'

'I had no idea, but it doesn't surprise me. Your writing is very engaging, Jamie.'

He wanted to throw Jan's words away, but instead he caught them, holding on before they flew away. She was Jan Goldstein after all.

'Susan Vincent is my mother's maiden name.' He paused, letting the name sink in.

Jan's eyes bulged as her face crinkled. 'I beg your pardon?'

'*Lie to Me*? The bestselling debut book?' Alice added.

'That's the one.'

'What are you doing here then?' she squeaked.

'No way!' said Alice, her mouth open. 'This is amazing!'

Simone tilted her head and said vaguely, 'I don't think I know it?'

'It was that book Jamie gave to me to read when we first got here,' said Beth. 'Such a gripping read. I can't wait to see what you write next,' she added, turning to him.

She was grinning ear to ear. He'd kiss her right now if they were alone. He had kissed her – no, devoured her, for most of the night.

Her eyes dropped to his lips and he wondered if she could read his thoughts. Alice tugged on his arm again, and reluctantly he turned towards her.

'Jamie, why didn't you tell us from the start?'

'I was too embarrassed. I'm a gym owner with a footy family, writing romance books doesn't really fit. I haven't told a soul.'

'Why would you need to come to a writing retreat then?' asked Simone.

'Good point,' he replied. 'Truth is, my publisher asked for my next book and I've drawn a blank. I've had massive writer's block. Fear of being a one-hit wonder. Fear of the next one tanking. Then this retreat popped up and I thought it might help.'

'God, I didn't think it'd be like that once you finally had a bestseller.' Alice pulled a face.

'This is nice.' Simone sat back in her chair and smiled at them all. 'I've never had friends like this to share stuff with. I like it.'

Jamie had a feeling it was more to do with the wine than anything, but then again, he was enjoying this little deep and meaningful too.

Alice agreed. 'It is nice. Sharing things with people you have no connection with.' She glanced sideways at Jamie. 'Well, you know, now.'

He chuckled. 'I know what you mean. I just hope my family are as supportive about my book.'

'They will be,' said Beth. 'I'd bet you anything they'll be surprised but over the moon.'

That could be interesting, he thought. 'How much do you want to bet?' he asked as he swirled the last of his wine around in his glass.

A cute little furrow line appeared on her forehead, interrupting the flow of her scar. 'Like, money?'

'Or dinner?'

'Dinner? With a child?' she asked.

'If you like. Bring your dad too. And if you're wrong you can cook me dinner,' he said with a wink.

Beth chuckled as she played with her necklace. 'I'm not sure I can fit that much food in my fridge.'

'Seems like a win–win kind of bet,' said Simone.

Jamie saw the looks Alice and Simone shared, sizing up the two of them and what all this meant. Jamie hoped Beth knew what it meant. After this retreat he wanted to see her again. He'd just decided, and the way his body reacted, he knew it was real.

'That could work, but you'd have to keep Hudson entertained so I could cook something nice.'

'I can entertain my brothers, so I'm sure Hudson will be a piece of cake.' He grinned like a fool, he couldn't help it. But even though Beth was smiling, he saw an uncertainty in her eyes. It was the same vibe he got when they first met – her wall was still up. That worried him. How could she sleep with him and not let him in? Was this about Hudson? A protective single-mother thing? Keep everyone at arm's length until they had proved their intentions were good?

Alice turned to face him, squinting up against the glare coming through the large side windows.

'What?' he asked.

She had the look of an eight-year-old who had a million questions and didn't know where to start.

'What's with you and Beth?'

That, he hadn't expected. Beth jerked away from him as if he was kryptonite.

'What do you mean?' she squeaked.

Simone frowned. 'What's going on?'

'You two just seem to hum when you're together,' said Alice. 'I was just wondering if I was reading into things or if I'm right.' She beamed, grinning like the Cheshire Cat.

Jamie felt like chuckling at Alice's keen observation, but Beth had turned red beside him and he didn't think she found being put on the spot as funny. Best defuse this bomb.

'We get on well.' He nudged her shoulder. 'We came together to nut out Jan's involvement in this story-stealing caper and discovered we make a surprisingly good team.'

Beth smiled, although he sensed it was forced.

'Jamie's been a huge help.' She nodded.

'Beth also worked out that I wrote the book I lent her, so we've shared a few things,' he added. It seemed weird to make light of what they'd done. Hot kisses in Jan's wardrobe, amazing sex in his bed. Even with wine, he wasn't about to share. If anything, he wanted to keep them close to his heart and all for himself.

Simone seemed to buy his excuse, but Alice still cast him a wary gaze.

Beth scooped up her hair and tied it into a ponytail. She was flustered, the skin behind her ears colouring pink . . . much like it had last night when he'd trailed kisses from her breast, along her collarbone and up to nibble on her ear.

'I'd like to share a few things about Jan,' said Beth, clearing her throat.

It may have been an obvious topic change but none of them could fault her for setting her sights on Jan. Somehow, she'd avoided any real retribution so far. Her trial was now in session as all eyes fell onto the white-haired lady sipping wine the colour of her lipstick.

Jan swallowed hard.

'I wondered when we'd get back to me.'

# 32

## Beth

THE ATMOSPHERE WAS STILL EXCEPT FOR THE CHURNING pool water. All eyes were on Jan as if the spinning bottle had finally rested in her direction.

The others seemed curious, not out for blood. Maybe the wine had softened the lynching party. Or maybe their own secrets and issues had changed the whole vibe to one more understanding and forgiving.

'I think we might all need a top-up before we get into it,' said Alice, opening another bottle and filling up glasses.

Simone finished the last of hers before holding her glass out. 'Maybe we should get some food?'

'There's a heap of cheeses and biscuits in my room – I'll go get them,' said Jan, standing up.

The group tensed suddenly.

Jan rolled her eyes. 'I promise I'll come back.' She took a few steps towards the gate and then paused. Turning back to them, she added, 'I think, like Simone, I've just been waiting for someone to find me out and put an end to all the lies.'

Jan's lips curled in a sad smile, then she turned and walked out of the pool house.

Beth opened her mouth but had no words.

'How weird is it that we can end up doing stuff we don't like, but can't seem to find our way out? And yet sometimes the solution is easy – just stop.' Simone sighed heavily. 'Why is stopping so hard?'

'Life isn't black and white, there are so many shades of grey. It's why we need lots of compassion,' said Alice.

'Yeah, but you don't want to get burnt from being too naive either,' Beth added. 'I've been burnt before. I'm not willing to go down that path again.'

'Who burnt you?'

Beth noticed Jamie hadn't shimmied his way closer to her on the seat; maybe the others had made him cautious, or maybe he'd thought otherwise since Alice had made comments about them? Decided to cool off?

'Hudson's father.' Beth said it clearly. Lots of self-reflection and work had gone into this part of her life. She wanted to tell Jamie so he understood her hesitation.

'What did he do?' he grumbled.

She spluttered out a laugh. 'It's more what he didn't do.'

Eagle-eyed, they waited on tenterhooks. Beth sighed.

'Adrien and I went to school together. He was like Jamie – the hot guy that everyone wanted to be with. He was popular and I used to like him, most of the girls did. We never dated but we knew each other through friends. Anyway, I ran into him at a party years later at my friend's house. I was out the back in the dark by the fairy lights, my fringe was longer back then and covered the worst of my scars. We got chatting and he remembered me, said he'd always thought I was gorgeous.' Beth scrunched her nose. 'Fast forward, and we end up in a dark sleep-out at the back of the house.'

'I don't like where this is going,' said Jamie.

'Shh,' warned Alice, shooting him daggers.

'As you can imagine, he hadn't heard about the crash, or if he had, he didn't remember. So when the sun came through the window that morning, he ran out of that room like I was the Bride of Frankenstein.'

'Oh Beth. What an arsehole.'

'Funny thing was, Alice, I half expected it. People always have a reaction. But the worst part – I ended up pregnant and Adrien wanted nothing to do with either of us. Let's just say he showed his true colours: an arrogant arsehole who was obviously hung up on looks and didn't want anything to do with me or his son. He told me to have an abortion and gave me some money.'

'That's so awful.' Simone winced.

'Does he know you didn't go through with it?' Jamie asked.

Beth couldn't look at him, and kept her eyes trained on her wineglass. 'He made his feelings clear. So no, I haven't told him. I don't want Hudson to have someone like that in his life, even if it means he loses a family and grandparents. Maybe Adrien's parents would be lovely, but I'm not sure I'm ready to risk my son's heart, or my own, on a maybe.'

'I can't believe he didn't want anything to do with you; you're *still* gorgeous,' Alice insisted.

'I think he was always a dipshit by the sounds of it. I know the type,' said Jamie, his voice catching. He turned towards the gate as Jan re-entered.

Jan staggered past with boxes of crackers, circles of cheese and tubs of dip and pâté. Simone sprang up to help her transfer it to the little table and together they started opening it all up.

'Wow, that's more than a snack,' said Beth.

'I like to put this and the wine out on the last night,' said Jan. 'But now seems fitting.'

Alice found a knife in the bar and within minutes they were all scoffing food like it was book club night.

'Great idea, Jan,' mumbled Simone.

'So, can you eat much, since your surgery?' Beth asked.

'Only small amounts at a time,' she said with a shrug. 'I try to stick to healthy shakes, but it gets hard, bad habits creep back in. But I don't want to go back to what I was. My mum had no idea about healthy eating, and I'm only just really understanding it.'

'Feeding your body right will solve so many issues,' said Jamie. 'Although a little treat here and there doesn't hurt either.' He popped a cracker loaded with cheese into his mouth.

They fell silent for a moment, all busy eating, but Beth watched Jan.

Jan was about to pop a dip-covered cracker into her mouth, caught Beth's gaze and with a sigh put the cracker down.

'Look, I truly am sorry for Poppy and you, and everyone else's stories.' Jan faced Beth, holding her gaze. 'I . . . I could offer to mentor Poppy? Or even introduce her to my publisher. I'm sure they'd be interested. Her work was brilliant.'

Again, Jan's composure was showing some cracks. Was she seeing an easy option out? Or was she genuinely embarrassed about her betrayals?

'Do you know the torment you have put her through?' Beth almost whispered. 'She has enough struggles in life without you adding to her burdens.'

Her hand shook, sloshing wine around her glass but her voice was strong.

The lines around Jan's eyes softened and she had the grace to look remorseful. Her voice soft, she admitted, 'I know. I'm sorry, Beth. I didn't think about how it would affect people. Actually, I tried not to think about it at all. I've been trying to shut the world out for a while now.'

Jan had lost the imposing, teacher facade and now looked like a frightened, fragile woman. Her wrinkles seemed more pronounced, as if the bravado had left her body, making it crumple in on itself.

Beth sighed and relaxed beside Jamie. She wasn't after a witch hunt; destroying Jan was not the answer, nor would it make her feel better.

'I'll be the first to admit I'm not perfect. I don't think I've been my true self for quite a while. That's why I'm so glad that you are owning your words, Jamie,' said Jan. 'Because you truly have a storytelling gift. You should be delighted at what you've achieved – getting published is no easy feat. Let alone writing a bestseller. You write delicious words, you *should* own them. I wish I could own my own.'

Jamie's eyes locked onto Jan. 'What do you mean? Some of them are still your words. Your first few books were amazing,' he said.

Jan's sigh was heavy enough to blow a yacht across an ocean. 'Indeed, those first few were my own words and I'm very proud of them.'

'Well, what happened?' asked Beth. Everyone had a story, a past that put them on a journey to their current spot. And she really needed to know how Jan had arrived at the point where she was stealing people's secrets.

'Did it get too hard?' Simone asked. 'Was stealing other people's secrets and memories easier?'

'No, I never intended to do any of this.'

Jan looked down at the cracker in her bony hand then fixed her gaze on the gate as if checking no one was about to come in – or else looking for an escape route, Beth couldn't decide which.

'I don't write anymore.'

'What?' said Alice, her hair cascading over her shoulder as she tilted towards Jan.

Simone scrunched up her button nose. 'How does that work?'

'I have a ghost writer.'

'What's a ghost writer?' asked Simone.

'Someone else writes the story under my name,' explained Jan.

Jamie sucked in a breath. 'So, you don't do any writing? At all?'

'I do a little,' Jan said. 'I edit, and help them shape the book. I don't send it off until I'm happy with it.' Her chest seemed to cave in on itself as she sank low in her chair. 'But yes, they write most of it.'

'And yet what you teach is so relevant,' said Alice. 'That quote you read out – "If the characters are having a good time, the reader is not. If it's going well, it's going nowhere." It all made sense. Ramp it up, create obstacles. Conflict and action.'

'You are exceptionally good at teaching writing,' Jamie agreed. 'You can't fake that. Which makes it even harder for me to understand why you'd steal these secrets.'

Jan stretched her fingers over her face, the bright red nails at odds with the wrinkled paper-thin skin.

'I'm not sure how I got to this point, to be honest.' She looked openly at them and shrugged.

Beth liked this version of Jan better: more relatable, more human, more accessible. She was letting her guard down, chipping away the hard exterior.

'We've all shared our stories with you,' Beth said. 'I think it's only fair you tell us yours. We have nowhere else to be.'

'Yes, I agree. It's your turn, Jan,' Simone chimed in.

Jan surveyed them all slowly before looking down at her hands. 'My muse was my husband. He was my biggest supporter, and when he got sick, then died, I lost my way.' She paused, closing her eyes. 'I lost the love of my life. I didn't know how to live. I struggled to get through a day let alone write a book. My publisher was calling constantly, I was under contract and needed to produce a book. They'd already given me so much time, and yet I had nothing. I spent days sitting at a blank screen. My Henry was the one to often guide me to the computer and say, "Time to type, my dear."'

Jan's eyes were large and sad, glistening with emotion. Beth felt the air change; every ounce of hostility had fizzled away completely.

'Henry would make me cups of tea, he'd fetch my crochet rug when it got cold or a hot-water bottle for my back. He'd ask me about the book and help me brainstorm when I got stuck.

I didn't realise how much he was a part of my writing process. Without Henry I didn't know where to start. My creativity had been rusted shut. I was lost without Henry. It went on for nearly two years, but I had to produce something. I started googling writing help and ghost writers came up. That's how I found Julia. She came in and took over. In a way, she pushed me into action. I came up with the idea of the classes, as I know the theory of writing, I'd just lost the passion to create. Some of the stories from my retreats were just too good to not use.' Jan glanced into her lap, face tinging pink. 'I've tried to write ideas down myself but they all seemed to vanish like smoke through my fingers. It's so bloody frustrating.'

'So you haven't written a book since then?' asked Jamie, but there was no anger in his voice.

It was hard to stay angry at someone when you understood their pain, where they were coming from. Beth had dealt with enough pain to know it affected everyone differently.

'I was only planning to have help for that book, but then somehow I've ended up here. Having a ghost writer made it easier. I took the coward's way out. I gave up.' Jan swallowed and whispered, 'Henry would be so ashamed of me.

'Have you ever tried writing another book by yourself?' asked Jamie.

She frowned. 'I've wanted to, ideas have come but I feel I've lost all confidence now. I'm not getting any younger. I have hardly any family and no children. Henry was my life. I haven't been able to feel whole again. I know that sounds sad, but I don't have any close friends. The few I had I lost touch with after Henry died.'

'By keeping Julia around you don't have the opportunity to find yourself or get your life back,' Alice said softly. 'I don't think you enjoy it; I feel like you know this isn't right.'

Jan pushed at her fringe. 'I don't like it. I feel like I'm living someone else's life. But I don't know how to get back to mine. It won't ever be the same, not without Henry. I don't know how to find the old Jan.'

'*I* know!' Simone darted from the pool room, only to return with a bright-coloured pen with yellow feathers on the end and a notepad. Passing them to Jan, she said breathlessly, 'It's your turn to write some emotional memories.'

'Oh, I like it,' agreed Jamie. 'Yes, you should write something emotional for yourself. Your words, your emotions.'

Beth and Alice nodded. It was totally ironic, and Beth loved it. 'Brilliant, Simone.'

'What? Now?' Jan sat up, alert but confused by the change of direction. But there was also something like hope glimmering in her eyes.

'No time like the present. Let's move your chair outside, give you some quiet space,' said Jamie.

Beth stood up and helped Jamie carry the chair out the pool gate to a shady spot under one of the big marri trees. 'We'll leave you here to write.'

Jan, who'd followed them like a lost puppy, looked at the pen and then the notepad as if it was foreign. 'Where do I start?'

'That's the beauty, it can be anywhere you want. Any memory. I'm sure you have loads. Just think of Henry and then start writing,' said Beth, glancing at Jamie with a smile. 'They are your memories, so you can't get them wrong or make a mistake. Go for it.'

Beth went to leave but Jan reached out and touched her arm. 'Thank you, Beth. I'm not sure I deserve your kindness.'

It was in that moment that Beth knew they were doing the right thing and that Poppy would approve wholeheartedly.

# 33

## Alice

THREE EMPTY WINE BOTTLES SAT AMONG CRACKER CRUMBS and tiny slivers of remaining cheese. Jumpers were discarded, pants had been rolled up so feet could dangle in the pool and as they moved around, Beth and Jamie always seemed to end up on the wicker two-seater together.

Conversation had been lively and animated but the moment the pool gate cracked open, they fell silent.

Jan appeared bleary-eyed, her cheeks shining and plump as if her tears had rehydrated her skin. Simone's notepad was clutched tightly to her chest, along with that ridiculously bright pen. It was obvious that she'd been crying and yet her eyes shone like diamonds.

'How did you go?' asked Jamie gently.

Jan took tentative steps towards them, papers rattling as she held the notepad out to Beth. 'Would you mind?' she asked quietly.

All eyes were on Beth, the group on pause, breaths held. Alice knew how important this was for both women.

'I'd be honoured,' replied Beth as she took the notepad from Jan's shaking hand.

Beth tucked a leg underneath her and began to read while Jan retrieved her wineglass and topped it up.

Finally, Beth finished and looked up. Alice sucked in a breath while Jan looked like she might pass out.

'Wow, Jan. You still write beautifully and emotionally. Thank you for letting me read it.' Beth smiled. 'How did it feel to write from the heart?'

Jan's body relaxed as she dropped and perched on the end of Simone's chair.

'It felt good. I don't know if I'm ready to write a whole story yet, but I think I'll keep writing more memories, for now.'

'I'm sure it will help, and hopefully get easier,' said Alice. 'I struggled at first. Some memories were painful, but then it became a way of unloading my burdens. It was like putting them on the page meant they couldn't hurt me anymore. I don't know, it was freeing.'

She knew that it might take Jan a while to get used to this change, something Alice knew only too well – feeling so far out of your depth, out of control, not knowing what would happen next. But sometimes a shake-up was exactly what was needed. To be pulled out of your trance. Some days, it was a lot like being stuck on railway tracks when you craved to be running wild through the trees. There was no simple way to get off those tracks; sometimes it was painful and fraught with fear, confusion and frustration.

*Things get worse before they get better.*

*You have to hit rock bottom before you can go up.*

So many mantras, and yet for Alice, they were all true.

Now she felt whole, she knew who this Alice was. She was proud of this Alice and what she had overcome. And she couldn't wait to get back to her family.

But she would stay in touch with these new acquaintances. Friends. Like a book club, they were all different, had different tastes, but all brought something new and unique to the table. Alice liked that challenge and she liked these people.

She was even starting to like Jan.

# 34

## *Beth*

IT WAS FINALLY TIME TO GO HOME. BACK TO HUDSON. BETH'S skin itched with the anticipation of holding him and breathing in his milky lavender scent.

And yet . . . she had only been here three nights but she felt nostalgic. Somehow this place and these people had wormed their way into her heart. Last night they'd got through most of the wine, the most Beth had drunk since having Hudson.

Like old friends they'd sat around sharing stories and discussing publishing and the world. Jan had let them all read her work. 'It's only fair,' she'd said.

It was a heartbreaking piece about caring for her husband while he was sick. It showed another side to Jan – the nurturer, the lover, the devoted wife. It was beautiful and tugged tears from Beth's eyes, which she'd blamed on the alcohol. That night she'd called Poppy, but told her she would explain about Jan when she got home. It didn't feel appropriate to be whispering Jan's backstory over the phone, knowing she was close by. Her sudden desire to do right by Jan was confusing, considering she'd arrived at this retreat with the opposite intention, but she knew it was best.

Now it was all coming to an end. No more waking up to Jamie next door. No accidental meetings in the hallway with him half-dressed, no more kissing in wardrobes. *Or sex in his bed!*

Oh how boring life would be without his steamy kisses. He'd awakened a yearning deep in her gut, one she'd so neatly tucked away and told herself she no longer needed now she had Hudson. Her life was complete. But that didn't mean there was no room left in it for more.

Last night she'd gone to bed alone . . . disappointed. Her mind kept trying to find reasons why. Had the night before been really bad? Was once enough for him? Had sneaking from his bed in the morning done its job and warned him off? Was that what he'd wanted? Fears bubbled up like a tar pit, making her so confused.

Beth didn't know what the future held. Friendship among the whole group? A regular catch-up? No contact at all? That dinner bet with Jamie – would he follow through on it or would his life return to the way it was, with Beth becoming a distant memory? Jamie was burned into her brain; she wouldn't forget him anytime soon.

But she didn't want to chase a man who might not feel the same and her life couldn't be put on hold for one. Hudson was too important.

Jamie's door was closed, not a sound behind it as she lingered for a moment. In the kitchen, she did a quick tidy up.

'Leave some for us,' said Alice, coming up behind her. 'Are you heading off?'

'Yeah, thought I'd get an early start.'

Alice threw her arms around her, the kind of hug she'd expect from a close friend. Genuine, tight, long.

'Bye. It was so lovely to meet you, Beth. Let's catch up for coffee as soon as you're free. I'd love to meet Hudson.'

'Sounds great. Thanks, Alice, it's been wonderful meeting you too.'

'Is Jamie up?' she asked, as if Beth should know.

'Um . . . I don't know,' she replied quickly. 'I'm not sure.'

Alice nodded, as if understanding the many layers to her statement. Gold bangles jingled on her arms and her expensive perfume lingered long after she'd pulled away.

'Is Simone up, do you know?' asked Beth.

'I tried to see if she wanted a coffee, but she was out cold,' Alice said with a laugh.

'I have her number, I'll say goodbye later,' she decided.

'Safe trip,' Alice added as Beth headed to the door with her bags slung over her shoulders.

She took slow, measured steps as she turned to bid the retreat home one last goodbye, and, admittedly, one last glance towards Jamie's door as if willing it to open.

Should she wait, or was that too much? If it was meant to be, then Beth was sure she would have run into him already. Maybe the universe was trying to tell her something?

All the cars were lined up, and Beth felt a pang of sadness. Was this it? Drive away and it was all over, just memories to forget? The sensation was strange in her belly. It was loss. She would miss this, miss the camaraderie.

Not wanting to dwell on it, she threw her bags in her car and grinned when she spotted Hudson's seat.

*Mummy will be home soon!*

'Beth, wait!'

Her hand was still on the car door, about to get in when Jamie's voice pushed through the thick morning air. White clouds like steam puffed from his mouth as he jogged towards her, sweat glistening on his skin.

Beth felt a rush of relief, her muscles releasing tension she didn't realise she was holding. Her face heated knowing how much she wanted to see him before she left. Maybe she was wrong about the universe. Maybe she was just impatient.

'Are you leaving?' he huffed as he drew closer.

'Yeah.'

'Without saying goodbye?' he said as he skidded to a halt.

The heat from his body radiated, warming her, but not as much as his caressing breath. Any closer and they would be nose to nose.

'I . . . I have to get back,' she said grasping for words. Her mind was wandering over his body, studying the way the sweat clung to his skin and his grey muscle T-shirt.

'Are you running away?' he asked, tilting his head slightly.

Beth frowned. 'No. What would I be running from?'

*Am I running?*

Jamie smiled. He was sinfully gorgeous when he smiled like that.

'Me?' he asked as his steel-blue eyes drank her in.

Beth couldn't form a reply. She was scared of him, scared she liked him far too much, scared of what that meant, and she didn't know what to do about it.

'I've been thinking,' said Jamie, stepping even closer to caress her cheek. 'Last night, I wanted to give you some space.'

Surprised, she nodded dumbly.

'Actually, I felt I had to tell you something before anything else happened.' Jamie withdrew his hands and kept space between them. 'Beth, I've been an idiot. And I know what idiots have done to you in the past, so I want you to have all the facts.'

Beth wasn't sure she liked where this was going. Not one bit. She already knew about his affair, what else could there be?

He flicked some sweat from his brow and headed to the shade by a huge marri tree behind the car park. She followed, leaning against the trunk, her nerves suddenly spiking.

Jamie kicked at the ground, breathed out heavily then set those blue eyes on her, causing her heart to spasm.

'I'm an Adrien,' he admitted. 'I was one of those self-serving pricks that dated all the hot chicks and treated them like entrees.'

Beth's lips parted but Jamie held up his hand.

Jamie ran his hand through his hair. 'Then Letisha came along, and I got a taste of my own medicine. Quite fitting, wasn't it?'

Beth pressed her lips together, holding in a smirk 'Just a bit.'

'Anyway, I sensed your wariness and I understand how you were hurt, but I want you to know I'd never do that to you. And I totally understand that you and Hudson are a package deal.'

Big blue eyes pleaded for her to search and find his truth. Beth didn't have to look far, the long weekend had been plenty of time to see that Jamie was nothing like Adrien. Nothing at all.

'Are you following me?' he asked.

Beth nodded.

'Good, because I want to make my intentions clear. I feel like I've been looking for someone like you my whole life. The women I've been with in the past have been shallow or had different priorities. I've just wanted to find that perfect woman, settle down and have a family. And I know we hardly know each other but Beth, you are the most real woman I've met in a long time. I don't want to let you go.'

With one swift move Beth was sandwiched between Jamie's warm body and the hard cold tree trunk. His lips found hers with a primal hunger that sent shivers down her spine. She felt like a goddess as he kissed her.

Beth clutched his damp muscular back above his perfect tight backside, fingers scrunching his shirt in need. His kiss deepened and she could taste the dewy morning on his tongue.

The world became nothing; there was only Jamie's hard body and divine kisses keeping her tethered to reality.

As he pulled away the weight of the world returned like a heavy woollen blanket. She had to blink against the light and the feeling that her soul had just come back to her body.

Beth smiled up at him, felt the throb of her swollen lips. As if reading her mind Jamie brushed his thumb gently over them, his gaze focused.

'Beth, I don't want to wait. I know what I want. I want you. I don't want to be friends and see how this ends up. I want you now.'

'But . . .' She couldn't calm her mind enough to form a coherent answer.

'I love how I feel when I'm with you. Honestly, I feel like you bring out the best part of me. You're kind and loving. I know it hasn't been very long,' he said pulling her back into his arms and kissing the top of her head, 'but it feels so right. Don't you think?'

Concern darted across his eyes. He was worried about her answer. That alone made her insides quiver with delight.

'I feel like I've known you my whole life,' she whispered.

'And . . . are you willing to have me in your life? I want to know everything about you, Beth. I want to meet your son, your dad and Poppy. I want to hear about your mum. I want to show you off to my family. I want you to be mine to kiss all day long,' he said dipping his head and fluttering kisses across her cheeks, nose and lips.

Beth brushed her fingers along his jaw and up into the mahogany strands behind his ear.

'Will you give us a chance? Will you let me come and see you tomorrow?'

She was giddy with the speed of his plans. He was ready to jump feet first. Maybe it was time she tried that too.

'Hmm,' she murmured as he nuzzled into her neck and brushed his lips along the delicate skin under her ear. 'Seeing as you put it so nicely, why not?'

His chuckle was swallowed up by their kiss, a sweet, sensual kiss filled with a promise.

'Now what?' she mumbled, still dazed.

'Well, you get in your car and I'll follow you all the way back to make sure you get home. Then I'll go home and dream about you until I can see you again. How's that sound?'

'Wonderful.'

'Just give me ten minutes to shower and pack.'

He stepped back, before grunting and pulling her back in for another kiss. Beth could drown in his strong arms.

'Damn,' he muttered, raking back her hair from her face. 'I want to kiss you all day long.'

Beth smiled. 'I'm not going anywhere.'

For once she wasn't worried about how her lips puckered against the scars, because in that moment, she felt beautiful.

# 35

## Six Months Later

BETH WALKED OUT OF MR RANARIE'S ROOM AT WILLOW'S Rest and followed the sound of Simone's voice to the communal area at the end of the corridor. Most of the rooms were empty, with most of the residents attending Simone's class.

Eight men and women stood, leaning on their walkers or sitting in wheelchairs, their attention focused on the bright orange and yellow vision that was Simone.

'Come on, Mrs Walker, I know you can shake those arms a little more.'

Music – a bit of old-time rock and roll – was playing from a portable speaker as Simone demonstrated dance movements for the residents to follow. Beth couldn't help but smile watching her as she filled the room with an infectious energy. In the three months Simone had been working here, Beth had noticed a vast improvement in the residents during their physio sessions. Not only their mobility, but their mental wellbeing. Simone doted on them all as if they were her own grandparents.

'Oh, Mr Park, that's some smooth moves. Is that how you wooed Mrs Park?'

Simone was doing hip circles and moved around to help Mr Peterson.

'Let go, feel the music,' she said, guiding his frail hips into gentle circles. 'That's better.'

The song ended and everyone cheered, from relief or enjoyment, Beth wasn't sure.

'Okay, you can all have a rest now. I'll go get the drinks cart and afterwards we can play some cards. Who's keen?'

Hands rose like thin paper kites in the breeze.

Simone beamed then spotted her. 'Hi Beth, want to join in?' she called out.

She shook her head. 'Great crowd,' said Beth as Simone bounced over.

'I know. They're a hoot.'

'Do you knock off soon?'

'Yeah, now. I'll play some cards and then I have to do some more edits,' she said.

'The book's coming along?'

Beth knew from the staff here that Simone worked more hours than she was paid for. She devoted her time to these people who often felt discarded by their loved ones and society. Simone brought them life and fun. It worked both ways, though – Simone simply glowed in their company.

'Yeah, I'm getting there.'

'Did you have many edits left?'

Simone screwed up her face. 'God, yeah. I'm only halfway. It's been a tough journey but rewarding at the same time, you know? And Jan has been an amazing help. I'm not sure I could have done it without her guidance. Oh, and all you guys too.'

Beth already knew the book was being dedicated to them all, which was lovely. She'd read bits of it and couldn't wait to read the final proof.

'They suggested that if I find my dad I can add an epilogue,' she huffed.

'Oh wow, how do you feel about that?' Beth walked alongside her as they headed to the kitchen for the drinks cart.

She shrugged. 'Honestly, I still don't know. My life is pretty great without him, why change it? But then I wonder if I might be missing out on things. He *is* family. He's still my dad.'

'Only you know the answer, Simone. It's a hundred per cent your decision,' said Beth.

'It does my head in. Some days I'm all, "Yes, let's find him," and others I'm, "Nah, not interested."' Simone stopped at the trolley, it was already laden with jugs of water. 'How's Jamie going on his book?'

Beth chuckled. 'I don't know how he gets any work done with Hudson around, but somehow he manages while he sleeps. I think he's over halfway on the next book. He won't let me read it until he's done. It's so frustrating.'

'But he's too gorgeous to stay mad at, I bet,' Simone teased.

'Doesn't he know it. He has everyone wrapped around his finger; he's worse than Hudson. He took Dad to dinner the other night because his brothers were over, so, as you can imagine, Dad was beside himself.'

'That's so sweet, though, that your families get on so nicely. Oh, did I tell you I met Mr Park's grandson Daniel yesterday? He's divine, and single. Mr Park is giving me the lowdown.'

Beth laughed at the way all the eligible grandsons were being paraded before Simone as if the old people had nothing better to do than play matchmaker.

'But I'm too busy for love at the moment,' she added, hardly stopping for breath. 'Oh, and I'm off to dinner at Alice's tomorrow night and then watching the kids on the weekend while they go on a dinner date.'

'How are those two? I wish I hadn't had to miss our last catch-up; can't predict a bout of toddler tummy bug, though.'

'Mia's a crack-up, and Abe is learning the guitar.' Simone pulled a face. 'Oh, you meant Alice and Dale? Yeah, they're great. Alice has two talks booked in at the mothers' clinic next week. Self-publishing has really worked for her.'

'Wow, more? That's really taken off. I guess you can read a book but it's more personal hearing it from the actual person.' Beth glanced at her watch. 'Damn, I better get home and sort some dinner.'

'Righto, it was great to see you. Oh, can you let Jamie know the stove is on the blink, please? He might be able to figure out what's wrong.' Simone threw her arms out and hugged Beth tight.

'Will do. See you soon.'

As Beth drove home, she thought about Simone and how full her life was. How full all their lives were since the writers' retreat.

Poppy reminded her constantly that she should be thanked for sending Beth to the retreat. Beth would never forget the moment Jamie came home for the first time to meet Poppy. He'd dressed up for the occasion, trendy jeans and a button-up black shirt that pulled tight around his biceps. Poppy's mouth had dropped open at the sight of him and she'd spent the night following him around like a puppy. Then they'd started talking books and that was the end of the night, Beth was nearly invisible except Jamie knew exactly where she was, his hand finding hers often. He'd be mid conversation with Poppy and then shoot her a wink or a smile.

Without even trying, Jamie had slotted into Beth's life like the missing piece of a puzzle. Poppy glowed in his company, or maybe she was just happier in general. She'd been spending a lot of time with Jan, working one-on-one with their books and somehow healing each other, it seemed. Through the flames had come a friendship, two kindred spirits who had lost so much and needed to find their way back to happiness. Poppy was writing more than ever, and a publisher was interested in one of her recent manuscripts. Beth couldn't be more delighted with the outcome, and really, everything had to do with Poppy. If she hadn't insisted Beth go on the retreat, none of this would have happened. Alice wouldn't have found closure, Simone wouldn't have embarked on a new life, Jan wouldn't be writing, Poppy wouldn't now be taking car rides to work, Jamie would still have writer's block . . . and Beth wouldn't have met Jamie.

Pulling up in front of the house, she parked behind Jamie's ute. A warm glow came from the windows.

'How're my boys?' she said, shutting the door and dropping her bag to the floor as she came inside.

Jamie sat on the floor of the play room while Hudson walked back and forth from the toy box, dropping each new item in Jamie's lap.

Beth stopped Hudson mid stride and planted a kiss on his head. He wriggled past to Jamie, who had become a favourite, but Beth could hardly blame him.

'Get much writing done today?' she asked. 'Can I read any yet?'

'Another chapter while the little man slept. Then we went for a walk around the park. Oh and no, you can't read any yet.'

Beth groaned as she sat on the floor next to him. 'You love to tease me.' At night he would sometimes read a passage for her. Lying there beside him, listening to him read was magical. But as for her reading any of it, he was making her wait until he got to 'the end'.

'Hey beautiful,' he said, leaning over and kissing her. 'How was your day?'

'I saw Mr Ranarie at Willow's Rest today and ran into Simone. Oh, that reminds me, she said the stove's not working.'

'Righto. I'll check on it tomorrow.'

Jamie had become Simone's landlord when she rented the small apartment above his gym. When she'd mentioned about how desperate she was to leave home he'd offered it to her. He had a big heart, that was for sure.

'Hudson, here, mate. Give this to Mummy,' said Jamie, popping a wooden box into Hudson's little chubby mitts.

'Is Dad here?' she asked as Hudson stepped towards her, his focus on the box.

'No, he's gone to Poppy's for dinner.'

'Oh, okay.' Beth tried not to feel left out from their regular dinners, but it was nice that they were spending more time together. It was helping them both.

'What have you got there, Hudson?'

He slapped the box into her hand and went back to collecting more blocks. Beth frowned; she didn't recognise this box from his collection. It was pine and plain with a flower painted on the top. Had Jamie brought it for him? She slid the lid off the box and blinked.

Tears welled in her eyes as she glanced at Jamie. He was grinning like a buffoon, eyes shining as he caught Hudson who stumbled on his leg.

'Will you marry me, Beth? You and Hudson?' Jamie sat Hudson on his lap, his arm around him protectively.

Heavy tears fell from her lashes and down her cheeks as she processed his words.

*Marry me.*

After the accident, her future felt like a barren wasteland of loneliness. Then Hudson had come along and she'd felt blessed and content. Until Jamie.

*Why can't I have the whole kit and caboodle?*

*Damn it, I want it all!*

Reaching over, he took the box from her and slipped the diamond ring out. He held it out to her, light dancing from its perfectly cut edges and gold band.

'Beth?' Her name faltered on his lips.

Panic flashed across his face. She needed to say something.

'Yes, of course, yes. Oh my God!'

'Jesus, you had me worried there for a minute,' he said, sliding the ring on her finger before Beth launched herself into his arms.

Poor Hudson was squished between them and fought his way out, crawling back to the toy box. But Beth was lost in their wet, teary kisses.

'I love you so much,' she whispered against his lips.

'I love you, too. You and the little man are my home.'

Jamie had his phone out, holding it out to her.

'Best FaceTime Poppy and your dad. I'm under strict instructions.'

'What? They know?'

He looked shocked. 'I had to ask your dad first.' He grinned. 'I buttered him up by bringing my brothers,' he said with a wink.

Beth threw her head back and laughed. She laughed so hard that Hudson stopped to watch her as tears of happiness and love streamed down her face.

'Mummy's gone mad,' Jamie said, pulling a face at Hudson before rolling Beth into his arms again.

Jamie's lips met the laughter on her lips as he kissed her.

'What about Dad?' she managed to mumble out.

'He can wait. The whole world can wait.'

The only one who didn't want to wait was Hudson. He pushed his way in and slapped his plump wet hands on her cheeks before smooshing his face against theirs.

*Dreams do come true.*

She would have to thank Poppy properly one day.

# EPILOGUE

## Acknowledgements

THIS BOOK WOULD NOT HAVE HAPPENED IF IT WASN'T FOR a group of special people I now call close friends: Jamie, Beth, Simone and Alice. I can't thank you enough for finding me when I was lost and setting me on a path to freedom. A path that led me back to my Henry. I thought I couldn't write without my love standing by my side, but the truth was he was beside me all along, and still is. Henry lives on in my heart and in every word I write. Thank you all for that realisation and for giving this old lady a second chance to right the wrongs. I treasure the days you drop in for our book club catch-ups and wine.

To Poppy, I wronged you and yet you have helped me with this journey. I can never thank you enough. Your forgiveness means the world, and from it, I have found a kindred spirit. I love your passion for writing, I love how it rubs off on me. I love that you have become a treasured friend.

I've had to find out who I am at this point in my life, and this book feels like a rebirth. I had to dig deep and tread through dark murky waters that I'd feared for so long. Thank you again, my wonderful friends. This book is for you all, and for Henry.

To my ever-patient publisher, copy editor, publicist, and everyone at Olive Books who has had a hand in the publication, thank you.

All my love to my little dog Charlie. You brighten my days and keep me company. I cherish our time together. Thank you, Simone, for such a thoughtful gift. I love him.

Lastly, to all my readers, thank you for hanging in there.

# Acknowledgements

TWO AWESOME PEOPLE HELPED MAKE THIS BOOK HAPPEN. To Anthea and Rach, thank you! I was in an empty space and you guys helped fill it up again. If I'd known how productive our writers' retreats would be – just add gin, chocolate, cheese and friends – I would have started these years ago! Thank you for listening, for the stellar advice, and the endless support one needs to be able to write. Also thanks to Leah for being at the very first retreat where the bones of this book were discussed. Your help and guidance on many book matters will never be forgotten. I am lucky to have such wonderful writing friends.

My family also need endless thanking and hugs. They love me regardless and support me, even if they think I try to do too much. Mum and Dad, bro, cousins, in-laws and aunts and uncles . . . you guys all rock.

To the Hachette family, thank you all for your amazing efforts, especially Rebecca. I don't know how you do it! To Claire and Di, thank you, I feel very special to have both of you work on the edits. Thanks to Karen for the read-throughs and sorting the edits. Thanks to Ailie for being a fabulous publicist and Lyn Tranter for being my wonderful agent of nearly ten years. Massive thanks to all those who have helped in any way on *The Long Weekend*. It's such a team effort.

And lastly, a huge thank you to the readers. You guys are the best. I'm sometimes too busy to keep up my social media platforms, especially with book news and writer information. If I could thank you all personally I would, but having another day job makes that tricky at times. So, thank you for sticking it out and not forgetting me. Happy reading!

Loved *The Long Weekend*?

READ ON for an extract from
Fiona Palmer's page-turning bestseller

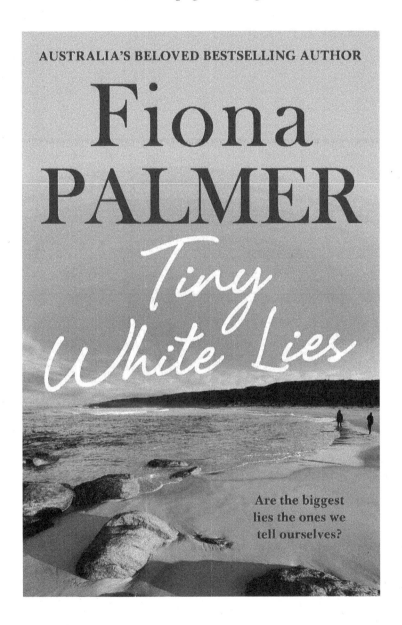

AUSTRALIA'S BELOVED BESTSELLING AUTHOR

# Fiona PALMER

*Tiny White Lies*

Are the biggest
lies the ones we
tell ourselves?

# 1

## *Ashley*

'U SKANKY BITCH*!!*'

'*Why do u bother coming to school, nobody likes you!!!*'

'*Stupid whore with a munted face like a dropped pie!! Go infect some other school.*'

Ashley's fingers were white as they gripped her daughter's iPad. Waves of nausea hit her like rough seas slapping against the side of a boat as she read message after message on her fifteen-year-old daughter's Instagram account. The more she scrolled through the obscene comments the more her face burned hot with rage.

Emily had begged to have an Instagram account last year and Ashley had allowed it, eventually. It was hard to resist her only child's charms and persistent nagging, but it came with the caveat that the password never be changed so Ashley could keep tabs. Which she did and found it all to be innocent friend chatter. But after a while the checks grew further apart until they stopped altogether. That was until today.

If Ashley Grisham allowed herself to be brutally honest, she had known for a while that something wasn't right with Emily. But they were both coming to terms with overwhelming changes and she was trying to give her daughter time and space to grieve, to heal. She thought Emily would come around in time. But more and more, Emily returned home from school quieter and quieter, moving slowly through life, shoulders drooped, head heavy and her eyes so sad it was breaking her mother's heart. And the distance, as if Em were on a boat drifting out to sea, seemed to grow between them with each passing day.

Of course Ashley had tried to talk with her, to check in, but Emily's reply was always, 'I'm fine, Mum.' Emily would flash her one of those smiles with her naturally red lips and straight teeth, the sort that could make the world believe she was the happiest, luckiest kid ever. Ash had been falling for it for too many years, or maybe she knew but was too scared to see the truth behind that smile. Because that smile was one Ash herself had worn on many occasions.

But it was in Em's eyes that the truth lay. She had Ash's blue centres but her father's large, almost almond shape. They were stunning, lending a pixie look to her narrow face and pointed chin. It was when those eyes sparkled that Ash could believe that Emily was really smiling.

Ash dropped her head against the iPad, ignoring the mess of red waves that got caught up in her fingers. Emily was lucky not to inherit her hair colour and freckles, even though her husband had loved both.

*Oh, Owen! Why did you have to leave us?*

Maybe Ashley had been leaning on Emily too much? Too much pressure for a fifteen year old? Emily had always been her rock, so much stronger and only still a teenager. Was it all just finally wearing her down?

Yesterday had been a turning point.

Em's brushed but still scraggly blonde hair had hung limp over her shoulders when she came home, but this time there was something stuck in it, smeared through it. Ashley had reached to pluck it out when the wet mess clung to her fingers.

'Oh, ew, Em, what *is* that?'

Emily had shrugged, making her oversized school polo shirt move like a flag in the wind. She hated clingy clothes and made Ash buy the next size up every time. If Ash even tried to buy something that would fit her nicely it would just end up kicked under her bed.

Ash had left her hand on Emily's shoulder until she finally spoke.

'It's banana.'

'How did banana end up in your hair?'

'Don't worry about it, Mum. It's nothing.'

Again she'd given that smile, the one that didn't reach her eyes.

'Emily?' Ash had taken her hand and held it between hers, eyes locked and waiting for the truth.

A huge sigh had escaped Emily's lips. 'It's nothing. Just some mean girls who like throwing food. I just got caught in the crossfire.'

That smile again.

'I'll go and have a shower.' Then Em had pulled away and headed off to her room in that slow, steady crawl.

Ashley knew she had only got a half-truth, just enough to 'Keep Mum Off My Back', and after stewing about it for most of the night and most of this morning she had finally remembered the Instagram account. And suddenly it was all coming together.

Emily was being bullied. Her beautiful, amazing daughter. Abuse was being hurled at her for no reason and she had been hiding it, putting on a brave face for her mum.

Ash lifted her head and touched the iPad again. She scrolled through more of the hurtful messages. Each one worse than the previous.

'If you died, no one would care.'

'Do it, do it, do it!!'

'Just kill yourself already u know u want too just like your daddy!!!!'

Clang!

The iPad smacked against the floor at her feet. Ash felt as if she were teetering on the edge of the cliff again, huge waves licking up the rocks reaching for her, pulling at her feet. The prickling on her skin started; the waves of dizziness.

'Oh god,' she murmured before collapsing back against the chair in the lounge room. It had been hard enough having to tell Emily how her father had died let alone see Owen's suicide being used to taunt her.

Count to five! she tried telling herself. But every time she tried to say 'One', those words raced past her eyes as the room turned dark.

'Just like your daddy!'

'Do it, do it, do it!'

A small part of her brain was trying to clutch onto reality. Ground yourself, the tiny voice whispered.

Ground yourself.

Ash started to move her feet on the floor while her hands searched beside her in the blackness. She could feel the material of the chair and the soft tassels of the yellow throw pillow. Her stomach rolled as she fought off the queasiness.

*Focus, Ash! Think of Emily as a baby, holding her in your arms, her sweet baby smell, her gentle coos.*

Distracting herself with her favourite memories usually helped, but it was a hard battle to overcome when the panic persisted. It felt like hours that she sat there in her own private hell. To some she probably looked like she was meditating but she could feel the slick sweat coating her skin as on the inside the war raged on.

It was probably ten minutes or more before Ashley felt herself gain control; before the room came into clear view and she could breathe again. She felt as if she had just run a marathon: her breath in heavy pants, her limbs and chest aching, her body frazzled and her brain like mush.

Pulling the black band from her wrist, she tied her auburn hair on top of her head, needing to free her neck from the constricting thickness of her waves. Her eyes caught the black shape of the iPad and she felt the prickle again, but she quickly glanced away, searching for something else to hold her thoughts. Anything.

A light-cedar-coloured acoustic guitar resting against the wall made her feel warm. She went over and picked it up, holding it against her chest as if she were about to play it. Her fingertips pressed against the strings one by one. Owen had taught Emily how to play on this guitar. She was just five when he had first propped her up on his knee, the guitar cradled against her small body while he helped her make her first chord. Then he got her to strum it, and the sound of it made her eyes shine so brightly. It was something they both loved and shared. Since her husband's death it had sat untouched. Hardly looked at. Avoided.

Eight months.

Ashley ran her fingers across the strings, the sound not quite right but still it filtered through her body like vines tethering her to the floor. It was the grounding she needed to bring her back to calm.

She strummed it absentmindedly while she sought out their family portrait that hung on the cream wall above the guitar. Owen with his blond scruffy hair at odd angles and his larger-than-life smile. His arms were around Ashley and Emily and they were all smiling as they watched the colourful butterflies around them. The sun had been out, shining through the butterfly enclosure, but ten-year-old Em had been watching her dad with delight. It had been a good day.

If only they'd had more like it.

With the instrument still clutched to her chest Ashley dared to think about Emily and the abuse she was getting online and at school. She doubted the banana incident had been an accident or a one-off. Kids could be so mean. Emily was a beautiful girl with a big, caring heart. Was that why she was a target? They were jealous of her stunning features? Or did it have more to do with her father's death?

It was common to hear Nirvana or Pearl Jam playing from Emily's room, or indeed her rendition of 'Thunderstruck' on the guitar, her fingertips having callused long ago. On weekends she lived in torn jeans and checked shirts. Anyone would think it was the early nineties and Kurt Cobain was still alive and grunge the in thing. Ashley had wondered if Owen's music influence on Emily had flared more since his death, and if she was finding ways to be closer to him.

Now, a million thoughts rushed through her mind. Should she call the school and make a complaint? Reply to all the messages and scold each child? Talk to Emily about it? Ash felt as if she were on a spinning carousel and didn't know how to get off.

'Oh crap!' Ashley caught sight of the clock on the wall. 'Bloody hell, I'll be late for work.'

She returned the guitar to its usual place and ran to the kitchen to collect her large black handbag and keys, all the while silently cursing her panic attacks and their ability to suck chunks of her life away. If only she could get control of her emotions. The coping techniques her therapist had given her were now her mantra, as well as the natural oils and calming sprays that at least gave her a small sense of control.

Ashley glanced around the house, checking everything was where it should be. Out of habit she adjusted the tea towel hanging on the oven door so it was straight, pushed in the two chairs around the dining table.

The iPad was still on the floor where she'd dropped it but she didn't have the strength to go and move it. The little prickle along her skin warned her to keep moving and leave the house; she couldn't afford another panic attack when she was already late for work. She knew how ridiculous it sounded, a grown woman scared of a square piece of technology, but in her mind it was a snake with fangs. The words it carried were venom. Ashley just couldn't handle thinking about those messages again, not yet. Maybe she was weak, she felt weak and silly most of the time; but Nikki, her best friend, always reassured her that she was none of those things.

Ashley pressed a hand down her navy skirt and checked for stains on her white shirt. When nothing else caught her eye she dashed from the house, locking it behind her, and then reached back to check it.

The morning traffic was in her favour and she arrived, not at work but at Emily's school.

She parked out the front, car running, and scanned the school. It was eerily quiet and empty, everyone inside, not even one kid loitering outside or taking a slow bathroom break. What had she hoped to get out of this visit? Spot the mean kids and go yell at them?

*You're too weak for that, Ash.*

Her little voice was right, she wasn't the confrontational type, but how she longed to be that strong mum who would stand up for their kid and give those horrible brats a good talking to.

'You're late for work, woman,' she chastised herself and set off for the shopping centre with no minutes to spare.

She parked quickly – at least the parking angel was on her side today – and with her handbag gripped tightly against her chest she walked like a kid wanting to run around the pool but knowing the watchful eyes of the lifeguard weren't far away. Inside the air-conditioned shopping centre music blared from the nearby hair salon, and in front of her four older women talked loudly as they shuffled slower than a wombat, forcing Ashley to weave around them and narrowly miss taking her hip out on the island Puffin Fresh Donut stand. Her eyes were drawn to the fashion boutique Designs on the right; two female mannequins wore stunning evening dresses in blue and lemon, but she couldn't see Nikki, who was the manager. She so desperately wanted to see her friend's face, to hear her reassuring voice, get her thoughts on this cyberbullying. On her break she would send a text to see if they could catch up for lunch.

Ashley felt her bladder swell as she passed the corridor to the public toilets but she tried to suppress it; there was no time to spare, and her boss Margie would give her a weighted stare all day if she was even a minute late.

'I'm here,' she practically shouted as she entered the pharmacy, which, luckily, seemed empty of customers.

Margie, in her pressed white shirt and blue pencil skirt, glanced at her watch before turning back to her task near the counter. 'Did you do your hair this morning, Ashley?' she said without looking up.

*Oh, damn!* She remembered scraping it up into a mess to cool her neck. Quickly she headed into the small room at the back where they kept their belongings and had their breaks. It doubled as a storage room, but it did have a small mirror on the wall, and as she caught her reflection she cringed. It was like a rather large rat had nested on her head. Her chest started to flutter, not in a good way, so she immediately reached into her bag for her balance oil and smeared it onto her wrists before fixing her hair.

'You okay, Ash?' asked Tim, leaning against the doorframe.

'Yep, nearly done.'

Ashley, happy with how her auburn waves now sat, headed towards Tim. 'It's been a horrible morning.'

He raised an eyebrow. 'Oh honey, you did look a bit dishevelled when you ran in. Careful, Margie's on the war path, but on the upside she's off in ten minutes for a meeting.'

'Really?'

The little diamond earring in his ear sparkled as his smile lit up his pale face. 'Gone for the rest of the day.' He did his signature 'spirit fingers' celebration. 'Oh, but she wants to see you before she goes,' he added with a grimace. 'Don't shoot the messenger,' he whispered as he left.

Ashley sighed heavily, then plastered on her biggest smile and went to find Margie.

Margie was in the corner at her desk next to the head pharmacist. Ash thought she resembled a stern old headmistress and that underneath her long pencil skirt she hid a cane, one she was dying to use. Margie would get a glint in her eye when she was about to deliver bad news or pain – and today, as she turned towards Ashley, that evil glimmer was there.

*Oh, great.*

'Ashley, I'm glad you could join us at work today. Please take a seat.'

Ash grinned like an idiot, trying to appease the woman when all she wanted to do was strangle that triumphant look from her face. The 'seat' Margie offered was the tiny stool she used to reach the higher shelves, but Ash sat on it with as much dignity as she could muster.

'I'll cut straight to the point, Ashley. I have been asked to tighten the budget and look at our staffing. I'm sorry to say that we no longer have a position for you here.'

Ash blinked, trying to understand Margie's words. 'Pardon?'

'Consider this your notice.'

Ash's mouth opened but no words came.

'Do you understand?' Margie continued, clearly preventing her lips from curling as if she took great delight in her power. 'We can't justify the extra staff and have made your position redundant, mainly because others have been here longer. Phil will go over your final pay and entitlements this afternoon.'

'I don't have a job?' Ash suddenly realised what this meant. 'I need a job.' Without Owen, there was no one else to pay the bills. Since his death, the cost of his funeral and dropping to one income meant that Ash was hardly making ends meet. She'd sold his ute, but that was only a quick fix. Ash gaped at Margie, then firmly closed her mouth. She would not play the recent-widow card.

'I'm sorry, I know it has been a hard year for you. We thank you for your service with us at the pharmacy. I'm sure someone will organise something for you on your last day.'

Then Margie fluttered her hand impatiently as if Ash were an annoying fly.

'Oh. Yes, okay,' muttered Ash as she tried to get up off the stool gracefully and failed. As she stood she felt a huge weight press against her chest, and in her muddled state of mind she did an awkward bow to Margie, as if she were the Queen of England, and left.

*You idiot.* She swore internally as she searched for Tim. She found him sorting the condom selection, his favourite task, and rushed almost into him.

'Hey, sweets. What did Hitler's mother want?'

'To fire me,' she huffed.

Tim's mouth and eyes flew open in his usual over-the-top flair but his shock made her feel a little better.

'Shut the front door!'

'I kid you not. Oh, Tim, what am I going to do now?'

Tim pulled her into a hug as a nearby customer watched them. Ashley didn't cry, she couldn't cry, she was in too much shock to muster up any tears.

Instead she felt the heaviness of her mind, like a throbbing volcano waiting to erupt. Visions of Emily and the constant worry of how she was going at school today were hard to ignore, and now the fact that she was jobless had just added to the weight on her shoulders. What *was* she going to do now?

# 2

## *Nikki*

NIKKI SUMMERSON GENTLY PULLED THE GREEN SILK DRESS over the hard cream mannequin. She paused at the breasts, the material pulling tight, and gently eased it over them. Her hand moved back to the breast, feeling its shape and its odd hardness. Even hard they were still better than hers.

*Stop it, Nikki!* she scolded herself and yet her gaze lingered on the breasts. At thirty-eight she was ogling breasts on a mannequin like a horny fifteen year old. It was ridiculous, she knew that, and yet here she was unable to stop admiring how perfect they looked and the way the dress moulded around them to show off the designer styling. Nikki would kill to be able to wear this dress.

'That dress is stunning, Nikki. Did it just come in?'

Heat burned up her throat and she took a moment before turning to reply to her assistant, Alice.

'Yes, six came in but I think this is my favourite.' Nikki smiled at twenty-two-year-old Alice, who had the spark of the young and a curvaceous body to match. Alice was a lovely size twelve, and knew how to wear her make-up to highlight her features, but it was her bubbly personality that had won her this position.

'You should try that one on, it's your colour, Nikki. Make those gorgeous emerald eyes of yours pop,' said Alice as she ran her fingers over the silky material.

Nikki would normally have jumped at the chance, but not now. All she felt now was a sense of loss and longing. Like a model past her prime, never to grace the catwalk again.

Lately it had been hard to come to work, to be surrounded by such beauty and still wear a smile when inside she felt like she was slowly rotting like one of her son's half-eaten apples left behind the couch.

'I might take it home one night,' she said, hoping that was enough to stop Alice before she began to insist Nikki try it on.

'Yes, you should. Once Chris sees you in that, look out.' Alice gave a little growl and wiggled her perfect brows.

Nikki's stomach jolted at the thought.

'Hey, were you going to take your lunch break now? Or did you want me to?' asked Alice.

Finally the escape Nikki needed. 'Oh yes, I'll go. Ashley wants to meet up for lunch today. Would you mind finishing up here and then we can start rearranging the front window.'

'Sounds great. I'll get things cleared away.'

While Alice fussed over the dress, Nikki darted to the back room for her bag and then set off into the shopping centre. She tucked her straight blonde hair behind her ear and twitched a bit as her bra rubbed against her skin. She was thankful for her chunky designer jumper, but soon it would be summer. Nikki shuddered at the thought.

The shops weren't especially busy today, so the short walk to the other end was painless. No dodging phone-consumed teens who didn't move or groups of mums with prams employed as battering rams, four abreast and hard to pass. Everything seemed to irritate Nikki these days, even Chris being extra helpful at home. She had a hot husband she couldn't bear to look at lately. And instead of getting better it was getting worse, because she knew he was waiting and wanting. The more he did nice things to try to win her over the more she felt like screaming and running the other way. Which was horrible, because she did love him. Was this what having a mid-life crisis felt like?

'Hi Nikki.'

She looked up as she entered the modern Expresso Bar. 'Hi James,' she said, waving to the owner, who wore a white-and-blue striped apron over his black clothes. His grey hair was always cropped short and tidy.

'Ashley's just arrived. I'll bring you both a coffee and take your orders.'

'Thanks, James.'

Ashley was sitting in the corner booth, staring at the opposite wall. Her shoulders were hunched over as if her gorgeous flaming locks were too heavy. She looked how Nikki felt.

'Hey Ash, you okay?' Nikki slid into the small booth opposite her. The black leather seat was worn but comfy.

Ash sighed heavily. Her face seemed paler than normal, making her freckles stand out. She was so down-to-earth gorgeous against Nikki's higher-maintenance, designer, always-look-amazing self and yet they had been fast friends these past four years since meeting when their girls started high school together.

'No, I don't think I am,' Ash finally replied.

Nikki's concern for her friend drowned out her own issues and she felt a little relieved to have a moment of breathing space; something she didn't seem to get much of these days.

'Is this why you wanted to meet up? What's wrong?'

Ashley's blue eyes, framed by ruby lashes, shone with tears as she looked up. 'It's ah . . . um . . . Sorry, it's been a shitty day so far.'

Nikki waited as Ash seemed to sort through her emotions and thoughts, all the while wondering what could possibly be wrong. She'd not long ago buried her husband – surely the universe could give her friend a break?

Taking a gulp of air, Ash exhaled her words in a rush. 'It's Emily. She's being bullied and abused.'

'What?' Nikki wasn't sure she'd heard right.

'Oh Nikki, I don't know what to do.'

Ash flung her hands to her wet face while Nikki dug through her bag for her little tissue packet and passed her one. 'Here,' she said, nudging the tissue into her fingers and waiting, letting Ash take the lead.

She pulled her hands from her face and dabbed herself dry. 'I'm sorry. I'm such a mess. But it's so awful. Has Chloe said anything?'

Nikki shook her head. She never got much out of Chloe unless she wanted money for new clothes or a beauty treatment; the rest of the time she was in her room and on her phone. Chloe was convinced she was going to be the next big Instagram sensation or YouTube star giving make-up tips. 'No, she's not mentioned anything about Emily. But I'll ask her tonight, just feel her out. What's been happening?'

Ashley sighed again just as James arrived with their coffees. 'Here you go, lovely ladies. What would you like for lunch?'

Nikki glanced at Ash, who was staring at the wall again. 'Um, can you decide for us today, please, James? Something comforting? One of our usuals.'

He squinted slightly, assessing them. 'I'll sort it, and some hot apple pie for dessert, I think.'

Nikki smiled. Now that did sound good. When James left she touched Ash's hand. 'Tell me everything.'

Ash pulled one of her tiny brown bottles from her bag and rubbed some oil on her wrist before she started from the beginning. She whispered the words she'd read from Emily's Instagram account but she couldn't bring herself to repeat the last one.

'*What?* They were telling her to take her own life?' Nikki sat back, appalled. 'That is disgusting, Ash, what kind of kid would say those things!' Nikki closed her eyes and hoped Chloe wouldn't ever get messages like that. Or even worse, that she wouldn't ever say horrible things like that. 'Were any from Chloe?' she suddenly asked, her heart in her throat.

'Oh no,' Ash said quickly. 'Chloe would never. They don't run in the same circles, but even so, I know Chloe's heart and she wouldn't be capable of that, Nikki, not to Emily. I'm positive.'

Ash smiled weakly and Nikki felt the pressure around her neck release. 'I hope you don't mind but I'll still be having a chat with Chloe regardless. It's just not on. She could be friends with these people for all I know. What are you going to do? Have you spoken to Emily?'

Ash shrugged as she picked up the coffee she'd just spotted in front of her. 'I honestly don't know what to do. I had a panic attack over it and have been in La La Land ever since. Should I go to the school? Are these people even in her school? Kids today have friends from all over the bloody country. How are we supposed to protect them?' She took a sip of her coffee. 'But I'll talk to her tonight. I feel so sick that she's been dealing with this on her own. Why didn't she come to me?'

Ash's blue eyes, rimmed red and glossy, skittered sideways, and Nikki felt like there was more to this story. Or maybe something else on her mind that she wasn't ready to share. 'I wish I knew, Ash. Maybe they don't want to worry us? I didn't tell my parents much either when I was that age. Remember what it was like as a teenager? I thought I was *so* grown up . . . But you don't realise until you really are an adult just how wrong you had it.' Nikki sighed. 'Sometimes I wish I could go back to those days and really enjoy them. They're supposed to be so carefree, but . . . This whole online world, and these phones concern me so much. I mean, Josh is a thirteen-year-old boy who has never climbed a tree. He sits on his phone or his PlayStation playing with other people online and I feel like I'm losing him. He's like a boarder, this boy who eats and sleeps with us, but there's no conversation, no interaction. And don't get me started on Chloe. She thinks she has to have a "presence" on social media to be popular. She wants to be famous. An influencer. I have a full-time job trying to stop her from going to school all made up like she's off to a ball. Sometimes the fights and battles just wear me down until I give in a little. And I hate that.'

'I know. What are we supposed to do? How am I supposed to help Emily? Take all her devices away so they can't touch her?'

They both leaned back as one of James's staff brought over their lunch. A Caesar salad and a creamy pasta dish. Nikki reached for the salad at the same time Ash took the pasta.

'Thank James for us please, Syd. He knows us too well.'

The young man nodded and replied that the dessert would be out in ten.

'I think putting her devices away would be good,' Nikki said. 'So she can't keep reading the messages and letting them consume her. But what about the banana in her hair? Go in and speak to the principal, just make him aware of it at least?'

Ash nodded. 'I think I need to. Surely a teacher has noticed something. Or if not I need to see that they're keeping an eye out.' Ash stabbed at her pasta. 'I feel so awful that I didn't find this out sooner. I'm her mum, I'm supposed to be able to protect her.'

'I don't think we can fully protect them from everything, Ash. Poor Emily. Don't they know she just lost her dad?'

Nikki watched as Ash moved her pasta around her plate, her face still so pale. The poor woman had been through hell, losing Owen the way she had and then trying to sort through the funeral and keep herself and Emily going. Nikki wasn't sure how she'd cope without Chris.

'One of them . . .' She took a breath. 'One of them mentioned Owen, and it implied they knew how he died.'

'Have you spoken with her?' said Nikki gently. 'It was bound to get out and go around the school. Kids love any sort of gossip.'

'No, not yet. She was already at school. We haven't spoken much about Owen's . . . death, except after it happened. Since then it's like neither of us wants to bring it up and open old wounds.'

'I understand. But Emily's a strong girl, Ash, don't forget that.' Nikki had seen firsthand the way Emily watched her mother, looking for signs of her panic attacks and knowing how to divert them or help her through them. Chris had once told her that he thought Emily had the eyes of a wise person who had been here before, mature beyond her age. And Nikki knew what he meant; she had seen Em pick up on emotions in a room, seemingly aware of things going on in the background while other kids were oblivious. Chloe seemed years younger at times in comparison and yet she had been born only four months after Emily.

'I know she is. Though I think that's mainly because I'm *not* strong.'

Nikki reached for her hand and squeezed it. After the funeral Ash had confided her despair at not realising Owen was suicidal and her pain at thinking she could have saved him. Nikki had heard the guilt in her friend's voice and held her while she'd cried and cried. She stayed the first few nights with Ash so she didn't have to be alone. She held her hand while she organised the funeral arrangements, hugged her when she fell to pieces and reassured her every day that she was not responsible.

'You are *not* to blame, Ash. For any of this. I'll keep reminding you of that for as long as I have to.' Nikki straightened up and put on a determined air. 'Now, let's work on how you'll approach Emily. We both know how difficult teenagers are to talk to,' she said, rolling her eyes.

Ash gave her a small smile, and took a bite of her lunch.

'We need to find a way for you to discuss the abuse without putting Emily offside or on the defensive. Especially when it's hard to guess which way she'll go,' said Nikki while filling her fork with salad.

'She'll probably deny the whole lot just so I won't worry. I don't want her to blow this off as nothing.'

'Agreed. It's a serious matter. I hate bullying.'

The apple pie with a side of ice-cream eventually arrived and both women pounced on it while the waiter took their half-eaten lunches away.

Ash brushed her hair back and fanned her face. 'Wow, it's so hot in here. How are you not boiling in that jumper, Nik?'

Nikki shrugged and hoped her red face and clammy skin weren't too noticeable. The truth was, she *was* hot. But they were nearly done and she would soon be back in the air-conditioned bliss.

'I wish I could be more help, Ash,' said Nikki, avoiding the jumper question; it was easier than lying. 'But I don't really know the best way either. This mothering gig is mostly guesswork and fear of getting it wrong. I wish I had the best answers.' She could see the despair written all over Ash's face, her neck tense and shoulders rolled forward, and wished there was some way to ease it.

'Me too. Thank you, Nik; just talking with you has made me feel better.'

'I'll help any way I can, you know that.'

'I know. I wouldn't have made it through Owen's funeral without you by my side and the days after,' Ash said softly. 'It works both ways too, you know.'

Nikki focused on cleaning up the last of the pie on her plate to avoid Ashley's words but it didn't stop them cutting through her. She felt as if she were betraying her closest friend, but she just couldn't confide in her, not yet. Maybe later when she'd got a grip on it herself. She just needed time to wrap her own head around it before she could talk to anyone. It was still too raw.

Also by Top Ten bestselling author Fiona Palmer

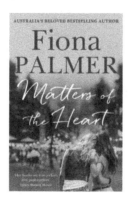

Western Australia, 2019: The **Bennets** are a farming family struggling to make ends meet. **Lizzy**, passionate about working the land, has little patience for her mother's focus on finding a suitable man for each of her five daughters.

When the dashing **Charles Bingley** buys the neighbouring property of Netherfield Park, Mrs Bennet and the entire district are atwitter with gossip and speculation. Charles and Lizzy's sister Jane form an instant connection, but it is Charlie's best friend, farming magnate **Will Darcy**, who leaves a lasting impression when he slights Lizzy, setting her against him.

Can Lizzy and Will put judgements and pride aside to each see the other for who they really are?

**Australia's bestselling storyteller Fiona Palmer reimagines Jane Austen's enduring love story in this very twenty-first-century novel about family, female empowerment and matters of the heart.**

'Ideal for those who love stories about romance, family dynamics and the value of friendship' – *Family Circle*

# hachette
AUSTRALIA

If you would like to find out more about Hachette Australia, our authors, upcoming events and new releases, you can visit our website or our social media channels:

hachette.com.au

 HachetteAustralia

 HachetteAus

Before becoming an author, **Fiona Palmer** was a speedway driver for seven years and now spends her days writing both women's and young adult fiction, working as a farmhand and caring for her two children in the tiny rural community of Pingaring, 350km from Perth. The books Fiona's passionate readers know and love contain engaging storylines, emotions and hearty characters. Her novels are consistently Top 10 national bestsellers.

**fionapalmer.com**  fiona_palmer

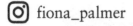 fiona_palmer  FionaPalmerAuthor

 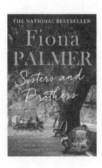  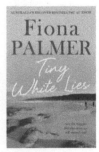